AUTHOR

Where the term City is used, it denotes the financial district
that is the City of London. When not capitalised, city refers
to the metropolis as a whole.

First published in the UK by Gibson Publishing

The Colour of London
Text copyright 2012 by Piers Treacher
Image copyright 2012 by Piers Treacher

A CIP catalogue record for this title is available from the British Library.

ISBN 9780-9-570811-47

This is a work of fiction. All the characters and events depicted in this book are
fictional and any resemblance to real people or occurrences is entirely co-incidental.
Some locations that appear in the story are real enough, and others have been used
rather fictitiously. For further information on these and other aspects of the story
please visit:
www.thecolouroflondon.com

For Alan and Pauline

The Colour of London

Piers Treacher

Gibson Publishing

Chapter One

Close. Oppressive. Unsettling. Those were the feelings that any living creature would have had in such a room. Its seven walls made sounds behave strangely, as if struggling to find their way around inside, not sure of where they were meant to go. Rough stone blocks made up the walls and floor, giving each surface a stifling solidity. Many of the stones were laid not quite true to the next and this unevenness made the walls seem tired. Some blocks jutted out, too exhausted from all the events they had witnessed to get back in line. Indeed, testimony to a grisly past, were the dark stains that casually spattered their surfaces.

There was but one door in the room, a squat, hefty oak affair with dull metallic bands bracing the wooden planks. The wood was dark from age but showed no signs of rot or insect attack. It looked substantial, yet a thin gap beneath it promised an escape to somewhere less uncomfortable.

There was no dust. Nor any cobwebs, spiders choosing to ply their trade elsewhere. The only thing there was, was light. Not much of it at first, just a diffuse red glow in the middle of the room. Although it had no discernible origin, no hot wiry filament at its core, there was a greater intensity at its centre that hinted at purpose. For a long time it seemed quite content, casting its soft and appropriately sinister illumination around the room.

Over time the brightness of the glow increased until discrete specks could be seen swirling near its core. They were not dust: there was no dust. Close inspection would have revealed these tiny motes absorbing the diffuse glow in their vicinity and re-emitting their own minute beacon of bright red light.

The number of these tiny specks grew slowly over time until they clustered so tightly that they formed a small sphere, about the size of a tennis ball. The sphere cast a glow of painful intensity that took delight in highlighting the stains upon the walls. For their part, the stains were more than happy to bask in the illumination.

After more time still, the surface of the sphere began to ripple. A small lump would appear and subsequently flatten. Then two lumps, one on either side, briefly tussled and then were gone again.

Something was trying to escape.

For a long time this struggle continued until eventually a speck on the surface fell inwards and disappeared. The tiny gap it left behind issued a fine light ray of staggering brightness.

More specks on the surface fell away, slowly at first but then faster and faster. The last few patches of the surface crumbled in a matter of seconds leaving only light. Pure, insanely intense, piercing red light.

Then nothing. Pitch darkness. Not even an afterglow. But there was sound, the sound of panting, the sound of something out of breath. The gasps got slower until whatever it was had itself under control.

Then silence.

"I suppose a fawning acolyte with a candle was too much to ask for."

The voice was resonant and lyrical with just a hint of annoyance.

Then footsteps, slow and controlled, the fifth of which was

followed by the sound of finger tips reaching stone. Carefully shuffling to the left, six and a bit walls were inspected before the door was located, just to the right of the initial point of contact.

"Hmph, typical," just a touch more annoyance from the voice.

The large iron ring on the door turned and the owner of the voice made its way into the corridor beyond. A rough stone passage led upwards, curling around the outside of the room. Some careful shuffling later, a faint line of light at floor level gave advance warning of another door. This one was locked but some groping around located a thin chain loop tethering a heavy key, hanging to one side of the door.

The next room was illuminated by a tepid and undersized fluorescent light strip on the ceiling. A rather too cramped collection of buckets, mops and floor polishing machines clustered in the middle, herded together by tall shelving stacks of cleaning equipment. The assortment of detergents and disinfectants gave the air an aroma of professional cleanliness. The voice picked its way forward towards another door, muttering quietly. A sharp exclamation was stifled as a rotary floor waxer gave insult to a shin.

Finally clear of the dangers posed by the broom cupboard, the voice's owner turned the cheap metal door knob and stepped through.

Bill Preston wasn't expecting this. Actually, he wasn't expecting much of anything, one of the things he liked best about being a security guard was that almost nothing ever happened. Or at least it never happened to him. This he was quite happy with, content even. So content that on this particular morning, towards the end of what had been a blissfully uneventful night shift, he had started to drift off. Not fall asleep you understand, that would be terribly unprofessional, and Bill was nothing if not professional. No, not sleep, but rather a delightfully relaxed state where everything felt comfortable and time passed easily.

He was much practised at achieving this state and was quite certain that should anything happen, and it never had, then he would be more than capable of being alert immediately and ready with a professional response.

It was in this state of lethargic preparedness that he sat at his desk in the rather grandiose lobby of one of the world's more successful investment houses. It was a big lobby, plenty of marble and expensive modern art. The reception desk from which Bill kept watch was set atop a plinth at the rear of the lobby. It gave him a good view of the main doors, a good view of the lifts and, quite by chance, a good view of the cleaning cupboard. And of the naked man who walked out of it.

To Bill's credit he did become fully awake in the briefest of instants, though his mouth opened in too slack-jawed a manner for him to have claimed he was anything other than completely unprepared for such an event. This was a shame because that instant was the first and potentially only opportunity of his career to demonstrate just how professional he was. Before he could do better than stunned disbelief, the naked man looked in Bill's direction and narrowed his eyes a little. Bill promptly toppled forward onto the keyboard in front of him; the indications were that he was either asleep or unconscious as his soft and rounded shoulders heaved gently.

The naked man scanned the lobby and his eyes came to rest on the large chrome letters set high on one wall.

AVAR INVESTMENTS
Getting you more of what you want

A tiny smirk played at the edges of his mouth before the first rays of dawn caught his attention as they spilled into the street outside the main doors. He stalked forwards and outside found the road empty in both directions. Standing tall and straight he waited as the sun rose enough to cover his face and then quickly down the rest of his body. Basking in the thin warmth he smiled broadly and took several long and deep breaths.

Further down the street a few early starters were beginning to show, eager to be the first at their desks. Seeing these in the distance the naked man stepped back close to the wall of the building and relaxed, his whole frame sinking an inch or so lower. The first person to walk past, a suited city gent, didn't even glance in the man's direction as he hurried off to his own temple of commerce further down the street.

Several more people passed on by until a cheerful young man in a high-visibility cycling outfit turned to go into the building. The naked man fell into step beside him and clasped a friendly arm around his shoulders.

"Good morning, I notice that you are early again. That is good son, that is very good."

"Thank you sir."

"I take it that you have a change of clothes though? It would not do to be at your desk all day like that now, would it?" the naked man's voice oozed paternal warmth.

"Of course not sir. I always keep several in the lockers."

"Really? How splendid."

On seeing the security guard slumped over his desk the cyclist broke step for a fraction of a second and was on the brink of saying something. A quick squeeze of his shoulder had him look straight ahead and walk unfazed through to the changing rooms at the back of the building.

The naked man was no longer quite so naked. He had a suit that fitted reasonably well and a pair of worn but well polished and expensive Oxfords. His shirt was wide open at the collar and his hair slightly ruffled. He had the rather predatory air of someone who had been up all night, only just returning home after a number of effortlessly successful conquests.

He strolled down a road that now bustled with busy city types. Everyone walked quickly and purposefully, concentrating intently on their own destination. Both men and women alike wore sharp looking suits, and many had little devices held to their ears, not wasting a precious minute that could be put to productive use.

Intrigued, the man reached out with his thoughts and located those of a middle aged woman walking in front of him with one such device. Her step faltered as he delved into her subconscious and tore out the information he was looking for. As he released her mind she shivered, resumed walking and continued barking instructions to a colleague about when to sell.

The man stopped outside a branch of one of the City's largest chains of coffee shops. He had already walked past several, but this particular venue held familiar connotations for him. He didn't recognise the shop itself, a modern and charmless effort straight from the franchise catalogue. Its decor was no doubt carefully designed to make you feel like staying just long enough to drink the product and then move on, making way for the next customer in need of refuelling. No, the man recognised it because he knew that a shop had stood on that site and served coffee for hundreds of years. Before the beloved bean it had supplied a changing but always popular choice of fermented drinks. The man remembered the wine it had sold particularly well, the continuity pleased him somehow. He smiled to himself and went in.

Sitting down with his gently steaming double espresso, the man pondered the tiny white china cup. Coffee had most definitely got smaller. It had also become more difficult to drink, the ridiculously inadequate handle proving to be of little practical use. After two aborted attempts to grasp the handle between thumb and forefinger, he picked the cup up by the rim instead. With it paused beneath his nose, he savoured the aroma and let distant memories be stirred by the familiar smell. The bitter taste that followed dried his throat and brought a further stream of recognition. He kept his eyes closed until he had finished reminiscing, and then happy that the present was where he wanted to be, he looked about him.

What struck him first was that although the shop was pretty much full, with relatively few empty seats at any of the tables, almost nobody was chatting to each other. There were a few people talking, but all into their phones and not to the people they were sitting with. The vast majority of patrons were also using their mobiles, but instead of talking were jabbing fingers at theirs, or tracing patterns on the screens. What was keeping people so absorbed that they were ignoring those around them?

The man was about to choose another unsuspecting donor of information when he realised he was in danger of getting lazy, and of weakening himself more than he needed to. Examining people's minds was not difficult, or at least most people's minds were not difficult to examine. However it did take a fair amount of energy to do, more so than many tasks, and should be avoided if possible. Having reminded himself of this, he instead leant over to the table next to him and gave the young brunette a warm smile.

"Good morning, my dear."

She looked up in irritation but instantly softened her expression.

"Good morning to you too."

Her voice sounded slightly dull and lacked the vivaciousness that her looks and demeanour otherwise suggested. The man narrowed his eyes and pressed on.

"How would you like to join me and tell me how that phone of yours works?"

"I'd like that very much."

She shuffled her chair closer and proceeded to show the man her smartphone and how it could be used for browsing the Internet. As the minutes passed she became more animated, her voice sounding brighter and more enthusiastic as she warmed to her subject. When she met his gaze it now seemed to energise rather than subdue her.

Long after both their coffee cups had gone cold the man looked at her again, lightly placing his hand over hers on the table.

"You do not need the phone any more, do you?"

She smiled with some degree of longing in her eyes and slid the brand new model across the table towards him.

The man stepped outside the coffee shop and was surprised to find it raining lightly. He glanced to his left and watched the brunette saunter off into the throng of busy workers. A very physical thought occurred to him and was promptly filed away for future attention. He now knew what his first steps would be. A new age had brought new tools with it, tools with so much potential that he couldn't help but grin.

He spread his arms wide and tilted his head back until the rain pattered onto his face. Eyes shut, he breathed deep and slow eleven times. People walked past and around him with not so much as a glance. Those going into the coffee shop swerved to avoid him yet didn't seem to register his presence otherwise.

Eventually the man awoke, took the smartphone from his pocket and leaned forward to shield it from the rain. His fingers traced expertly across its screen as he navigated social networking sites and search engines. By the time the rain stopped a half hour later, he was exhausted but extremely pleased with his progress. He locked and stowed the phone, then set off down the road, quickly disappearing into the anonymous masses that were lining the streets of London.

Chapter Two

Sitting quietly on Gordon Street was a rather anonymous building that housed the Department of Physics & Astronomy of University College London. It was a long and practical structure with stairwells at each end connected by corridors running its full length. Lecture rooms, teaching labs, offices and research teams were housed over four floors above ground and two below.

The lower of the two basement floors was where many of the post-graduate experimental researchers were kept. Some of the less respectful undergraduates quipped that this was in recognition of the academic hierarchy involved. Faculty staff at the top, which was generally true as many of their offices were on the higher floors. Undergraduates frequented the central part of the building, and post-graduates skulked along the two basement floors where they belonged. The theory went further, suggesting that within the genus of post-graduate – or doctoral candidate as they were also known, the 'candidate' sobriquet hinting strongly that many wouldn't survive – there were two species: theorists and experimentalists.

Theorists most definitely considered themselves the superior breed and many of the undergraduate population also subscribed to this classification. Their contribution to science was more worthy, their efforts more noble. Success came directly from the raw power of their own intellect and nothing else.

Experimentalists in contrast were usually thought of as somewhat second class. Yes they were physicists, but they relied on machines and equipment to generate their success, and by virtue of getting their hands dirty with practical endeavours they were only one short step away from being engineers. Shudder.

In reality this viewpoint was a bit naive. It ignored the fact that many of the great physicists so revered during lecture courses were first and foremost experimentalists. It also failed to recognise that physics had always been, and by necessity was, a partnership between theory and proof. Just as experiments were often designed to investigate a theory, many theories were inspired by experiments.

Whatever the merits of the undergraduate view on post-grads, and those conducting practical investigation in particular, they were dead wrong as to why they were located in the lower basement.

It was actually because many of the experiments being run within the department were quite sensitive to vibration, light and temperature. The basement substructure was sunk far enough into the ground so as to avoid the worst of the heavy London traffic. The Circle line trains passing through nearby Euston Square station were still a problem, so some rooms were built with vibration isolated floors to minimise their impact. The temperature below ground was relatively stable and meant the air conditioning didn't have to work too hard to keep a steady 19°C. The lack of windows meant no uncontrolled lighting conditions and also no sunshine to heat rooms during the day. In short, the basement was the best place for experiments.

Given the majority of experiments in the department were run on a day-to-day basis by post-grads, it wasn't surprising therefore that they could be found most commonly down in the sub-basement laboratories. The communal post-grad office space was located on the upper basement floor for convenience, where theorists and experimentalists alike were expected to live cheek by jowl.

Another view the undergraduates held, and much more accurately this time, was that those working towards their doctorates were really little more than cannon fodder for the big guns in the faculty. Be they theoretician or experimentalist, they would be worked like pack animals by their academic supervisors for the three or four years it would take to accumulate enough novel research with which to write a defendable thesis. Some professors or lecturers would actively engage with the research and help direct it, whilst others would send their wards off into the intellectual wilderness and expect them back only when they had something worth publishing. Either way, it was a trade of sorts where the supervisor provided the resources and the opportunity, and the grad-student the graft and determination.

If all went well then a worthy thesis would result and be milked for journal papers, lifeblood to the academic that would help secure funding for their next avenue of research. The grad-student might even go on to become an academic themselves and thus become a useful ally to the supervisor.

Sometimes the research would not go so well and the objective would become purely to complete a thesis that would survive examination. The grad-student would leave with a certificate and the right to add some letters to their business card, and the supervisor would get a tick in the box for having managed another successful candidate.

It was in room B2-3, a fluids laboratory in the sub-basement, that Jack Eastwood was experiencing the grad-student equivalent of hitting the wall. He would gladly have run a marathon if it would have helped his research.

He was sitting in the dark at a flimsy desk on which perched both a computer that whirred loudly and a large, expensive and inactive display screen. An old and rather dirty keyboard sat in front of him, its predecessor that had come with the computer having been borrowed and subsequently lost by one of the other post-grads. Jack didn't mind this, a keyboard was a keyboard, except in this instance the grimy replacement had an 's' key with a tendency to get stuck. He could either remember to jab forcefully at it, or risk generating interesting new wordsssss signalling the need to prise up the key with the paperclip that sat embedded in Blu-tack above the row of "F" keys. Quite why Jack hadn't replaced or cleaned the keyboard was just one of the many questions he couldn't answer at that moment in time. It was also most decidedly the least important.

The most important question in his professional life was why the hell was his experiment not working as he predicted it should? He rubbed his eyes with the heels of his hands and leant back in his swivel chair. Just as he took his hands away the bright ceiling lights snapped on, glaring right down at his face. Cursing, he span round and tried to glower at the intruder, but the bright lights made him squint so much he could barely make out the outline of a tall gangly shape.

"Alright Jack, thought I'd find you here."

"Sam! Do you by any chance remember the chat we had last week?"

"What chat?"

"The one which ended with you promising not to enter when the red light's on?"

"What red ... oh."

Jack's eyes had adjusted enough to be able to see Sam's gaunt figure duck its head out the door and return just a little more slouched than before.

"I'm sorry mate, really didn't see it. Were you in the middle of a run?"

"Yep," Jack battled to keep the frustration out of his voice, "but it's all bollocks anyway, so don't worry. What can I do for you?"

"OK, sure. Erm, your bike, can I borrow it?"

Sam rubbed his hands together and managed a fragile grin. He was also demonstrating his habit of hopping very slightly from one foot to the other, which gave the unnerving impression that he was desperately in need of a toilet. Jack couldn't help but feel sorry for the guy, he had never seen him look relaxed. Even when drunk he was an awkward bundle of nerves.

Jack sighed.

"Again? You still not got a new one?"

Sam's bike had been stolen five weeks previously from the racks outside the department.

"Can't afford it, and turns out my insurance wouldn't cover it."

Sam looked at his shoes.

Jack gave in. He always did.

"Yeah, of course you can. Just use your own helmet this time, alright?"

"Sure. Erm yeah, OK. Thanks mate. I owe you."

Jack fished his keys from a pocket and worked the one for his bike lock off the ring. He tossed it to Sam and pointed towards his head.

"Your helmet, remember?"

"Sure, see ya."

Jack turned the screen back on and shut down the automated cycle the experiment had been running. The interruption had cost him about an hour's worth of data, but he knew he was kidding himself. It wasn't working, no matter how many times he ran it.

His head was hurting so he turned the room lights back off and sat down at his desk. Pushing the keyboard away he laid his head down on his folded arms and tried to let some of the tension drain away.

Apart from the monitor, the only illumination in the room was coming from a glass case sat on top of a very large and solid metal bench. The case was approximately half a meter on each side and pointing at it were two laser sources. Each beam was spread by a lens into a sheet of green light that was focused into the centre of the box. Two pairs of what resembled CCTV cameras also pointed at various angles toward the case, carefully positioned so as to avoid the jungle of tubes and wires which emerged from it and snaked away to other bits of equipment located nearby.

Inside the case was a circular glass tank of precisely 300mm diameter. The top few centimetres of the tank was not glass like the rest, but rather a metal ring that was able to be rotated by a series of motors and gears mounted above the case. The space between the tank and the case was filled with water, the purpose being twofold. Firstly, it was supplied by a heating bath which ensured the whole experiment stayed at a constant temperature. Secondly, it kept changes in refractive index of the experimental chamber to a minimum so that light passing in and out suffered as little distortion as possible.

The tank itself was filled with a clear fluid that was mostly water but also a small percentage of glycerine. This increased the viscosity of the fluid to the exact value Jack wanted. The other thing the fluid contained was a huge number of extremely small glass beads, so tiny that in the green sheets of laser light they looked like fine dust suspended in the liquid. This was exactly their purpose.

As the test fluid moved within the tank, driven by the rotating ring at its top, the beads travelled with the flow and sparkled every time they passed through the light sheets. The cameras pointing at the experiment recorded images hundreds of times a second, tracking the path of each glass bead for the duration of its passage through the light sheets. The large computer sitting on Jack's desk then processed the pictures and generated a map of the flow in the illuminated portion of the experiment.

Rather sensibly, and this wasn't always the case within the world of obscure academic research, the technique was known as Particle Image Velocimetry. Even more sensibly its users only ever called it PIV.

What Jack had been calling it the previous few months didn't bear repeating. It just wasn't working. If pressed he would have conceded that the PIV system was working exactly as its manufacturers had intended, it was his experiment that wasn't. This was a reality which Jack had been struggling with for a while; Sam's intervention had been but a minor frustration in a long series of disappointments, dead ends and unfruitful ideas. He had already spent two years designing and building the tank and its complicated rotation system. He had tried numerous subtly different configurations to try to prompt the behaviour he was looking for, yet to date he hadn't seen even a glimmer of what his theory had predicted.

Jack was one of the rare breed of physicists who were equally at home with the convoluted mathematics of the theorists or the invention and repetitive attention to detail required of the experimentalists. He understood the friction between the two camps but found it petty and distracting. He had already published articles with professors of each flavour whilst still an undergraduate at Oxford, a rather unusual feat in itself. He was disappointed by the way each had tried to convince him to take a research path exclusively one way or the other, he was interested in both. What Jack possibly didn't appreciate was just how rare his ability was to be able to think and contribute in both ways.

He had eventually found a place he felt comfortable with when put in touch with the Q-Institute. The QI was a research group based primarily within UCL's Department of Physics & Astronomy but whose membership spread to a number of other faculties, including medicine, engineering and chemistry, and even some other universities. It was funded by the Qwilleran Foundation, an American philanthropic body that provided the money for several such inter-disciplinary centres around the world.

Jack had brought his own idea with him for a research

project. His academic record from Oxford coupled with already having published related results made it an easy decision for the board of the QI. Jack was a researcher with real potential and it was a minor coup to prise him away from Oxford. It also took Dr Ratliffe no time at all to agree to be his supervisor; he was a minimal hassle post-grad if ever there was one.

His experiment was the final step in proving a theory he had developed, a theory that concerned the concept of universality. For the last few decades scientists from all sorts of disciplines had started to realise that the same phenomena occurred in completely unrelated systems. You could take two situations as disparate as the rhythm of a beating heart and the weather. Despite their intrinsically different natures, when you studied data that measured the way each system behaved – its 'dynamics' – under certain circumstances they looked identical. Researchers had drawn these parallels between a range of systems and identified some fundamental laws. The presence of similar behaviour in seemingly dissimilar systems had become known as universality.

Jack's theory had been born during his undergraduate days at Oxford. To earn a little extra money he had undertaken to help a professor in the economics department sort through some historical data on cotton prices in India. Over a period of decades the market rate for cotton had fluctuated in a way that nobody had been able to account for. Intuition, hard work and some luck had led Jack to spot a pattern to the way the price behaved immediately before it underwent a sudden fall. This type of behaviour was already known in physics as a Hof-del Pino instability, but it was a theoretical concept and had never been observed in real physical systems. Finding it in cotton prices was of some interest to the scientific community and Jack quickly had his name on several published articles.

By the time he took his finals at Oxford, Jack was convinced HDP instabilities existed in many other systems and that he knew how to find them. His proposal to the Q-Institute board was to look for them in two further systems unrelated to each other – or cotton prices – and develop the theoretical framework that would explain their universality.

He had spent his first year at the Institute working with a biologist and a neurologist at UCL, Doctors Bayliss and McKie. They had provided him with brain activity data from twenty four patients that had undergone epileptic seizures. Jack helped them develop a model that described the neuron cascade preceding the seizure and in the process identified the same HDP instability within the data. He then set out to find the third example, this time within a simple fluid system in a desktop experiment. It turned out not to be quite so simple.

Whilst designing and building the experiment, he had worked with two eminent mathematicians at the Institute, Professors Shipton and Hewitt. Between the three of them they had developed the theoretical framework describing why the instabilities were found so universally. The theory was almost ready to publish and they were convinced it would be big news, maybe even worthy of reaching the cover of Nature, that most august of scientific publications. However, the two examples they had to back it up were both 'after the fact'. Critics – and there were always many when making assertions of substance – would accuse them of just searching through enough data until they found what they were looking for and ignoring all the rest. If they could publish and include an experimental example where the instability had first been predicted by the theory, then the whole argument would be significantly stronger. It was under this weight of holding back from publishing that the experiment had been worked on day and night for so many months.

Jack knew he had just slept by the slick of drool that clung to his wrist. He checked his watch and was surprised to find less than an hour had passed. He fetched himself a can of Coke from the fridge in the post-grad office and sat down there to rethink his strategy. For inspiration he selected a stack of research papers he hadn't got around to looking at and started to work his way through them. He said goodnight as his various colleagues headed off home and carried on reading. He was determined to find something useful before calling it a night.

By half past one in the morning he admitted defeat and left the office. Angry with himself for not stopping earlier, and angrier still for not finding even a morsel with which to build on, he slunk out the back door to the department. He walked round to the front and stopped short. His bike was gone.

Sam.

He rubbed his eyes, failed to dislodge the grit which seemed to be coating them, and set off down Gordon Street. On his bike the journey home at night would have taken barely twenty minutes, but with the Tube well past its bedtime he knew that London's night buses were his best bet. He could walk it, but the first and only time he'd done so had resulted in a trek over an hour long.

It took him fifteen minutes to get to Tottenham Court Road and about the same again to ride the N98 to the corner of Hall Road and Maida Vale. Less than a minute later he was turning the key to the front door of his lodgings in Hamilton Terrace. He closed the door gingerly behind him and listened intently for signs that his landlady might still be up and about. He was scared stiff of the predatory Miss Giovanni and had no desire whatsoever to have to deal with her when so tired and off his guard.

Satisfied that all was quiet he tiptoed to his room on the second floor. Five minutes later he was in bed, two minutes after that he was asleep.

It was almost 09:00 and Jack was back at the Institute. He had been asleep for barely five hours when his alarm had called time on what had been much welcomed rest.

His first stop was the coffee machine in the academic lounge, which he refilled to make a wickedly strong half jug. Pouring all of it into an oversized mug he set off for the department office on the ground floor. He'd rescued his post from the pigeon hole and was heading back out the door when one of the ladies from the admin pool spotted him.

"Not so fast Mr Eastwood," Irene's voice was a laser beam that had burned more than a few ears in her time.

"Whatever it is, it can't have been me Mrs Goodrich." Jack felt the back of his neck start to prickle and redden. What had he forgotten? He turned and smiled at the late middle-age dreadnought heading his way. He actually quite liked Mrs Goodrich, as indeed he liked all the secretarial staff. Their office was a welcome oasis of honest common sense in what otherwise was a rather self obsessed building. Disappointing Mrs Goodrich produced the same sense of guilt that Jack got from disappointing his parents.

"What time is it now young man?"

"A little after nine?"

"Correct. And what time did you leave last night?"

"Sometime after midnight. Did I leave a door open or something?"

"No, you did not. But according to the exit logs you swiped out at twenty five minutes to two. You may not realise it but I have to review those logs every morning, and I've been keeping a track of you."

Jack felt the heat spread from the back of his neck, up his cheeks and all over his face. Where the hell was this going?

"In the last two months you have left the building before midnight on just seven occasions, and before two o'clock just thirteen times."

"Mrs Goodrich, there's ..."

"I haven't finished young man," she cut him off abruptly.

"You leave late, yet you always seem to be in first thing the next day. In short, you're working too hard and it's not good for you." He was taken aback, no one had questioned his work ethic before.

"I don't know what to say," he offered.

"How about you promise me that you'll start going home at a sensible time? That pretty girl of yours must be wondering what's happened to you."

"Mandy? I'm fairly sure my hours don't bother her. Anyway, I'm seeing her tonight. I'm really not turning into a dull boy Mrs Goodrich. Honest."

"Just see that you don't. And remember, I'm watching you."

He couldn't make out whether it was genuine reproach in her eyes or friendly concern. As he left the office he caught sight of one of the younger ladies grinning conspiratorially at him, so he presumed it was the latter.

He struggled through the rest of the day, even regular dosing with coffee and Coke didn't help very much. Mrs Goodrich's well meaning scolding had pulled the plug from his reserve of concentration. He'd stayed focused so intently for such a long stretch that he'd ignored the accumulation of fatigue. Now that it had been pointed out to him, he really understood how drained he was. He'd gone well past the point of simply feeling tired, his weariness had become ingrained. He felt squeezed at a cellular level, every bit of his body would need sustained rest in order to recover its energy. Still, that was the price you had to pay. He'd seen it in the faces of the post-grads when he started at the Institute. You had to push yourself to the limits, exclude everything else so that your narrow area of research could fill up your whole being. When you reached the point of saturation was when real progress was made. Jack was there, he could feel it. He had given as much as he could to his experiment and desperately needed it to work soon. Failure was not an option.

As it happened, Mrs Goodrich's concerns were soon addressed. Jack had a date that evening with the beautiful Mandy, something he'd been looking forward to for the last couple of weeks as their diaries kept them apart. She was Jack's age but looked younger than her twenty-five years, had perfect skin and shiny dark hair that hung long and straight. In the picture Jack carried as the wallpaper on his smartphone, her cheeks were rosy as she smiled brilliantly on a cold winter's day. By most standards, she was absolutely gorgeous. An impartial observer however, whilst admitting that she was indeed very attractive might also have commented that she knew exactly how pretty she was. There was a dangerous confidence in her eyes that sometimes unnerved Jack, and often led him to question why such a stunning girl had chosen to be with him.

He sat down with his pint of London Pride on one of the aged pews in The Northumberland Arms and took two large gulps. The beer tasted good, it was his first in over a week. The pub was busy and he'd been extremely lucky to get a seat on a Friday night. He savoured the rounded flavour of malt against hops and smiled.

Twenty minutes later and his smile had started to fade. His pint was almost finished and no sign of Mandy. He checked his phone. No text message, no missed call. This wasn't the first time she had been late however, her attitude towards time keeping was certainly her own. Jack ordered another pint and sat back down, though rather more self consciously this time. He leafed through one of the newspapers from the end of the bar but took no interest in the stories within.

He glanced up from the table frequently, expecting to see her. Several times he sensed someone approaching, but each time it proved to be another drinker seeking the spare chair at his small table. He politely said he was waiting for someone, the confidence in his voice weakening a little more with every repetition.

Forty minutes after he had first sat down, Jack finished his second pint. Still no word from Mandy. He went outside to try phoning and was answered on the sixth ring. There was a lot of noise in the background, it sounded like a busy bar and Jack struggled to make out her words.

"Hi pet, can't talk, it's manic in here."

"Where are you?" Jack shouted back.

"Got to go, I'll text you later," and the line went dead.

Jack stared at the handset in disbelief. His breathing was quick and his heart pounding, the redness of his face a mixture of humiliation and alcohol. He took a step towards the door of the pub but stopped from going back in. He'd had enough of drinking alone and didn't want to face the pitying stares from the other patrons. Making a point of turning off his phone he headed home.

Jack was angry. The date had been in her diary for a couple of weeks, and she cancelled him for what? After work drinks? She hadn't even had the courtesy to let him know, just left him sitting in a pub looking like an idiot.

Then he was confused. Why would she do that? With both their work commitments time together was at a premium. Surely she realised how much seeing her meant to him.

Disappointment followed. Was this a true reflection of how much he meant to her? They had been together nearly a year and yet she apparently thought nothing of casually standing him up.

And finally exhaustion. The fatigue weighed heavy, compounded by his unfulfilled expectations for the evening. The beery glow had faded and all that remained was profound tiredness.

Chapter Three

"Will you stop your fucking whining," Henrietta snapped at her twin brother.

"But what if no-one comes? It'll be like last year Hetty – that was so embarrassing."

Fernando looked at the mountain of booze on the table and wondered how many people it would take to make a noticeable dent in it. Quite a few he guessed.

"Yes, well fortunately I organised things this time so it'll be just fine. Why don't you go and clean something Ferren? It's what you're good at."

The sneering tone in her voice was enough to send her brother scurrying from the room, he knew better than to stay around when she started to sound like that. She'd needled him from an early age, ever since they'd learned to talk. Even his name was a result of her taunting. When he'd tried to pronounce Fernando, it had first come out as Ferren, his eighteen month old mouth not able to manage the complications of Fernando. Henrietta taunted him for being stupid, repeatedly chanting "Ferren! Ferren!" By the time he could manage his full name, the diminutive version had stuck. In his early teens he had tried to get people to stop using it, but his twin had made sure that never lasted for long. His tacit acceptance of the nickname had become an admission of her superiority over him. He hadn't challenged her in years, and had even come to draw a measure of security from his sister's continued domination of him. He felt safer knowing that her strength was close at hand, even if the aggression it spawned was sometimes directed at him.

Henrietta checked downstairs – nothing breakable was out, nothing that any of their friends could knock over. Having spent the previous nine months getting the house into shape, she would be damned if she was going to let one of those idiots mess it up. Henrietta had done the interior design and managed the workmen, obliquely putting her degree in art history to use. She wasn't quite sure what Fernando had contributed, other than to get the money from their parents. It had started off as an investment project, to be sold on at a profit as soon as possible, but by the time it was ready for sale they'd become attached to the house and wanted to keep it. A timely dip in property prices had given them a temporary excuse to blunt their father's insistence that they treat it like the business opportunity it was meant to be.

A bell sounded and Henrietta just beat Fernando to opening the door onto the fashionable Regency street in Pimlico. A young couple bustled in.

"Darlings!" Henrietta ushered them inside.

"Happy birthday Hett," the man replied as he air kissed her cheek.

"This is for you."

The woman presented a gaudily wrapped box. She pulled a second slimmer package from her bag.

"And this is for Ferren. Here you go sweetie," she pressed it into Fernando's hands.

"Drinks are through the back, help yourselves," Henrietta called as they disappeared towards the kitchen. She ordered her brother upstairs with the coats and muttered something less than complimentary as she opened her present. The designer handbag was discarded on the hall table as she opened the door to a small group who had all come bearing gifts.

"Darlings!"

The house had filled up quickly, most of the guests knew both the twins, though there were a few that Fernando had cultivated on his own. A pair of couples held an animated conversation in the hall, with arms being waved expansively to punctuate the points being made.

"I don't understand, why would they think they could make money out of it? For sure they've done it up nicely, but I can't believe that adds much to the value," said one man.

"Hello, because they didn't pay for it in the first place. It's all Daddy's money, so anything they sell it for is pure profit," countered his fiancée. The second man couldn't stop himself and chimed in.

"No way! He just gave it to them? Unbelievable!" he spilled his wine as he slammed his glass down in exasperation on an expensive sideboard.

"Well good on them," his girlfriend said, "if I could squeeze a free house from my parents I'd do it in a heartbeat. They're loaded, why not help me out now when I need it rather than waiting until I inherit it all anyway?"

"I suppose," said the first man, "but if they want to make a living doing this then shouldn't they have at least tried to do it profitably? That bathroom must have cost a small fortune and it doesn't add much to the price."

"But it is spectacular," said the fiancée.

"Yes it is, but that's not the point. They should have spent as little as possible to make it acceptable, not gone all in with marble and gold taps. I'll be amazed if they ever sell it for more than they paid. Sorry, more than Daddy paid."

One of the women raised her glass and toasted,

"To Daddy!"

The other three snorted.

*

It was a couple of hours into the joint birthday party when the doorbell sounded a double ring. The twins were both in the hallway, but it was Fernando who was closest and answered the door. He opened it to find a handsome man standing on the doormat, concentrating intently on a smartphone in his hands. Fernando smiled nervously at the man but he didn't look up. Several seconds passed and Fernando started to feel uncomfortable.

"Erm, hello? I'm sorry to interrupt ..."

Suddenly the man looked up, his face deadly serious at first but a large and warm smile quickly broke out.

"Ferren! How wonderful to see you again. One moment." The man went back to his phone for a good few seconds and then put it away in the pocket of his Paul Smith jacket. He stepped forward and grabbed Fernando in a bear hug, then held him at arms' length to take a good look at him.

"You are all grown up my boy. Marvellous! And where is that beautiful sister of yours?"

Henrietta had approached the pair of them, curious as to the new guest. She didn't recognise the man but there was definitely something familiar about him. His voice was rich and languid, a continental accent, something Mediterranean perhaps? His skin was well tanned and he radiated good health, his thick, dark hair shiny with scented oil. She couldn't even begin to place his age. He could be barely older than her mid-twenties or well into middle age. She instinctively looked at his hands. No sign of a wedding ring, not that a ring would have mattered, but its absence pleased her.

"Ah, Hetty my dear. You also have grown into a fine young woman."

To her surprise, Henrietta blushed at the compliment, then tried to regain the initiative.

"You seem to have the advantage sir. I'm not sure we've met

have we?"

"Forgive me, it has been some time. My name is Avaro, I am a friend of your cousin Nathalie, we used to babysit when you two were little. I heard that you were celebrating so I thought I would drop by."

"Nathalie? I thought she was in Italy these days?" asked Henrietta.

"Indeed she is, but I am in London for a while on business and could not pass up the opportunity to see you both, and your lovely house."

The man eyed the other guests as he sauntered into the large hallway. Almost at the short passage that led to the kitchen, he turned and called to the twins, neither of whom had moved.

"We will talk later, but first a drink. This is a party is it not? And I am very good at parties."

He disappeared amongst the guests as Henrietta stared after him, her curiosity raised. He must be in his early forties, assuming he was close to her cousin's age. His presence was palpable, he seemed to fill the hall and it had felt empty as soon as he stepped out of it. Fernando was looking expectantly at her, waiting for a lead to follow. She shrugged and went in search of a drink of her own.

It was near to midnight and the party had really got going, so well in fact that the house was teeming with revellers. Fernando was pretty sure he didn't know half the people there, many were friends of friends presumably. He'd been worried at first when gatecrashers started turning up. He just couldn't find the words to turn them away, so they all pushed straight on past him. Henrietta didn't seem bothered by them though, so he had turned his attention to the rapidly dwindling stash of drink. What had once seemed a vast quantity was running dangerously low by the middle of the evening, and on his sister's instruction he headed out for more supplies. Figuring that spirits had the highest alcohol to weight ratio, he returned having cleaned out the nearest corner shop of vodka, rum and gin. By midnight, they too had started to run dry but by that point had obviously had their effect.

The first floor lounge was littered with people in various states of undress, happy victims in a drinking game where stripping was the penalty shot. Bodies intertwined on sofas and standing couples wrapped themselves around each other, swaying in time to the 'post-grunge' discharging from the Bang and Olufsen system.

The kitchen had seen the worst of the action, including a vodka snorting boat race. Two lines of participants had faced off and each team mate had taken it in turn to sniff a shot up their nostrils. Their glass was turned upside down when finished to trigger the next in line to begin. Several people had collapsed, two had got vodka in their eyes and started screaming, one person had started bleeding. Despite the apparent side effects, there were plenty of volunteers for a second round. By the time the vodka ran out, everyone involved was hurting to some degree. Most were so far gone they didn't care.

By three o'clock Henrietta was too tired and too drunk to care what happened, so she sloped off to get some sleep. She had been smart enough to lock the door to her room so had an empty bed to retreat to. She was disappointed to be sleeping alone, but her cousin's partner was the only interesting man there. She had no qualms about trying something on with him, despite the family connection, but Avaro had quickly acquired a gaggle of followers that she couldn't prise away from him. Silly bitches might have taken the not so subtle hints she'd dropped, it was her birthday after all. Still, at least she had a bed. She'd seen her brother curled up on the floor of the study, too scared to kick out whoever had made use of his room. She was out within seconds of lying down.

The next morning Fernando woke to pain. Pain in his head from drinking more than he was used to, which admittedly wasn't very much. Pain in his neck from having used a small scatter cushion as an inadequate pillow, and pain most other places from having slept on a thin and rather chilly carpet. He stood up slowly and wondered if he was going to be sick. He swayed momentarily but decided that no, he wasn't going to throw up. He felt a little better once he started to move around, though his respite was short lived. As soon as he got down the stairs and saw the state of the hall his pulse started to quicken. Glasses and bottles lay discarded at the sides of the floor, and were strewn over every surface. A pale stain on the parquet floor looked like white wine. He was dismayed to see it had soaked in and raised the grain of the wood.

He checked the other rooms and apart from more glasses and bottles, and a few bodies asleep on sofas, the ground and first floor were remarkably free from further disruption. The kitchen would take a major clean but there wasn't as much damage over all as he'd braced himself for.

He made coffee and sipped it gratefully, his hangover beaten back by the caffeine. He knew that a shower was the next step on the road to feeling human again so headed upstairs. He couldn't remember why he had slept in the study, but his question was answered as soon as he opened the door to his room. Laying naked on his bed were his cousin's friend and three women, the covers lay discarded on the floor. Avaro was in the middle, a woman draped over him from either side with the third curled up submissively at his feet. Fernando's bed was a super king but it was still some going to get four people into it.

He stood with his mouth open, completely lost for words. His cheeks reddened as he blushed at the sight of the women. He recognised the one on the left as Jennifer, a friend of his sister's from school that he'd fantasised about countless times during his adolescence.

Avaro smiled as he caught Fernando staring at her shapely

breasts.

"Ferren, good morning to you."

"Yes, erm, yes. Good morning."

He could hardly get the words out and glanced guiltily at the older man before focusing his gaze out the window, choosing a large red pillar box to fixate on.

Avaro extricated himself from the embrace of the women, got out of the bed and walked over to Fernando, who was visibly intimidated by the older man's unabashed nakedness.

"My boy, we have a lot to talk about," he said as he clasped a friendly arm about Fernando's shoulder.

"Get your sister up and give me twenty minutes to say goodbye to them," he gestured towards the bed.

"I will take you both to eat. You are hungry, yes? Then we can discuss your birthday present, I think I may be able to help with your new business."

He smiled knowingly at Fernando and then pushed him out the bedroom door, closing it straight away.

Fernando sat in the kitchen and tentatively sipped a second cup of coffee. He felt distinctly uncomfortable wearing his clothes from the party. The shower had helped wash away the last of the soreness from the night on the floor, but he couldn't bring himself to venture back to his room for a clean change. He had heard one of the girls leave his room just as he was about to exit the bathroom. He'd held back and quietly relocked the door, desperately hoping he wouldn't have to speak to her. To his relief she had gone straight past and down the stairs, the front door sounding moments later.

Henrietta joined her brother in the kitchen, taking his mug rather than getting her own.

"So I'm up. Happy now? This better be worth getting out of bed for."

It had required quite an effort on Fernando's part to rouse his sister. Not because she had a hangover, she was one of those lucky people who never seemed to get them no matter how much she drank, but she was tired. Fernando knew that a tired Henrietta would need cajoling and on that morning it was only the mention of Avaro and his mysterious present that finally got her up and about.

"You were talking to him for long enough last night, didn't he mention anything?" Fernando asked.

"Something about knowing a guy who has a property that he wants to redevelop. Works in the City I think. Sounds quite large scale so it's probably worth speaking to him I guess."

"That would be great Hett, a fresh project, might keep Dad off our backs about this place?"

"That's what I was thinking. And if we play our cards right we might be able to get some cash out of it in the process."

She stopped and looked up as Avaro came into the kitchen. He looked just as suave and assured as he had the previous evening. Even his clothes looked immaculate, not at all creased from a night strewn on the floor of Fernando's room. He smiled warmly.

"Now food, and the best presents I could possibly give you."

The three of them walked into the expansive lobby of Avar Investments, the twins excited after what they had heard at breakfast. Avaro had outlined the proposal over coffee and croissants and then taken them into the City to meet the other party. The proposition was that a close personal friend of his and their partner had a large run-down building in Notting Hill. They were looking for someone to redevelop the property by splitting it into a set of luxury flats. They would agree a budget and a percentage of the profit would go to whoever managed the project through to completion. Having heard about and then seen the twins' great work at the Pimlico house, Avaro assured them that they were just what his friends were looking for.

It sounded like the perfect arrangement to Fernando and Henrietta, who were both keen to hear more details of their next potential goldmine. The man was very busy with work but could spare the time to meet if they went to him.

They were chatting enthusiastically as Avaro went over to the side of the entrance hall where a door proudly displayed its shiny new lock. The bored receptionist ignored them completely as Avaro unlocked the door and ushered them into what was now a rather plain and small office.

"Anthony works downstairs in the old part of the building. Go through, but mind your step."

Avaro used a heavy key to open the rather more substantial door at the back of the office and indicated for the twins to lead the way. A rough stone passage led downwards, it was lit by freshly installed wall lights with a single cable sagging slightly between each of the lamps. Henrietta was in front, her confident footsteps resounding off the bare stone. Her brother was more cautious and twice was given a hurrying nudge from behind. The twins' conversation had ground to a halt, the weighty antiquity of their surroundings quietened them both. It wasn't until they reached the open heavy oak door that either of them thought to question why this friend of Avaro's would be working in a cellar. By then it was too late.

Fernando yelped as the pair of them were pushed forcefully through the doorway into the seven sided room. As he tumbled to the floor he caught sight of his sister on her hands and knees beside him, a look of incomprehension on her face. The room was illuminated by two of the new wall lights, one either side of the opening they had just been thrown through.

"What on earth are you doing?" Henrietta cried.

Avaro closed the door, his silhouette looming over the twins.

"Giving you each your present, as I promised."

The continental lilt in his voice had been replaced with something harder, something older.

He walked to the centre of the room, raised his arms out in front of him and started to murmur, too quietly for the twins to make out what he was saying. Both Fernando and Henrietta picked themselves up and made for the door. The large iron ring wouldn't budge at all, not even swing up and down in its binding. It was as if it had rusted fast.

"Hetty, what do we do?" the panic was evident in Fernando's voice.

"He must have the key, we'll have to fight the bastard for it."

She snarled the last few words and launched herself forwards. She was about two metres from Avaro when she suddenly had great trouble moving. There was something surrounding him that she couldn't get through. It was malleable yet ultimately unyielding, as soon as she pressed in one place another bit of it pushed her back. It was also invisible. She stared at her hands. She could feel them moving as if through thick mud, yet there was nothing there. She stepped back, paused for a moment and tried moving forwards again. She met the same resistance.

She looked at Avaro and loathing burned in her eyes. He smiled back at her as she started beating futilely at the invisible barrier again.

Fernando was back by the door. He slid down until sitting on the floor and whimpered. His sobs became even more desperate as he saw his sister's useless attempts to reach Avaro. Tears ran down his face as he tried and failed to reconcile the impossibility of their situation.

Avaro started to move his hands in front of him, weaving them in patterns as if performing an agitated tai chi exercise. Red light began to appear and a dull crackling noise could be heard as the light started to arc around his forearms like static electricity. It built quickly until his lower arms were covered in jumping ribbons of red light.

He raised his voice to a loud and forceful incantation in a guttural language, the sound a visceral stream of short vicious barks. He pointed his left hand at Henrietta and a flash of energy leaped from his arm and hit her square in the chest. Her body convulsed a couple of inches into the air and fell limp to the stone floor. He aimed his right hand at Fernando and the remainder of the energy shot into him, his head slammed back against the door as he lost consciousness.

Avaro stood bent over with hands on his knees, breathing heavily, the wall lights picking out the perspiration on his face. He spoke through a huge and manic grin, as much to himself as to the bodies in front of him.

"Welcome back my friends, we have so much to do."

Avaro stood close to the glass and gestured out across London. The view from the 33rd floor bar at the top of Centre Point was magnificent. The sun had set and the city was now a sea of tiny lights before him.

"As you can see, a lot has changed since we were last here together. It is much bigger, with so much more energy."

Hetty and Ferren joined him at the window, they both looked out with anticipation on their faces.

"It has a similar feel though," said Hetty.

"But the energy is different, more ambiguous, it's not so clear cut as last time," countered her brother.

"Is that just perception though? A carry over from these bodies? I can feel a whole load of conflicting thoughts and emotions that I'm pretty sure aren't mine."

"That is normal," said Avaro, "it is different when you do not take form directly. You will always be influenced to a degree. That is why I chose your hosts so carefully."

"How did you do that exactly?"

"It is called social networking," Avaro enunciated the words with precision, "people these days live their lives in public, they share every detail openly. In such a society it is quite straightforward to find whatever type of person you choose. You can learn everything about them without even meeting them. They invite you into their lives with the most cursory of examination."

"They are more trusting?" Hetty asked with disdain.

"Naive."

Avaro sat back down in his chair and waited until the others had joined him before he continued.

"It is a different era. The values are less certain, which is good news for us. There is also technology."

He tapped the smartphone that sat next to his glass.

"We still have much work to do, but there is potential enough for each of us in this city. A toast – to London."

"To London!" replied the twins.

They drained their glasses and ordered another bottle of champagne.

Chapter Four

It was nearly a week since Jack had been left to sit on his own at The Northumberland Arms. The incident had played on his mind almost continuously, rarely leaving his thoughts for more than five or ten minutes at a time. Occasionally he had managed to block it out for long enough to do some concentrated work in the lab, but he knew it had become a serious distraction.

He'd got as far as selecting Mandy's number on his phone, but his pride stopped him from actually ringing her. He was feeling hurt, and to be the one to call first would be too much like a kicked dog running expectantly back to its master. By the middle of the week he had become obsessive about checking his phone and email for word from Mandy. It had become an increasingly frequent cycle of anticipation and disappointment, repeated several times an hour.

Why the hell hadn't she got in touch? Had something happened to her? Maybe he should call? No, it was just her being thoughtless. She would call when she missed him. But how long would that be? The cycle of questions went round and round in Jack's head, the subject torturing him further with each pass.

*

By the end of the week, Jack's behaviour started to draw comment. His friends at work knew what had happened to him, telling them helped him lessen some of the neurotic intensity. They'd been sympathetic, but when Jack sat down at his office desk for the ninth time that morning, Sam and a final year post-grad called Mikhail exchanged glances. Sam shrugged and looked down at his hands, Mikhail tackled the issue.

"Jack. What are you doing? That must be twenty times you check your email today, and we have not been to lunch yet. Why not just call her?"

"And say what? If I sound casual she'll think I'm happy to be treated like that. If I try and be angry it'll probably just turn into a row."

"And what is wrong with that? A row can be good, clears the air. And then you make up," Mikhail said with a knowing grin.

"Yeah well, Mandy's a lot better at arguing than I am. Besides, the last time we rowed we didn't speak for ages, and that's already the problem."

"Maybe she wants to break up?" Sam interjected. The other two turned in their chairs to face him.

"Say what?" asked Jack.

Sam blushed and his gaze flicked rapidly between his two friends.

"I was, erm, just meaning that maybe, just a possibility, that she doesn't want to see you anymore. The last time I was dumped, I was just sort of ignored."

Jack looked in disbelief at Mikhail, who shrugged, and then back at Sam.

"Leaving aside the brutality of that suggestion for a minute. You were ignored?"

"Yeah, she just stopped returning calls and emails. Never saw her again."

The three of them sat in silence for a few moments, each contemplating a different angle.

"Anyway," said Mikhail, "maybe he is right Jack. Is not

pleasant, but maybe true. Only way to find out, is to call her."

"Thanks, you too?"

Silence fell again between the three of them. Eventually Jack conceded the point and slouched a little lower in his seat.

"Yeah, maybe, it's not something I'd really wanted to consider."

He sighed.

"OK, I'll find out."

It took Jack nearly ten minutes to construct a polite but neutrally worded enquiry as to Mandy's wellbeing and availability for the weekend. He had a text message reply by the time he got back to the office with a fresh cup of coffee.

```
2moro @ 11am charlies tcr
```

No pleasantries, none of Mandy's customary sparkle. Jack's heart sank until it was nestling uncomfortably just above the hollow pit in his stomach. At least he knew Charlie's though, a fifties' styled American diner on Tottenham Court Road.

"You were right, looks like an invitation to an 'it's not you, it's me' conversation," Jack muttered as he turned his phone over to Mikhail and Sam. They handed it back sympathetically and retreated quietly to their desks.

Although the bright sunshine rendered the neon sign mute, the chrome panelling behind it shone brilliantly on the Saturday morning. Unsuspecting shoppers flinched as the glare reflected into their faces as they passed below.

Jack was already nervous when he pushed open the swing doors and entered the busy diner some minutes before eleven. His heart raced a fraction faster when he saw Mandy sitting quietly at a table in a small booth. She was never early, and seldom on time. Her punctuality was ominous.

He shuffled onto the red leatherette seat opposite her and hid his hands under the table, wary of them shaking. He looked up and forced a smile.

"Hi hon."

Mandy smiled warmly and leaned across the table, she held a kiss on Jack's lips for a couple of seconds. As she sat back down Jack's mind raced. Surely that's not how you greet someone you're about to dump? What was she playing at? Had it all been a misunderstanding? The wave of relief turned rapidly into confusion.

"Morning," Jack managed warily, "so what happened to you last week?"

A blank look crossed Mandy's face.

"What do you mean?"

"Well, we were supposed to have a date on the Tuesday, you were going to meet me at the Northumberland remember?"

"Oh that!" she smiled in recognition, "yeah, sorry. Some clients whose account I work on were in the office, so our bosses took us all out for drinks. Things got a bit boozy, just lost track of time I'm afraid. Good night though, one of them knew some really cool bars."

Jack felt the familiar heat at the back of his neck as his confusion crystallised into humiliation.

"And you didn't think to let me know you were cancelling on me?"

"I'm so sorry pet, I must have forgotten. But hey, you phoned didn't you?"

"After I'd been sitting on my own for nearly an hour!"

"Well call sooner next time."

She was still smiling but Jack couldn't decide if she was being serious. Before he could respond a waitress sporting an apron appeared at their booth. Her features and voice suggested she was more Eastern European than authentic American. She took two orders for coffee and hurried off, grateful not to have to witness the sparring she had intruded upon. Round two kicked off as soon as she stepped away.

"So let me get this straight," Jack began in a measured tone, "we don't see each other for two weeks, mostly because you're busy with work. Which I don't mind, because I respect you needing to build your career. The one evening we do plan to meet, you not only pass me over for people from work, you leave me sitting like a fucking idiot in a pub."

Jack had built up some momentum and ploughed straight on before Mandy could respond.

"A pub that you chose! And then, as if I'm not feeling shit enough already, I don't hear anything from you for more than a week, and only then because I get in touch with you."

"Are you finished?" Mandy asked impassively. Jack's momentum disappeared. He sat mutely.

"Firstly, you know full well I have to make sacrifices for work. If that sometimes means I prioritise it over you then I'm sorry, but that's the way it is right now."

As always seemed to happen, Jack felt the initiative slipping away.

"Secondly, whilst I should have let you know I couldn't make it, and again I'm sorry I forgot, there was nothing to stop you calling me – which you did. Eventually. It wasn't my fault you sat stewing. I have a mobile, honey, use it."

"Lastly, we each have our own lives, but yours is so full of your precious research that I'm amazed we get to see each other at all. Be realistic, it's not like you make that much time for me is it?"

Jack paused for thought whilst their coffee arrived. He knew there was an element of truth in Mandy's view of things, but no more than an element surely? He was almost certain she was the one showing a lack of respect for their relationship, he just couldn't find the words to say it.

Mandy took Jack's prolonged silence for acceptance, and brightened considerably.

"Come on pet, you know that arguing doesn't suit us. When we've finished our coffee why don't you come back to mine and I'll remind you why you love me so much."

The look she gave Jack was a practiced blend of innocence and desire. Despite the misgivings he had about the way he thought he'd been treated, he knew he couldn't refuse. He wanted her so badly.

Ten minutes later they headed back to her flat for what would turn into an entire afternoon in bed. The physical side of their relationship had always been superb, and on that occasion they made the most of it, putting any other differences aside so they could enjoy each other's bodies.

By the time Jack left in the early evening, he was both exhausted and refreshed. Mikhail had been right. He was acutely aware however, that since leaving the diner they hadn't said another word about their relationship, and the avoidance had left Jack feeling uneasy. He knew things weren't right, no matter how good the sex was, and that fact continued to play on his mind.

It was late on Sunday and Jack was still in the lab. In the wake of Saturday's reunion with Mandy he'd had some good ideas about how to alter the experiment, and was pressing on into the night to get the new configuration up and running. The lab work also gave him ample time for reflection, there not being much else for him to do during the hour long automated runs.

He thought back over their year together and pondered how much the relationship had changed. Strangely he'd felt closer to her at the beginning. She started off doing simple things like calling by the lab to say hello or being the one to get in touch after a few days apart. Recently though, he'd felt like he was the one doing all the running, the one making the effort.

He'd interpreted the change in Mandy's behaviour as a lack of fondness on her part, but maybe it was the opposite. Maybe it wasn't her taking him for granted, maybe she just felt more comfortable and assured about the strength of the bond between them. She was trusting their feelings for each other.

Although it may have bloody well felt like it, Jack wondered whether he hadn't been stood up deliberately after all. She'd been under pressure from work, had to go out drinking, lost track of time, things slipped her mind. Plausible? If so, it raised her question of why hadn't he called her sooner? Why had he sat there torturing himself, feeding the part of his psyche that had always doubted Mandy's interest in him?

As for him being the one not making time for them, she'd never complained before about the evenings and weekends he spent in the lab. But maybe that was the point; she had never complained. She'd just been quietly supportive of his dedication to his work, not getting stroppy and insecure that he didn't want to spend time with her.

He was brought out of his reflective meanderings by the alarm sounding the end of a measurement cycle. He quickly set the analytic package in motion to convert the multitude of data points into something that could be displayed and interpreted visually. Despite the power of the dedicated work station it still took a few minutes so he went to the ground floor vending machine for a drink. He was about to press the button for his usual Coke, but on a whim chose a bottle of water instead. Drinking half of it straight down he headed back to the lab to see what the new configuration had delivered.

He brought the data up on screen, and started sorting through the three dimensional plots of the flow in the vortex chamber. In effect, the rotating ring created something not dissimilar to a mini tornado. As the flow speed was increased the vortex would become unsteady, and at a critical point it'd break down into disordered flow. The Hof-del Pino instability that Jack was searching for lay right at the point of collapse. The PIV system had been mapping the flow in that region over repeated occurrences during its hour run.

What presented itself to Jack on screen was a series of animated slices through the flow, each one showing what happened in a slightly different plane as the breakdown occurred. When viewed together they gave a quick and dirty way of seeing what was taking place in the flow. Jack filled the screen with sixteen consecutive slices from the centre of the vortex, and set the animations to run on a synchronised continuous loop. He hadn't switched the main lights on in the lab, and as he leant forwards the glare from the screen absorbed his field of vision.

He stared, hoping to see direct signs of the particular instability he had been searching for.

And he stared.

After a length of time Jack could not have put an estimate to, a dull awareness crept up on him that he couldn't take his eyes from the screen. Not because anything was stopping him, but rather he simply wasn't staring at the screen anymore. He was looking directly at the traces themselves as if sitting right inside the experiment. The sensation confused Jack, not least because it wasn't logically consistent. The experiment didn't have discrete lines in it, they were an artificial construct generated by the PIV system to represent what was happening in the flow. The experimental chamber just had colourless liquid and glass beads so small they required a laser to pick them up. The lines had also changed from the polychromatic spread of the animations to a narrow range of bright purple hues.

Despite the inconsistencies, Jack knew he was inside the flow itself, and he could see the lines right in front of him. He risked a glance to the side. He saw the long flowing streaks there as well. He was definitely in the experiment, or in some weird abstraction of it.

At the back of his mind there was something trying to make itself heard, a forgotten fact desperate to be remembered. Jack couldn't focus on what it was, he was too intrigued by the lines he saw in front of him.

They swirled all around, and in places started to waver rhythmically before quickly going back to their smooth paths. The onset of the instability was close, he could feel it. The ripples were not something the maths had predicted but he instinctively knew they were the key to the problem. Jack leaned forward to get a closer look at one of the ripples and suddenly found himself standing on one of the flow lines. It was moving quickly and started to drag him along its course. He tried to resist its motion and felt himself having to run to stay still. He ran faster and faster until he could feel the flow outrace him. It started to pull him down. He urged the muscles burning in his legs for more speed but a ripple formed under his feet and tripped him up.

The flow caught him full in the chest and he travelled with it, spiralling deeper and deeper down the core of the vortex. He was spinning fast, so fast that the lines around him blurred into a cocoon of brilliant purple light.

Then he was back at his desk. He was aware of the walls around him again, the familiar hum of the computer, the precise green light of the lasers and the glow of the monitor.

Jack stood up carefully, his hands clasped to the desk for support. He was OK, a little light headed perhaps. He knew he'd not been asleep, so what the hell had just happened? He glanced suspiciously around his lab, as if expecting to find the answer hiding behind one of the many pieces of equipment. Obeying a sudden urge to be anywhere but where he was standing, he walked straight out the lab, got his coat and bag, and went home. His experiment was left ticking over in standby mode, the animations looping again and again and again.

That Sunday night Jack slept fitfully for a long time, waking later than usual and not at all rested. His dreams had been filled with strange sensations and images. He was thankful he didn't remember much about them, just the lingering feeling of confusion.

When he got into work, his lab seemed more familiar and nothing like as uncomfortable as when he'd left. Despite the lack of daylight, just knowing the sun shone outside reassured him.

He was going about his work quite happily, resetting the experiment for another run, when mid-morning an image flashed across his eyes. It was so brief that he couldn't resolve what it was, the indistinct memory faded rapidly. It was akin to when he'd glanced at the sun by mistake as a child, a fantastically bright image that quickly disappeared as the eyes recovered themselves. All he could make out was a few wavy lines clustered around an amorphous shape. He rubbed his eyes hard with the palms of his hands and got on with his work.

Late in the afternoon he experienced another image. The same bright flash, the same rapid dissipation, though he sensed the picture itself was different this time. Lines and shapes in a new formation. This time he went for a quick walk round the UCL campus, maybe he had been spending too much time cooped up in his laboratory.

The visions kept coming over the next few days, and although their frequency increased Jack couldn't find any pattern to their occurrence. Having searched the Internet and come up with a wide variety of possible causes, many of them rather sinister, he decided to attend the Friday drop-in session at the university's student medical centre.

He sat down in the general practitioner's shabby consulting room, and looked at the late middle-aged Doctor Shepperton. He was typing using a solitary finger, each key being attacked precisely. He didn't look up as he addressed his patient.

"What can we do for you today," he paused briefly whilst he found Jack's name on the screen before going back to the keyboard, "Mr Eastwood?"

Jack told him straightforwardly about the initial hallucination and the subsequent flashes of images. He had never had a problem talking to physicians, he reasoned the more information he gave them, the better they could do their job.

"So what are you studying?" the doctor asked routinely, he still hadn't looked up.

"I'm a grad-student at the Q-Institute, mathematical and

experimental physics. It's mostly lab work at the moment."

"So you're working long hours?"

"I guess so."

"And how much exercise do you get?"

"I cycle to work quite often, but not much else. I used to do more but finding the time is difficult."

The doctor finally looked up.

"It's stress. Work fewer hours and get more exercise. You'll be fine Mr Eastwood."

He smiled in what he thought was a paternal manner, he was entirely unaware that most of his patients found it condescending, Jack included.

"OK. Thanks. And if the visions persist?"

The doctor was already looking down at his keyboard.

"They won't. But if they do, just come back and see me."

Jack left the surgery only marginally reassured.

In deference to the advice he'd been given, Jack took a Saturday off for once and went to Regent's Park. He hadn't used his rollerblades in over a year and although initially unsteady on his feat, the confidence soon came back. His choppy stride wasn't elegant but it got him up to speed quickly. He glided in long shallow arcs, getting used to the inside and outside edge of each skate during the crossovers and outside turns.

He was disappointed that far from reducing in frequency, by the end of the day the visions were coming less than an hour apart. Jack's increasing concern for their cause was tempered only by the familiarity he now felt with them, though their lack of novelty brought only a tiny degree of comfort.

He considered backing out of his plans for the evening with Mandy, but mindful of her comment about him being the one who wasn't making time for them he dutifully attended. The Bloomsbury Lanes, a small bowling alley just off Tavistock Square, was one of his favourite haunts. Its antiquated overhead return tracks and nostalgic decor gave it a singular charm. He also quite liked bowling, there being something inherently satisfying about sliding down onto one knee as the ball was launched. He wasn't very good but he generally got better after a beer or two.

After shoeing up, he got himself a bottle of Budweiser and sat down on the seat between Mandy and her friend Linda. There were six of them in total – Mandy never had trouble rallying her troops. She gave Jack a quick peck on the cheek and then concentrated on the game. It amused Jack the way she took so much care in selecting a ball, and then waited patiently to use it every time. It seemed out of character with her carefree attitude to almost everything else.

Jack didn't dislike her friends, but he didn't feel great affinity for them either. Linda and Pete were colleagues at the advertising firm Mandy worked for and spent most of the evening talking shop with her. Their partners Steve and Gail had broader conversational tastes but somehow Jack couldn't really warm to them. Nice people, he just didn't feel like he had much in common with them.

Jack sat down cheerfully after hitting a 4–10 split and drained the last of his second beer. He looked up at Mandy getting ready to take her go and felt conflicted. What he saw was a beautiful, curvaceous woman that he thought he loved. Thought? Surely he should know! What was it holding him back? A tight knot of self doubt had stopped him from trusting her words when she'd said she loved him. He could feel his insecurities gnawing from the inside out. How could he let them go and trust in his feelings for her, and in hers for him?

She caught him staring at her, smiled and leaned down to him as she came back from her second ball.

"Hey pet, you coming back to mine after this?"

"Erm, maybe. Not sure, bit of a headache."

She squeezed past the scoring table to straddle him playfully, arms wrapped around his neck for support.

"I'll make it worth your while," she breathed into his ear.

She leaned back so that their faces met and smiled coyly at him.

He returned the gesture, desperately wanting to believe the look of sincerity on her face.

"OK, back to yours it is. I'll get some more drinks in."

Later that night Jack lay awake in Mandy's bed, physically satisfied but still confused and uncertain. Another instantaneous image flashed across his mind. He shut his eyes so tightly that kaleidoscopic patterns quickly blotted out the afterglow. Once his vision had adjusted back to the dark, he glanced across at Mandy's peaceful sleeping form. Still nothing. He turned events of the past few weeks over in his mind. The experiment. The hallucination. Mandy. The images. Nothing resolved itself, each train of thought jumping to the next before he was able to organise it. He eventually fell asleep just as the sun began to rise.

Jack worked the Sunday and managed virtually no sleep that night, the images a constant interruption. By Monday morning he was exhausted and booked an appointment at the medical centre for the following day. To cheer himself up he went for lunch at his favourite noodle bar, The Ever Filling Bowl on New Oxford Street. Its all-you-can-eat midday offer was popular with many of the post-grads. Mikhail and Sam both tagged along.

The big Russian made Sam budge over as he sat down, steam rising from the pile of udon noodles with chicken that he had selected.

"So, you are still having these images?"

Jack put his chopsticks down and wiped a dribble of broth from his chin.

"Yep. They're getting worse, three or four an hour. I don't know what ... sorry, there goes another one."

"Do they hurt?" asked Sam.

"No, but they break my concentration, and I'm finding it

impossible to sleep through them now."

"Wow, that sucks."

"Too right. I spend half my time waiting for the next one to occur, a bit like a sneeze you know is about to happen."

"Drink more. Preferably vodka," Mikhail offered between mouthfuls. Jack chuckled.

"I may just do that, alcohol does seem to help a bit ... bugger. That was another."

The other two stared at him in concern.

"And another. I've never had them that close ..."

Jack stopped, his mouth slightly open, his eyes staring down at the table.

"Misha, erm, what's going on?" Sam's voice quivered.

Mikhail passed a hand back and forth in front of Jack's face. No effect, not a flicker. Sam started to reach over the table towards Jack's shoulder, but the Russian stopped him.

"Wait. Do not touch. I have a brother who walks in sleep. If this is similar then better to leave him until he ..."

"Oh boy," said Jack.

Sam visibly jumped in his seat.

"That was weird. I've just seen Misha's lunch, well, get up and dance." The other two looked perplexed.

"No, seriously. I was looking at your noodles and all of a sudden I thought I recognised something."

"I do have udon with chicken every time we come here," interjected Mikhail.

"Funny. No, I mean a pattern, something about the way they were arranged. As soon as I saw it, the strands starting rising off your plate and swaying. Like the belly dancer at that north African place we went to last month."

"OK, now you take the piss."

"Well that's what I saw. This is getting ridiculous."

"And scary," added Sam.

"I think we follow my plan," said Mikhail.

"What plan?"

"You see a doctor tomorrow, correct? OK. So we start drinking now. By the end of today you will be out like light switch, get some sleep at least. Doctor sends you for tests and you are not our responsibility anymore."

The Russian grinned at his logic and Sam nodded in agreement. Jack felt a surge of affection for his two friends.

"Thanks guys, I appreciate it."

Mikhail leaned back and ordered three beers from the passing waiter. They arrived ice cold, condensation streaking down their sides.

"Na zdarovye!"

Jack's second trip to the medical centre was much more successful in his view. The younger female medic he saw had quizzed him extensively, her concern increased by the explanation of his obvious hangover. Anytime you started drinking to solve a problem, you knew it was a big problem to solve she had said.

Jack was quite impressed when she twice took books off her shelves to look up points she wasn't certain of. He'd always been suspicious of doctors who never referred to anything, relying solely on what knowledge they could store in their head. He dealt with systems vastly less complicated than the human body, and he was by most accounts pretty smart, yet he wouldn't dream of trying to do everything from memory alone. He also knew a bit about the psychology of 'perception of probability'. He was convinced that some doctors must suffer terribly from being influenced by the particular mix of cases they had seen previously. A trained physician using a diagnostic database made more sense to Jack than a trained physician alone.

He had left with the promise of a referral to a neurologist for the investigation of 'possible migrainous phenomena' and a prescription for some pills that would lower his level of brain activity. The benzodiazepines would 'zonk him out' the doctor had said, Jack presumed this was a non-medical term, but it would certainly help him sleep.

He then felt he had a rather awkward choice to make. Carry on battling the images and visions for as long as it took to complete this phase of his research, and he knew that the breakthrough he had worked so hard for was close at hand. Or, take the pills and get some much needed rest, but in all probability put his research on hold. Having checked the listed side-effects on the Internet he had no doubt the medication would make it impossible for him to concentrate. There were probably health and safety rules against using lasers whilst under the influence anyway.

He put off making a decision by going to the pub for the evening. After five pints he managed a night of intermittent snatches of poor sleep, but sleep nonetheless.

By Wednesday afternoon, Jack knew that the crunch time had come. The images had appeared about every ten minutes during the morning and the afterglows were lasting longer, as if they'd started to burn themselves into his retina. He picked up the prescription, bought a bottle of water and retreated to Russell Square Gardens to contemplate what he was about to do.

Since moving to London, it had become Jack's favourite place to go when he'd serious thinking to do. He had cracked the toughest parts of the mathematical portion of his research whilst sitting on one of the many benches that offered a seat to those wishing to rest or contemplate.

The geometry of the paths appealed to Jack's scientific mind, a square perimeter with intersecting diagonals, overlaid by a tear drop that looped around the centre, reaching as far as one of the boundaries at its tail. Beautifully tended flower beds punctuated the grassy areas, and a staggered ring of huge London plane trees hopped either side of the main loop of path, offering shade on hot days. In the centre was a fountain that intrigued Jack every time he saw it. Set level to the ground, it was all but invisible when off. Suddenly the barrage of jets would erupt, the central one reaching over twelve feet high, the peripheral ones only four or two, depending on their place in the pattern. The water drained quickly into a discrete grill.

Jack sat down on one of the benches near the fountain and took several deep breaths to try and clear his mind. He concentrated on blocking out the images. He couldn't tell if it actually made any difference to their frequency, but the very act of trying to resist made him feel better, a little more in control.

Not to take the pills or to take the pills, that was the question.

A bright flash seared across his vision.

He winced, not at the pain, the images didn't hurt, but rather at the rude interruption to his thoughts. He knew that he probably should take the pills. He desperately needed proper sleep, his eyeballs were practically crawling in their sockets. He also needed a break from the relentlessness of the images. They were becoming a part of him, changing who he was. What would he become if he let them continue? He could take some time out, regroup, let the doctors find out what the problem was, get it cured, and then come back stronger. His work would still be there.

Another image momentarily blinded him.

Though actually it might not be. If he stopped his work, Bayliss and McKie might go ahead and publish what the three of them already had. The experiment he'd devoted two years to would likely be lost in the maelstrom of other papers that would follow. Detractors and supporters would look for proof one way or the other, his efforts would by then be far behind the bow wave of opinion. He could be passing up a career-defining opportunity if he backed down now.

Searing purple lines streaked across his retinas.

He didn't know what to do, so he concentrated on relaxing, breathing in the warm spring air and enjoying the peacefulness of the gardens. He watched a young Asian family playing Frisbee, the tiny son laughing with his slightly larger sister as they tumbled to the ground, both with their hands on the plastic disc their father had thrown to them.

Bright swirling patterns flickered and faded.

He watched a noble looking Caribbean man cheerfully emptying the overflowing bins, his orange hi-vis waistcoat flapping open in the gentle breeze. He bent down with the grace of a dancer to pick up surplus litter from the floor.

An image so bright it made him sway in his seat.

A young couple, probably UCL students, lying entwined on the grass. The girl wore a stretchy blue and white striped dress that accentuated her sculpted curves as she wriggled playfully atop her bearded boyfriend. Jack decided they looked French and chuckled wryly as he remembered back to the previous summer when he and Mandy had lain not far away, blissfully enjoying the newness of their intimacy.

His chuckling ceased instantly as another image crashed into his mind.

Close by, a pair of pigeons were patrolling the grass, seeking small remnants of discarded food. Marching in lock-step, they looked just like any other devoted couple.

Flash.

The images came faster and faster, the next appeared only moments after its predecessor had faded.

Bam.

Jack desperately looked around for help, his hand reaching to the packet of pills lurking inside his jacket.

Scream.

As his hand closed on the medication, he caught sight of a young man who was strolling past wearing a Star Wars T-shirt. Jack's gaze had moved on when all of a sudden he did a double take, realising there was something odd about the T-shirt. As he looked again the man seemed to slow, as did everything else in the gardens. A Frisbee hung completely static in the air, the water of the fountain stood frozen mid cascade, looking for all the world like an ancient stalagmite.

"Over here my boy."

Jack looked back to the man, he was motionless. Then he saw the T-shirt, the two figures had stepped off the fabric and stood fully three-dimensional, hovering in space just yards from Jack.

"That's right," said Obi-Wan, a gentle smile on the old man's face, "we've been waiting for you."

"Yes, waiting have we been," cackled the little green figure of Yoda.

The tiredness drained away and Jack felt alert and alive.

"Whoah! Now if I'm going to hallucinate, this is more like it."

"Are you certain that's what we are Jack? Hallucinations?"

"Well what else could you be? You're fictional characters, played by Alec Guinness and Frank Oz, and yet you're standing here talking to me. Moments ago you were on that guy's T-shirt. Sounds pretty much like a hallucination to me."

"Well, when you put it like that, it does sound a little odd, but then these are strange times for you Jack, important times."

"No kidding. Look, give it to me straight. Am I dying right now? Did I think you up to make it all easier?"

"Yes, understand he does," Yoda hobbled excitedly on the spot.

"And no," said Obi-Wan, looking disapprovingly down at his companion.

"No Jack, you are not dying in the sense that you mean. But you do have a choice to make, and whatever you choose a part of you will die as a result."

"So is that good or bad then?"

"Neither it is, there is no good or bad," chirped Yoda.

"OK guys, let me take this from the beginning. You're products of my imagination, right?"

"Correct," admitted Obi-Wan.

"And I'm not dying in the 'about to have a massive brain haemorrhage' sense?"

"No, you are not."

"OK, that sounds better. So why did I ... why am I imagining you two?"

"Why do you think?"

"Because I needed guidance and you happened to be passing?" Jack asked tentatively.

"That sounds a reasonable explanation, why not go with that."

"So what's your advice then?"

"To an answer rushes he does, yet simple the truth is not."

"Look, if this is my hallucination, would you mind Master Yoda if Obi-Wan does the talking? I'm not in the mood for riddles and to be honest, I've never found your syntax particularly convincing."

"Hmph! Never so insulted have I been. Help you, I will not," he crossed his arms in disgust and stared off to the side.

"Anyway, Obi-Wan, what are you here to tell me?"

"Only what you already know Jack."

"Oh please, don't you start too."

"What did you expect? If we are constructs of your imagination, then we can only say things that come from within yourself."

"Point taken. So what is it that I've missed? What is it that I need a psychotic episode in order to understand?"

"What is your greatest concern?"

"Right now? That when I snap out of this I'm only moments away from a fatal seizure."

"I have already said you aren't about to die."

"Yes, but as you also pointed out, you can't have knowledge beyond what I already know, so you reassuring me is likely just wishful thinking on my part."

"Hmm, I hadn't thought of that," admitted Obi-Wan, "still, what is the cause of your concern of imminent death?"

"Images, visions, you being here. Sorry, but it's true."

"And what have you been trying to do about these occurrences?"

"I went to see a doctor."

"And what else?"

"I've tried to block them out. By getting drunk or just sort of concentrating."

"And what has happened to them?"

"They've got more frequent."

"So what else might you try doing?"

Jack paused. All of a sudden it seemed so obvious, so natural. "Oh, I see. I hadn't thought of that."

"Evidently," sniped Yoda, "great mind, much potential you have, yet stupid you are."

Jack smiled at the aged character, and despite his gruffness, a thin smirk played at the edges of Yoda's mouth.

"Thank you Obi-Wan, and you too Master Yoda."

"We will always be with you Jack."

As they retreated back into the two dimensions of the T-shirt, Jack could see them discussing something, but he couldn't make out the words.

He was suddenly aware of the world around him in motion again. The young man walked on, the Frisbee landed and the melted fountain tumbled back to the ground.

He could feel the next image about to arrive. He breathed out to relax, cleared his mind to make space for its appearance and welcomed it. A brief flash and as it faded he clung to it desperately. The image persisted longer than before, time enough for him to register its complex form. He felt the next approach and did his best to usher it in. A different pattern scorched across his vision, one that lasted longer still and was joined by the next before it had faded. The staccato of the flashes increased at an exponential rate, each superimposing itself on the previous. Faster and faster they came, until they were so rapid Jack saw every one of them instantaneously. All the patterns he had seen, all the patterns that existed, were held in his mind at the same time. Jack had a profound sensation of his consciousness expanding in every direction, encompassing the infinite. There were no boundaries to his being. He was the universe.

*

Then he awoke.

It was getting dark, the gardens were almost empty, just a few stragglers picking themselves up off the grass to head off for the evening. Jack looked down.

A small wiry dog of indeterminable breeding was looking up at him as it urinated on his left trouser leg. He smiled at it. He understood the astonishing intricacy of the way the warm liquid flew through the air, and as it spattered the fabric of his jeans. He appreciated the myriad of chemical reactions and biological constructions that formed the little animal, the beauty of the complexity was breathtaking. The dog returned his stare until it had finished and then trotted away.

Jack looked at his own hands and marvelled at the feat of entropy he witnessed before him. So much order.

Everywhere he looked he could sense the fundamental structure of what he saw, he felt in tune with the physical laws that governed all around him. He knew his eyes had been opened to a new reality, a truer reality. He sat there in serene contemplation, intoxicated by the sense of freedom and majesty that coursed through him.

Chapter Five

Avaro juggled pans off and onto the Fisher and Paykel hob, careful to keep the delicately flavoured sauces from becoming burned.

"No, we need to keep adding new content at least every other day, it is crucial the momentum is maintained."

His voice was raised so as to overcome the various bubbling and sizzling noises coming from the food. Every time he leaned over the cooker to inspect progress, the in-ear wireless headset threatened to fall and become one of the ingredients. The indicator light on his smartphone blinked smugly from the safety of the dresser by the door.

"Yes, that is true, but it is those who are already hooked who are critical to recruiting new users, we must keep their interest at a maximum. Besides, the new areas will be necessary to soak up the increase in users."

He splashed a liberal dose of Chianti into a shallow copper pan and a billow of rich vapour headed for the ceiling.

"Say that again?"

A splash of balsamic vinegar joined the wine.

"Yes, the prize money is in the account. Do not worry about that. And have the lead programmer re-check the control parameters. We want at least two big winners in the next week to generate publicity."

Finely chopped fruits were added to the pan.

"Good. So get back to me with their details as soon as you know them."

Avaro removed the headset and turned back to his cooking. The last three of the dishes were near to completion, the other six lay ready on the table or ticking over in the oven.

With a theatrical flourish the sauces were poured from height onto their meats and the final plates brought to table. He stepped back for a moment to admire his handiwork, poured himself a large glass of vintage Barolo from the decanter, and set about demolishing the feast he had prepared.

Hetty drained her glass and smiled enticingly at the man on the other side of the table. John Abrahms was thirty-eight years old, divorced and he lapped up the attention of the younger woman. In addition to the prospect of getting her into bed, he was also intrigued by her suggestions. She was clearly much more than just a pretty face. Someone attractive and good on policy? He would have to work out a way of keeping this one close to hand.

"Another?"

"Are you trying to get me drunk?" Hetty asked coyly.

"And if I am ..." Abrahms left the suggestion hanging.

"And if you are, you're out of luck tonight. I need to get going. Next time maybe."

Hetty tilted her head to the side and ran a hand through her hair. She took the opportunity to glance around and check once again they weren't being observed.

Gordo's was an understated wine bar set below street level, a regular haunt of politicians and Whitehall bureaucrats. Near to St James's Park Tube station it was close enough to Westminster to be convenient, but far enough removed to offer a degree of privacy for its clientele. Abrahms was a government special advisor, less high profile than the minister he worked with but it still paid to be discreet. He was also significantly more influential than his elected counterpart.

"So there will be a next time?" he asked.

"I would think so, assuming you like what you've heard."

"Absolutely, and what I've seen."

Hetty knew then that she had him. It had been tricky work, to make the manipulation subtle enough so as not to change his character blatantly, yet sufficiently deep that in due course he would feel compelled to act. She had used sexual tension to help break in initially, and the anticipation would also keep driving his motivation forwards. She was pleased she hadn't lost her touch.

Abrahms would go home convinced the girl's insights into the current discrimination legislation were correct, and that radical reform was necessary. A programme of changes that heavily favoured minority ethnic groups would be a tactical masterstroke for his minister and position the party perfectly for the election the following year.

Hetty got up, kissed him on the cheek and put her jacket on.

"I'll call you," she promised, and promptly hurried off up the stairs leaving Abrahms well and truly hooked.

Hetty hailed a taxi and jumped into the back of the black cab. As she leaned forward to give the Pimlico address, she spotted a small Union Flag sticker on the dashboard and decided to test the water.

"So what do you think of this new idea of the Government's then? It must make things harder for you guys surely."

"What's that then miss?"

"This proposal to give preference to Asians and the like when employers recruit. Companies will have to meet quotas for non-white British workers."

"Haven't heard about that, but it doesn't bloody surprise me," he practically spat the words out.

"I mean, I'm not racist or anything, but if politicians spent less time worrying about keeping all the immigrants happy then maybe they'd realise what the British majority are going through."

Hetty leaned back in her seat and smiled as the cabby carried on venting. She ignored the words and breathed in the passion of the invective, its frustration and grievance. The aggression refreshed her and she felt some of the fatigue lift from her tricky evening at Gordo's. It took only a few minutes for the taxi to reach Alderney Street, but by that time she was quite upbeat. She tipped the cabby well and trotted inside.

In the kitchen she found Avaro tucking into the first of his dessert courses, empty plates and bowls indicating the enormous amount already consumed. Delighted to find food already laid out, Hetty sat down and pulled a dish of baked apples over to her side of the table.

"Do not even contemplate it," said Avaro.

Hetty paused, a large serving spoon held midair, ready to be deployed.

"Are you serious?"

"Never more so," his face was implacable.

Hetty put the spoon down as Avaro pulled the dish back over to him. As their eyes met she saw the steely look and thought better of pushing the matter.

"Suit yourself, but we're going out tonight then. I'm starving and have cause for celebration."

"I take it your chance meeting went well then?" Avaro looked up with interest.

"Yes it did actually. That brother of mine's a useless shit most of the time but it wasn't a bad idea of his. Speaking of which ..." she cocked an ear at the sound of the front door closing. A moment later Ferren dragged himself into the kitchen and sat down heavily in one of the empty chairs.

"Evening Het, Av."

He leaned forward to smell the last remaining untouched dish.

"Don't go there, the old man isn't in a sharing mood," Hetty warned.

"Pity, would have made up for the rubbish time I've had.

Eleven more candidates I saw today, every one of them a fantasist, those chat rooms are full of them."

"Stick with it, it's just a numbers game. You'll find the right one eventually," Hetty encouraged. Ferren was slightly taken aback, it wasn't normal for his sister to be supportive.

"What's with you?"

"Ah well, that idea you had about using Abrahms looks like it might work. I've got him just where I want him."

"Great," Ferren said with sarcasm, "I'm so pleased for you."

"Why you pissy little ..."

"Enough!" Avaro spoke through the final mouthful of his dinner. He swallowed and put his fork down.

"Go and get changed, both of you, we are going out. You can eat and we all can drink."

The twins glared at each other as they rose sulkily from the table and headed off upstairs. Avaro watched them go and then looked back at the empty plates.

He smiled.

The three of them turned off Oxford Street and started to walk up a cobbled side road. Their destination was an exclusive venue that Hetty had been to a few times called 'Stiletto'. It was more a bar than a nightclub, though there was an intimate dance floor upstairs.

Ferren had to sidestep a vagrant sitting in one of the doorways whose legs protruded onto the narrow pavement. He quickened his step briefly, but Avaro put a hand gently on his arm and stopped. He turned round and walked back to the filthy tramp, his rough beard matted and rancid. Avaro produced a wallet and slipped a twenty pound note into the hands of the unfortunate wretch on the floor. The man stared back up and mumbled his gratitude.

Both Ferren and Hetty looked at their companion in disbelief. He returned their unspoken enquiry with a gentle smile, and winked at Ferren as he walked back past them and on towards the giant bronze doors of the bar. The twins followed him in, baffled by what they'd just seen.

The ground floor was punctuated by unevenly spaced very thin columns. Square in section they tapered gently before flaring to form arches with each other as they reached the ceiling. The lack of regularity in their placement made it hard for a patron to judge perspective as they looked through to the mirrored wall at the back, the bar taking up the whole of the right hand side. What looked like genuine flaming sconces were high enough up the walls so as to be out of reach and were the only source of illumination. Coupled with the blood red walls and furniture it made for a very dark room with a striking and powerful ambience, either seductive or intimidating depending on the nature of the guest in question.

The three of them took a table towards the middle, the twins being quick to request food as soon as the sparsely dressed waitress attended them. They raised eyebrows when Avaro added another couple of dishes to the order, but thought better of questioning it.

It took a few rounds of drinks for them all to unwind, and after they'd finished off the last of the food Avaro ordered the house speciality from a passing waitress, a vodka tower. Whilst waiting for it to arrive, Ferren enquired with genuine interest as to how one of Avaro's projects had been going.

"Streets? Or rather Streets of Gold which is what I decided upon in the end. It is not yet live for all smartphone platforms, but those it has been released for have seen excellent take-up, much better than even I had hoped for."

"What does it do?"

"In essence it is not dissimilar to the other massive multi-player online games available. Each player, or user as my developers call them, has a unique character that travels around a three-dimensional virtual London. It started with just the City, but we have already expanded coverage to much of central London. There is a currency called 'gold' that the character has to acquire in order for them to unlock new areas to explore.

They can get it in a variety of ways, but principally by stealing it from other characters by force or by guile. They also earn experience with which they increase their character's level and become stronger and more powerful."

"So it's just a computer game?"

"Well yes and no," Avaro looked a little perturbed.

"It does have many standard features that help to get and keep humans addicted. The stratified progression system to work their way up and the acquisition of an arbitrary currency being two examples. However, there are some differences too."

Avaro paused to drain the last of his drink before continuing. "Firstly, if the player is actually in the physical vicinity of where the character is within the game, then they gain access to unique abilities."

"How does the game know where they are?"

"The GPS on the phone, or the IP address or repeater it is routing through. This encourages those actually in the capital to play, and also means it is likely that two people coming into conflict online may well actually be within sight of each other."

"Oh, I see."

"Exactly. Secondly, there are regular monetary prizes dropped into the game which cause frenzies as players rush to get their hands on them. The character then has to carry the money to safety before it can be claimed thus making them a target for everyone else."

"Lastly, I personally have helped with the design of the game. There are certain images, phrases and sounds used that promote particular thought patterns, such as selfishness, ruthlessness, addiction and the burning desire to accumulate more 'wealth'. In the past one could influence a whole room in such a way, or maybe a gathered mob. Thanks to technology though, an entire city is just the beginning of what is possible."

Avaro grinned confidently at the twins.

"Anyway, enough of all this. Here comes our drink."

What was brought to the table was an ice sculpture fully two feet high. It was in the form of a tall round tower, with a hollow at its top in which lay a reservoir of very high grade Swedish vodka. Through the ice could be seen a narrow winding channel that exited about half way down the side of the sculpture. A small chrome tap was plugged into the tower to control the flow. It took a pair of waiters to lift it from the trolley and put it safely on a rotating mount on the table.

"Me first."

Avaro put his mouth directly below the silver tap and turned it on full. It was four seconds before he came up for air, his eyes wide and nostrils flared.

"You two have got to try that!"

They left the bar, all three of them slightly unsteady on their feet as arm-in-arm they set off down the road. Ferren had started to sound melancholy.

"It's alright for you guys, but I'm going nowhere. I'm never going to find the right candidate. I've searched everywhere, still not a hint."

"Then stop trying so hard," replied Avaro, "and I am sure things will work out." He winked conspiratorially at Hetty, who tried to wink back but managed an unsightly leer instead.

"Hello, what's this?" said Ferren as he brought them up short. They recognised the homeless man lying on the floor, a pair of paramedics crouched over his form. Drunk as they were, they could tell he was dead, the ambulance crew were now just tidying up the body. As they walked on past they saw two empty bottles of cheap whisky lying nearby.

"How do you do it?" asked Ferren.

"Experience," said Avaro, "I told you, people have not changed. Not really."

Hetty stepped into the road to hail a cab, and was pulled back by the older of her companions.

"No, we take the Underground tonight, you will see."

The three of them walked on to Oxford Circus and descended into the Tube to wait for a Victoria line train. As one arrived and the doors opened, Avaro graciously stepped aside to make room for a young lady who was clearly pregnant. As they followed her onto the busy train, Avaro whispered to the twins.

"You may need to concentrate now."

He briefly passed a hand in front of their faces and their eyes widened as they sobered up considerably, the effects of a small fortune in high grade alcohol disappearing in an instant.

"What do you see Ferren, what can you feel?" he asked quietly.

Ferren looked about him cautiously, and his eyes settled on a plain looking middle-aged man standing a few metres down the carriage. The man glared at a young woman in a business suit who was sitting in the priority seat nearest the door, right next to where the pregnant woman stood.

"Why doesn't he say something?" whispered Ferren.

"It is not in his nature. Take a closer look."

Ferren let his eye lids droop as he reached out to the man. Seconds later they flew wide open.

"Bloody hell!"

He managed to keep his voice quiet but he was visibly excited.

"I hope I've got enough time for this."

He closed his eyes and concentrated, holding onto a handrail to steady himself as the carriage ground to a halt. No-one got off at the stop and only one squeezed on. Ferren spoke through gritted teeth.

"Het, can you help me please?"

She took hold of his hand, narrowed her eyes and concentrated on supplying energy through to him. Sweat ran down his brow, the effort compounded by the warmth of the train. His face twitched several times, and then he opened his eyes to glance across at the man. He was quiet and still, but the emotion continued to radiate from him like a furnace. Ferren turned excitedly to Hetty and Avaro.

"I think I've done it. Let's follow."

The doors opened at Victoria and the woman in the suit got off, followed by the seething man, and then the three observers. They hung back a little but Avaro cloaked them just in case, no-one would notice them. They followed the man along the platform as he kept pace behind his prey, up the escalators to the ticket hall, and on into the rail terminal. She headed towards a stopping train bound for Sutton. The man looked up at the departure board and then bought a ticket from a machine using a ten pound note. He used a circuitous route to avoid the multitude of CCTV cameras and calmly boarded the same train as his target.

"Yes!" exclaimed Ferren in delight. Avaro had started to chuckle, quietly at first and then louder until it was a deep belly laugh. He clasped a hand on Ferren's shoulder.

"Good work my boy. That is priceless."

Ferren joined in the laughter, until he too was doubled up.

"What? What is it? What's so funny?" Hetty implored.

The laughter blew itself out and her brother straightened up, his face flushed.

"Well, I've been having no luck for weeks now, and we bump into this guy by accident."

Avaro raised a sceptical eyebrow but held his tongue.

"And what's more, he works just along the road from us. It's perfect!"

"OK, I get you've found the candidate you were looking for, but what's with where he works?" a frustrated Hetty demanded. Ferren responded with a ring of triumph in his voice.

"He works in Millbank, at Thames House. Het, he's MI5. I haven't just got myself a potential serial killer, I've got a James Bond calibre psychopath."

Chapter Six

Jack stared at the flow in the experiment as it cycled through yet another collapse of the vortex. He'd lost count of the number of times it had done so that day, and still he couldn't regain the intimate understanding he had felt previously.

He leaned back in his chair and tried to encourage the frustration to ebb away, he knew getting tense wouldn't help. Everything he had experienced since that afternoon in the gardens convinced him that a form of relaxed concentration was what he needed to aim for.

Immediately following what he'd come to think of as his revelation, he had seen everything very clearly to begin with. Every surface glistened slightly, as if coated in an extremely thin layer of moisture. The ground, buildings, plants, people, even his own skin, everywhere he looked seemed to be covered in a sheen. When he concentrated on looking at the faint iridescence, as opposed to looking at the object it covered, he could see that actually there were two surfaces lying together, each superimposed on the other. One was a shade of red, the other a sort of purple. The two appeared to lie in exactly the same place, in mathematical terms they would be two co-incident planes he thought.

He didn't know how long he had sat there marvelling at the

sight around him, but in short order the clarity had started to fade. Within minutes he couldn't resolve the two distinct layers, and then the sheen itself evaporated. What had remained were dull hues to various objects, a few mainly red, some predominantly purple and most a mixture of the two. A man who walked past had an indistinct aura, a faint smoky haze that surrounded him. When Jack concentrated hard on looking at him, the haze resolved into swirls of red and purple smoke that enveloped the man. They shifted and flowed, intermingling with each other, as if competing for the right to surround their source.

Jack had risen from the bench and set off back to his lodgings. He'd gone up through Tavistock Square and paused at the northern corner by Upper Woburn Place, intrigued by the cloud that surrounded it. The roadway outside the British Medical Association building was an intense dull red that spread out for some metres in every direction. Above it hung a thick mist of the same colour. Jack hadn't been in London in 2005, but he remembered the tragedy of the bus bombing, one of the 7/7 attacks. When he got close he had felt a chill from the mist, his body shivering. He'd hurried on past and up to Euston Road.

He'd reached St Pancras Parish Church just as the congregation were leaving after evensong. Jack had stood and watched as people poured out of the giant central doors and down the steps, purple hues predominating amongst the worshippers. A family with three young children had come out, the little boys and girl were shining especially brightly. Jack had looked closely at their auras and seen only the faintest of red strands woven in. He'd waited until the priest had finished saying goodbye to his parishioners and then followed him inside. Jack had sat respectfully on a pew near the back and watched quietly as the church wardens cleared up after the service. The whole building had an underlying purple hue to it, the walls gently radiating a violet mist. The semi-circular altar area was backstopped by six huge Ionic columns. That entire end of the church gleamed brightly, the area much thicker with fog.

Jack was not by nature a religious individual. He had never been to a church service save for weddings and funerals, yet he'd sat there and marvelled at the glory before him. As he looked at the dense purple mist it had seemed to reach out to him, to make a connection. He'd felt his whole being swell with the majesty of his surroundings. Somewhat intoxicated he'd got up and hurried out, confused by the feeling of elation that had surged through him.

He'd carried on west along Euston Road, past the tip of Regent's Park and on down Marylebone Road. On reaching the Royal Academy of Music he'd stopped and watched a group of students leave. Their auras were noticeably brighter than most other people in the street, two in particular seemed to glow. When he looked closely he could see that they were predominantly purple in hue, but again with red strands of smoke hiding within the violet swirls. He was intrigued to see some of their instruments radiate a faint purple colour from their cases.

He had continued on past Madame Tussauds and then turned north-west towards Maida Vale. On rounding a corner he'd encountered an unpleasant scene already underway, where a man stood on a pedestrian crossing shouting at a woman in a car. She sat hands clasped to the steering wheel, not daring to look at him. He was inches from the front of the car and gesticulated repeatedly at her, berating her in vicious terms for trying to run the crossing. Jack had seen red mist tumbling from the man, spreading out and dissipating as it hit the ground. The inside of the car had also filled with a red fog as the woman trembled in fright.

Before Jack had a chance to intervene, the man had stepped to one side to move closer to the driver's window, and she had driven off leaving him swearing profusely at her. As Jack approached he felt the influence of the man's turbulent aura, it had been hot and prickly. He made a conscious effort to ignore it as he walked past.

By the time Jack reached his house he was exhausted and had gone straight to bed, sleeping deep and long for the first time in months.

In the days since, Jack had taken to investigating his new found view on the world as if it were a scientific study. He'd spent time wandering the streets, observing people and their behaviour in particular. He had seen red be the predominant aura of those who were displaying the more negative of human traits – jealousy, anxiety, selfishness and anger. Purple had tended to be associated with more positive aspects such as generosity, kindness, compassion and creativity. He hadn't found a single person whose aura did not on close examination contain at least some strands of both type. He had also seen people change from one day to the next, their balance shifting with their mood and attitudes.

He'd observed that all living things possessed auras of some description. All the animals and plants he'd seen had a purple tinge to them, and though the mist surrounding them was generally very faint, it was always there.

He'd seen that many buildings possessed a kind of aura too, either in part or the structure as a whole. He had walked past churches, mosques and synagogues, all seeming to shine like violet beacons. Most other buildings were less strong and consistent, more residual, with patches of red as common as not. It was religious buildings though that Jack had spent most time considering. Were they like that because religion was inherently positive or because they were frequented by positive people?

Back in the lab, Jack hoped to regain the initial level of pure clarity by focusing on his experiment. Having already had one vision where he'd felt he was part of the structure of the flow itself, maybe he could recapture that degree of understanding by looking at it again. He'd spent the whole day trying to both concentrate and relax but to no avail. He just couldn't get the background sheens to resolve again. It felt like trying to see the image hidden in a stereogram, he could sense they were there and that they would be seen if only he could look in the correct way. Despite his efforts they remained elusive.

The alarm on Jack's phone went off and he looked up in surprise. He noticed the dinner jacket hanging on the back of the door to the laboratory. It was time to get going, so he put the frustration of his new type of lab work to one side and went to get changed.

Jack looked at his reflection in the giant mirror and smiled a little childishly at himself. The person that grinned back had no aura, but then neither did any of the other guests standing behind him. It was evidently a property that didn't follow the normal laws of optical physics, which suggested to him that it wasn't actual red or purple light that he had been seeing. Maybe he was sensing it somehow and interpreting it as colour? Was it a new type of energy not known to conventional science that didn't function in the same manner as electromagnetic radiation? Whilst he was curious and indeed keen to observe and learn, he was strangely relaxed about its nature. The obsessive desire he normally felt when it came to scientific problems wasn't as strong with this, maybe because he'd already found out that he needed to relax into it, rather than try too hard.

He watched Mandy walk up beside him and grinned at her too. She frowned back before stepping between him and the mirror, forcing him to focus on her.

"You're in a good mood tonight. I didn't realise these corporate things were so your cup of tea."

"Never been better," Jack replied, "free booze, beautiful women and more art than I can shake a stick at."

He gestured around him with the thin stemmed glass in his hand at the pictures covering the walls. The Saatchi Gallery was one of London's premier contemporary art venues, and Mandy's firm was sponsoring the new exhibition. Not having heard from Jack in days she'd been nervous about whether he would actually turn up.

"So which do you like best?" she began leadingly, "the art, the wine or the women?"

Jack looked closely at her swirling aura, she was an interesting mix of a number of large and intense positive strands interwoven with a smaller number of weaker negatives. As she asked the question, one of the red wisps of smoke pulsed a little and the tiniest hint of crimson mist was shed into the air around her. Jack was in a playful mood and decided to experiment.

"Well the wine is excellent, and I haven't had much of a chance to look at the art yet, but there are some fabulous looking women here."

He did his best to keep his tone ambiguous, and a little too calculatingly stole a lingering glance at two ladies standing some yards away. Mandy turned slightly to follow his line of sight, just in time to see one of the women meet Jack's gaze and smile back at him.

He regretted it straight away. The same thin red strand in Mandy's aura pulsed strongly and seemed to constrict around one of the larger purple ones. More red mist oozed steadily outwards which Jack was surprised to see joined by a similar colour flowing from himself. A haze was building up between them, encouraging the negative in each. Jack could feel its effects ripple towards him, increasing his belligerence and feeding his stubbornness. He knew he should stop, he wanted to stop, but he couldn't.

"Darling, are you jealous?" he asked.

Mandy was still fuming and didn't reply. Jack couldn't help a cutting tone creeping into his voice.

"Because I don't think I've ever seen you jealous before. But then maybe you've not needed to be."

"Bastard," she whispered, visibly hurt.

Mandy hurried off into the crowd.

Jack felt slightly unsteady on his feet and had to fix his vision on a single point to help him keep his balance. What the hell just happened? He'd never been deliberately cruel to her before, and yet he hadn't been able to stop himself.

He thought about going after her but couldn't work out which way she'd gone. Anyway, he wanted a chance to calm down and regroup so he wandered into one of the adjacent rooms to take a look at the pictures.

The exhibition was a retrospective of the celebrated Colombian artist Carlos Ramírez. Jack thought he was quite traditional by modern standards, a tendency towards representation. What was on display was mostly painting but a few pieces of sculpture were included. Jack was intrigued to see that most of the paintings radiated a strong positive aura, some very strong indeed. He was no expert on art, but when he stopped to contemplate the works he could see why they were so full of energy. They were in turn both beautiful and inspiring, great artistry and passion had clearly gone into them, and any viewer would feel this straight away.

Two pictures in particular caught his attention. The first was a version of The Crucifixion. Despite the inherent brutality and viciousness of the act, Ramírez had managed to convey the figure on the cross as being possessed of pure and complete love for humanity. Even Jack's own absence of faith couldn't stop him from needing to wipe tears from his eyes, such was the power of the work and the intensity of feeling it inspired.

The other was a life sized painting of two men dancing with two women. The first of the couples were gracefully proportioned and classically beautiful, though the expressions on their faces were severe and devoid of warmth. The other couple were grotesques, their limbs incorrectly proportioned and twisted, their faces disfigured, but yet they were smiling with content. The contrast between the two couples gave Jack an overwhelming sense of the beauty inherent in all humanity. Just to look at the picture made his heart ache, it shed violet mist in rolls that washed over him feeding his love of life, his love of being.

*

Having found himself another drink, Jack went to look for Mandy. He didn't find her in the first few rooms he tried, and he paused when he came upon a surprising set of pictures. Each of them had red mixed into their aura, four in particular had very strong negative components. He felt himself become nervous just by approaching them.

The first was of disjointed body parts. Initially taking it to be cubist, Jack then realised they were actually severed limbs desperately trying to find a way of assembling themselves so as to make a whole. The futility was intense.

The second was a messy array of black and very dark red brush strokes that completely covered the canvas. There was a hint of perspective running away towards the centre and as Jack studied it a powerful sense of infinity gripped him. He could feel panic start to creep in at the edges of his consciousness and he managed to force his eyes away and moved to the next picture.

The third was of a little boy sitting on the floor with three simple wooden toys in front of him. He was playing with only one of them and sorrow filled his eyes. The red smoke flowing from it brought a feeling of crippling loss and great pain.

The fourth was quite abstract and Jack had trouble making out the subject, he thought it possibly a fist. He couldn't intellectualise or rationalise the image, he simply didn't understand it. He did however experience an acute sense of malice from the painting, as if it detested him, which in turn prompted helplessness within himself.

Jack stepped back from the group of intimidating pictures and breathed out slowly, trying to shake off their influence.

"And what do they say to you?" a short dark haired man was standing next to Jack. The man sipped his red wine and waited for an answer. Jack took a few seconds to consider before replying, he turned to face the man and was about to speak when he was taken aback by the man's aura. He was wreathed in many very bright swirls of purple smoke, several of which were wrapped so tightly around a flame red strand that it barely shone through.

"That my heart goes out to the artist. To suffer that much, to be in such intense pain must be unbearable."

Jack looked closely at the man.

"But then you know that, don't you Mr Ramírez. I am truly sorry."

Jack felt his eyes well up as he sensed the pain buried within the artist. He could see a billow of purple mist flowing from himself to the diminutive gentleman before him.

"Thank you sir," honest gratitude lit up the man's eyes, "these are all from a very bad time in my life. Fifteen years ago my brother and sister were both murdered back in Colombia, victims in a trade union dispute. Yes, it happens. I was indeed in great pain and for a time I lost my love for the world."

"How did you find it again?"

"Through my family, and through my faith. Are you a religious man, Mr ...?"

"Eastwood, Jack Eastwood," he shook Ramírez's hand, "no sir, I am not. Or at least not yet."

The older man looked curious but didn't enquire further.

"Well, I was very angry with my God, I could not forgive him for what he had allowed to happen. In time though, I came to realise that it was not his place to require my forgiveness, for it was man and not God that had done these terrible things."

"But surely if man is a creation of your God, then is that not the same thing?"

"No, for God gave man free will. Although that betrayed my brother and sister, it is the one gift that defines us as human, the most essential of qualities that we possess. We could not exist without it, so we must live with it."

The artist raised his glass and Jack returned the toast.

"Thank you signor Ramirez. If you will excuse me, there is someone that I owe an apology to."

*

Jack found Mandy standing with a group of what he recognised as work colleagues. He interrupted politely, took her hand and ushered her over to one side. She made a point of putting up some resistance but let herself be led away. Jack held her hands in his and waited until she met his eyes. He concentrated on the fondness he felt for her and tried to direct it her way. He felt and saw the positivity flow through his hands to hers, and go on to surround her. The negative parts of her aura were enveloped and their glow dimmed.

"Forgive me, I was being an idiot. Do you honestly think I'm interested in anyone but you? In anyone but the woman I love?"

She looked back at him for some time without speaking, her face a mixture of confusion and suspicion. Jack saw her indecision enacted out through the tussling of the components of her aura. When at last he saw the red swirls subdued, he knew what the answer would be. The dangerous look in her eyes had gone, replaced by genuine longing and affection. She put her arms around his neck and pulled him into a lengthy embrace.

"Take me home Jack."

Again he lay awake in Mandy's bed, though this time he was far from feeling uncertain. Their love making had been a profound experience, one that he knew they had both shared. Their auras had joined, giving each a sensation of total openness and honesty with the other. They had peered into each other's souls and welcomed what they'd found.

Jack looked down at Mandy's naked body, part draped over him, her head on his chest rose and fell with his breathing. He smiled to himself, knowing that he'd moved forward. She loved him, he understood that now. She could be a little thoughtless at times, but for the most part it had been his insecurities holding them back. Now that he'd let them go, there was a balance to their relationship that had been missing before. He drifted off to sleep in relaxed anticipation about what the future held for them both.

*

It was several days later and Jack was back in his laboratory. He'd carried on staring at the flows in the measuring chamber, lasers off, just trying to feel what was happening. He hadn't managed to see the co-incident surface sheens again, but he had achieved an understanding of the Hof-del Pino instability that had been so elusive. It was there in the experiment, he could feel it, it just occurred at a much faster rate than he'd previously expected. The frequency cascade was in a higher range than the equipment had been set up to detect. A few weeks reconfiguring the sensors and it should be easy to observe experimentally. He wanted to kick himself, it seemed so obvious now, such a trivial problem. He needed to share the good news.

He shut the experiment down and checked his watch. It was just after eight in the evening but his supervisor Dr Ratliff would most likely still be in the building. She was preparing for a major international conference and had practically lived in her office the past couple of weeks.

He headed up the staircase and was turning the corner between the second and third floors, when he almost ran into someone coming the other way. He pulled up, stepped to the side and raised his head to apologise. He saw two things.

The first was a smartly dressed man of possibly Mediterranean origin. He wore a sharp suit and had a long coat draped on his right arm.

The second was the man's aura. It was by far the strongest he had seen yet and a deep, intense red. Jack instinctively looked closer at it and was confused and unnerved by what he saw. The aura did not consist of swirls of red mist encircling the man's body as he had expected, but rather appeared as a continuous glowing surface, very bright in places, dull in others. It was as if he were made of lava, some patches having cooled almost to black.

The man looked at Jack, then smiled and continued on downwards. Jack paused, unsure what to do. He stood transfixed by the rhythm of the man's footsteps as they descended the stairs. He heard the tempo change as the man reached the ground floor and presumably headed straight out the department. Jack made up his mind and raced after him. He reached the lobby just in time to see the man already the other side of the big glass doors. He was about to round the corner and disappear into the main quad. Jack ran for the exit and made to reach for the handle when there was a crash to his right hand side. He glanced across to see a picture frame fallen from the wall and smashed on the floor. Shards of glass lay unevenly, distorting the image in the photograph beneath. Again Jack paused. He knew the picture, it was a signed photo of Albert Einstein. It had been screwed very securely onto the wall to stop it being stolen. It could not have just fallen off. Something niggled at the back of his mind. He took his hand away from the door and decided to go no further.

He was about to inspect the picture to see why it had come down when he noticed that the man had left a faint red trail behind him. It was already starting to fade so he followed it back up the stairs before it disappeared altogether. He got as far as the fourth floor when it went off down the main corridor. He followed it to the third door on the left, Professor Linthorp's office. Jack knocked on the door and waited. The seconds passed and no answer came. He went in.

Jack knew straight away that the professor was dead. Linthorp's aging body lay slumped over a cheap institutional desk, his aura residual. Just a dull glow and some mist wafting around it in an indistinct cloud. What was left of his essence was purple, all except for his head, which was an intense red. Jack stepped forward and took a closer look at the body. A dark trickle of blood ran from the right ear and formed a small pool on the wood-effect laminate. It had reached a wire bound notebook, the side of which had turned a deep crimson. Jack took out his mobile and dialled the police.

Chapter Seven

The carriage rocked from side to side as it rattled down the track, the lights of domestic west London sparkling outside in the twilight. An unremarkable man in a beige raincoat sat quietly as he stared straight ahead of him, looking like just another tired commuter returning home late after a relentless day at the office. In the periphery of his vision was a thirty-something woman, her clothes suggested she'd also been at work in an office. The flush of her face hinted that she'd had more than one drink afterwards as well.

The brakes squealed in discomfort as the Tube train slowed into Turnham Green station, but it was the jolt as it finally came to rest that prised the woman from her thoughts. She exited the carriage and walked along the platform, failing to register the man in the raincoat some twenty paces behind her. She swiped her wallet at the barriers and headed out into the pretty tree-lined streets of Chiswick. It took only a few minutes before she rang the bell of a sizeable terraced house. An exasperated middle-aged woman answered the door.

"Finally. This really isn't acceptable Mrs Chanley, we finished for the day more than two hours ago."

"I'm so terribly sorry Margaret, I was caught up at work," the younger woman's voice was either sincere or well practiced at making excuses.

"Isabella is fine," the older woman brought out a push chair that contained a tiny pink-clad occupant, "but if you collect her this late again then you'll have to make other arrangements. I'm not a charity Mrs Chanley."

"I promise this won't happen again, you're a life saver Margaret. See you tomorrow."

The older woman shook her head in resigned disbelief and went back inside whilst Isabella's mother manoeuvred the buggy around and hurried off down the street. She didn't see the man step out from the shadows of a nearby front garden and resume his pace at a discrete distance behind her.

It was just under five minutes later that she turned onto the short garden path of an attractively sized mid-street property. The tiny front garden was surrounded by a high privet hedge that was so overgrown it blocked out much of the dim illumination provided by the street lamps. She walked the few paces towards the front door whilst the poorly maintained security light above it failed to come on. After fumbling for several seconds trying to find her keys in the large handbag that swung from the back of the push chair, she then proceeded to struggle to get the correct key in the lock, quietly cursing the darkness of the porch area. She eventually succeeded in opening the door, then struggled the buggy up the two steps and into the generous hallway.

As she turned to close the door a gloved hand knifed forward and struck her in the throat. She staggered back and fell to the floor, gasping for air, her crushed larynx producing no more than a brittle rasp. The man stepped into the hall and calmly closed the door behind him. He grabbed her by the hair with one hand and ignored the thrashing of her legs as he dragged her to the plush lounge-diner at the back of the house. He dropped her to the floor, crouched down over her and delivered a short and powerful punch to the right side of her lower back. She writhed on the thick cream carpet as her kidney screamed in agony.

The man circled the room, keeping one eye on the woman

whilst he first closed the curtains and then gathered a long length of speaker cable that had been attached to the Bose television's surround sound system. He lifted the woman up onto a dining chair and deftly wrapped the cable around her until she was secure. He checked his work and on finding it satisfactory he switched a table lamp on, its low energy bulb providing little illumination through its thick fabric shade.

He kept his back turned to the woman as he left the room and headed for the kitchen. From her seat in the lounge, she could hear the slow and careful strokes of an edge being drawn against a sharpening steel. As the man came back into the room the woman's eyes opened wide as she saw light glinting off the middle blade from her set of five Sabatiers. She glanced up to see the man had tied a scarf around his face so that only his eyes stared back at her. He lent down and carefully placed the knife in her lap, she tried to scream but managed only a dull croak as he walked out to the hall. She shook with impotent hysteria as he returned pushing the buggy, leaving it just a few feet away from her. Isabella murmured gently.

The man carefully cut away most of the woman's clothing and then took less than two minutes to administer fifty nine expert wounds that bled little but caused searing pain. Many were calculated to make struggling against her bonds agonising in the extreme. By the time he crouched down and brought his eyes level with hers, she could feel the fire across her entire body, only the areas next to the chair having been spared. The man paused for a moment and assessed the rapidity of her breathing. Confident that he had got the balance just about correct he plunged the knife into her for the sixtieth and final time, giving her a gut wound that he knew would prove fatal within the hour. He left the rosewood handle protruding from her abdomen and stepped back. He checked himself methodically, his eyes smiling when he found no trace of blood.

He calmly looked through her handbag until he found her wallet. He extracted the Oyster card and slipped it into his pocket. The woman struggled as she saw the man lean down and peer closely at the tiny child in the buggy. He raised his head and made eye contact with the woman.

"Cute kid."

The woman watched him leave the room for the hallway, and after a short pause she heard the door latch click open and shut. She panted and whispered incoherently for the next forty seven minutes, the blood pooling in her lap before dripping onto the reddening carpet. As she drew her last breath Isabella began to cry.

Chapter Eight

Hetty traipsed down the stairs in her dressing gown and slippers, pausing when she got to the kitchen doorway to rub the sleep from her eyes.

"Morning sis," said her brother, "another late one was it?"

She didn't bother to cover her yawn and instead made straight for the coffee machine, a pot of thick dark liquid sat two thirds full.

"Certainly was, but I think I've found what I've been looking for."

She poured a mug full and sat down wearily at the table, her hair hanging in messy tangles around her face. Ferren got up and used a tea towel to take a plate of croissants out of the oven, which he put it down in front of his sister.

"Good for you. Now try eating something."

Hetty made a start on her breakfast whilst her brother sat skim reading a tabloid newspaper. When he finished it, Ferren placed it on top of three others he'd already read. He moved onto the broadsheets.

"You know what I don't get?"

"Don't tempt me," replied his sister. He ignored her.

"Is why so little coverage? I'd have thought by now he would be front page news."

"Because, my friend, the police are not releasing all the facts."

Avaro draped his coat over a chair and sat down at the end of the table. Ferren obediently got up and poured the remainder of the coffee for him.

"They are deliberately concealing the details that suggest all the deaths are at the hands of one man. They are also not reporting their suspicions as to where or how he selects his victims."

"On the plus side, he's smart enough not to get caught for a while, so the details will come out eventually," said Hetty.

"Not good enough," retorted Avaro, "Ferren, you did very well to mould him but now you must maximise your return. Suitable members of the media need to be identified whom leads can be passed to."

"Yeah, you could pose as one of the investigating officers, concerned that the public get all the info they need to protect themselves," Hetty smiled at her own suggestion.

"Actually," replied Avaro, "I was thinking you could both do with making friends of some journalists. They are very influential in how people think in this age. Perception is more important than reality."

Hetty grimaced to herself at the older man's aphorism but kept her silence. They all sat quietly for a few moments until Ferren's eyes lit up.

"Oh, now here's a thing Av. This is a nice piece about your *Streets of Gold,* a full page in the Guardian's technology supplement."

"Let me see."

The older man grabbed the pages from him and quickly scanned the relevant article. He chuckled to himself.

"Idiots, they completely miss the point, but that is good. I had thought maybe it would not be subtle enough, too obvious in its structure and intent. But they are treating it purely as advertised, I must congratulate the developer."

"Have you got it on all the major platforms now?"

"Yes, the final one was released two days ago after the compatibility issues were resolved. It is now available for any smartphone or portable computer with a wireless connection. The number of regular players is also increasing faster than I had hoped. I am confident now that it will serve its purpose."

"Which means little brother, that we need to start getting some results of our own," Hetty grinned at Ferren before heading upstairs for a shower.

She sat quietly in her seat and resisted the urge to scratch the itch brought on by the jumper she was wearing. Hetty regretted the discomfort but it did give her the look she was aiming for. Together with the jeans and sensible shoes she appeared a practical, straightforward and attractive young woman.

She relaxed and let her senses reach out across the carriage. Once her body had settled into the rhythm of the swaying she could feel quite clearly the bilious anger flowing from her target. She checked his aura and stared for some time at the hypnotic swirls that circled him, two thick bands of red smoke dominating the rest of his personality.

She brought her concentration back to the physical world around her and examined in turn each of the occupants at that end of the carriage.

An old lady, probably in her late seventies, had a crinkled and time-ravaged face that was no doubt well accustomed to the scowl it wore. A floral dress poked out the bottom of the thick brown coat that covered her. Her lips moved from time to time but made no sound as she carried on a conversation that only she took part in.

Next was a city type, a nice suit and modern, rather than traditional, shoes. He looked in his late twenties and had a handsome face that was characterised by somewhat bony features.

A Muslim woman in a burqa sat with a young Arabic boy by

her side. He kicked his heels gently against the panel below the seat whilst his mother sat impassive and unreadable, only her eyes and hands visible for interpretation. One of the latter was clenched tightly about the boy's arm.

The last of the passengers was also the most demonstrative. It was hard to judge his age but Hetty guessed most people would say early thirties. He wore large black Dr Martens boots, a pair of blue, black and white tie-dyed combat pants and an olive green bomber jacket. His piggy face was heavily pock marked and the rest of his head was recently shaven.

Hetty reached back out with her senses and reassured herself that her plan would work. She wanted to avoid using direct influence on her mark until as late as possible. It would make any manipulation so much stronger in the long run. She also wanted those superfluous to her plans out the way so she nudged two minds, suggesting it was time for them to alight. As the train slowed and reached its next stop, the old woman got up stiffly and hobbled her way to the doors. Before she reached them the skinhead jumped up and offered her his arm, patiently helping her onto the platform as the doors started beeping. They closed behind him and the train moved on. Hetty now had her cast assembled.

She stared across at the young mother and began.

"What are you looking at?"

"Nothing. I was not looking at anything."

The mother spoke English well but with a heavy accent, loaded with anxiety.

"Yes you were, you were looking at me. Do you fancy me or something?"

The woman looked back at her, the whites of her eyes showing and the folds of her garments trembling slightly.

"Is that why you came over here, to stare at nice white girls? Is that not allowed back home?"

At this the man in the suit stood up and put himself almost between the two women.

"Excuse me miss, is this woman bothering you?"

He winked at Hetty and turned to face the mother.

"Because she's fucking well bothering me."

He spat the words out over her, tiny specks of spittle showing briefly against the black cloth of her garments. She dragged her child off his seat and ducked their way past the man standing over her. She walked quickly past the other three occupants in the second half of the carriage, none of whom so much as looked up, and stood by the door at the far end of the carriage. She was careful to keep her gaze directed downwards and her child behind her.

"That's right, run away and find someone else's taxes to sponge off," Hetty called, adding "fucking pakis" under her breath.

The man sat down opposite Hetty and leaned forward confidently.

"Tom. Nice to meet you."

"Samantha, and you."

By the time they got off the Tube at Plaistow, Hetty was sure she had him hooked, and she hadn't even influenced him directly. Some subtle manipulation later on in the evening to embed what he already felt, and he would be hers for as long as she wanted. They walked in jovial conversation from the station to the hall where the meeting was due to be held. It was just a local branch meeting but Tom tried to impress her with his status as national treasurer, Hetty acted suitably surprised and fed him the details from the background story she'd prepared. When he suggested they might go for a drink afterwards she smiled genuinely, though not for the reason he took it for.

They rounded the corner and came upon the entranceway to the hall, the light spilling out of it inviting them straight in. The sandwich board standing proudly on the pavement outside announced the hosts of the evening as being the Albion Patriotic Alliance.

Chapter Nine

"And please stop wasting police time Mr Eastwood."

Detective Sergeant Valerie Tucker got up and held the door for Jack, eager to get rid of the nuisance witness before an entire morning slipped by. Her family had hardly seen her since the investigation started and she was damn well going to get home on time that day.

Jack bit his lip and avoided making eye contact with the investigating officer. He left the police station without saying another word.

The days since the incident had been difficult for Jack. When the police first arrived on the scene they'd listened with interest to his description of the Mediterranean man. He enhanced the truth a little by saying he'd actually seen the man exit Professor Linthorp's office, he'd figured he couldn't really tell them how he knew the man had come from there.

Shortly afterwards the officer had returned and asked very carefully about the route the man had taken. She made Jack clarify it several times and it was then that he started to suspect something was wrong, or at least more wrong than what he'd already seen.

Eventually the police woman had told him that the CCTV footage covering the exit into the main quad showed no such man. Just to be sure, they had checked hours either side of the time Jack made his phone call to the emergency operator. There was also nothing on the camera from the front of the department. No sign of him at all.

Jack had persisted with his version of events, but he knew he'd been labelled a fantasist. He was certain the post mortem would indicate natural causes – most probably a brain haemorrhage – and then the case would be closed.

To make matters worse, rumours circulating in the department had got back to him of the different theories for why he'd made the story up. The more generous cited work-related stress, the nastier ones blamed desperate attention seeking, or a ruse to distract from his failed attempt at stealing the signed photograph.

To keep the peace in the post-grad office he'd conceded that maybe he was mistaken, the shock of unexpectedly finding a dead body having thrown him. Only Sam and Mikhail seemed to accept his initial word on the matter, though he suspected they too had been avoiding him.

The department had reacted with great sadness at Professor Linthorp's death. He was a kindly and popular figure who had devoted as much of his considerable enthusiasm to teaching and helping students as to his research. A collection of flowers and cards of remembrance had quickly built up in the lobby. With Linthorp not having any known relatives the department had been the focal point for people to pay their respects.

Jack was puzzled as to why anyone would want to kill the gentle old man, assuming that he had indeed been killed, so he set about looking into the various projects the professor had been working on.

He went from the police station straight to the main library, not so much for access to reference material – he could get pretty much everything he wanted online – but rather for some peace and quiet away from the whisperings of the gossip mongers. It was past lunchtime before he walked back to his office, notebook in hand. His phone rang as he got to the north cloister, it was Mandy.

"Hi pet, how are you holding up?"

"Good thanks, though I took another ear bashing from that police officer this morning. Even I'm starting to doubt what I saw. Maybe it was all just stress or something."

"Well I believe in you. Why don't I take you out for dinner tonight and we can work on de-stressing you afterwards, how does that sound?"

"Jack? Jack?"

He had stopped at the doors to the department, fascinated by the two figures he saw standing on the opposite side of the lobby area. A man and a woman, their auras were both vivid hues of violet, brighter and larger than even that of Carlos Ramírez. Instinctively he inspected them closer and drew breath at what he saw. The ends of the thick positive swirls that surrounded them flicked out periodically at the air, as if tasting it.

"Jack? Are you still there?" Mandy asked urgently.

"Er, yes love, but I think I'd better call you back. Tonight sounds great though, see you later."

He ended the call and cautiously opened the glass doors.

They had already turned to face him, the man looked curious, the woman surprised. Jack was sure he knew who the man was, but couldn't place him at first. Slim of build and expensively dressed, his demeanour spoke of relaxed confidence. When recognition hit, Jack was baffled. The man was Sabir Chadili, creative midfielder for Arsenal Football Club and Moroccan international. What the hell?

The woman holding his hand was a bit older than Jack, very pretty and carrying a bunch of flowers. Jack almost did a double take when he saw she was wearing a priest's collar.

"This cannot be coincidence," Chadili said to his companion, his voice held only the faintest hint of a North African accent.

The pair of them returned Jack's stunned expression with friendly smiles, then walked over and each offered a hand.

"I am Sabir, and this is Rebecca. We have come to pay our respects to Professor Linthorp, but I suspect this is going to become a long conversation."

"Well I have got a few questions."

"I bet you have," said Rebecca. "Why don't we go somewhere quieter?"

The three of them sat down at the cafe in the Welcome Collection. Though only two minutes walk from his office, Jack had never been there before. He and Sabir tucked into their lunches whilst Rebecca made do with tea.

"So how did you know the Professor? No offence, but you two don't seem the types to be interested in high temperature superconductor research."

Sabir sat chewing whilst Rebecca answered.

"I used to be the chaplain at St Pancras Parish Church, and Arthur was one of my congregation. I'd got to know him and his wife very well over the years, they were both active in the church and very supportive to myself as a young priest. When she died about three years ago, he was absolutely devastated, poor man. I stayed in touch when I moved to my new position at Westminster Abbey, I'm a minor canon there."

"What do I call you then? Reverend?"

"Rebecca is fine," she laughed.

"And you two are a couple then?"

"Two years now," chimed Sabir, in between mouthfuls.

"Good for you, though that must be hard with being famous and all."

"Not really. It does have its moments, but I tend to keep a low profile and I have always kept my private life exactly that."

Sabir put his knife down to pick up his orange juice. He paused before drinking.

"I sense though you are more interested in other matters. Would you like to go first?"

The invitation was all that was needed to open the floodgate.

For several weeks Jack had by necessity kept his own counsel on the changes he'd experienced. It was such a relief to talk to someone that he went on for nearly an hour without either of the others needing to say more than a few words. He described in turn the first hallucination, the repeated visions, and the way they increased in frequency until the revelatory experience in the park. He went on to cover his seeing the glistening sheens and then everything he had subsequently deduced about auras and their nature. He stopped short of mentioning what he'd seen the evening of Linthorp's death.

"So what's going on then?" Jack finished, aware that his mouth was dry from all the talking. The other two looked at each other and decided Rebecca would start.

"Well firstly Jack, you're not alone. As far as I can tell you're like Sabir and myself, or at least you have begun a similar journey."

"Are there many more like us?"

"Apart from you, me and Sabir, there are two more in London that I know of. There are others elsewhere in the world, though I'm not sure how many."

"So what are we? What's happened to me?"

Rebecca took time to choose her words carefully.

"You've been awakened to the greater reality of the universe."

"You mean God?" Jack was conscious of Rebecca's status.

She looked to Sabir for help, he shrugged wryly, "you are the theologian, my love."

Rebecca turned back to Jack.

"Well, I don't think it's as simple as that. As you've already discovered, the wider reality is governed by positive and negative energies. If you were looking from a religious viewpoint, then you may very well call the positive side God, and the negative side evil or perhaps the Devil."

"And if I weren't religious?"

"Then maybe just good and evil, or right and wrong. My point is that short of being a sociopath, most people would understand the difference between the two, whatever the labels applied to them."

"But I thought the defining aspect of God was that he, she or it is a singular intelligence. Making humans in his own image and all that."

"Whether or not there is a singular intelligence as you put it, driving either type of energy I don't know. We tend to just refer to them as positive and negative energy."

"But you're a priest! Surely you don't say that in sermons."

"Funny. No of course not, but I interpret what I do know to be true and put it into a form that others can understand."

Sabir smiled.

"Rebecca and I have had this conversation a few times before." She frowned at him and returned to Jack.

"As long as I can help people move closer to the positive side then I'm happy with my work."

"So what about heaven and hell?" asked Jack.

"Ah," Sabir leaned back in his chair, "that is where the veils come in."

"Veils?"

"The two glistening surfaces you saw at first. They are the boundaries between the physical world and the positive and negative energies. It is across the veils that humans draw energy as a result of their intentions, emotions and actions. It then appears as the purple or red smoke."

"But when I look closely at people's auras they seem to be made of distinct strands, yet objects or places are more diffuse."

"I think that is because human emotions and intentions shape and hold energies to a form, aligning them with concepts. I am not really an expert in this kind of stuff though, I just play football."

He winked conspiratorially at Jack.

"It's OK," said Rebecca, "there's another of us here in London who knows a lot more about all this,"

"Two," corrected Sabir, which produced a frown from

Rebecca before she continued.

"One other that we'll introduce you to. He'll be better able to answer your questions, and hopefully help you finish your awakening."

"Finish? What else is there to come?"

"Sorry, a poor choice of words. I mean explore your new situation, work out what you are capable of."

"What do you mean?"

"Well," Sabir took over, "as far as I know everyone who is awakened can not only draw more easily from the veils, but can normally learn to manipulate the energy in some way."

Jack raised his eyebrows in scepticism.

"Like as in magic powers?"

"There are thirty-seven people in this cafe, including us and the serving staff. There are four more in the kitchen. The lady buying her food right now is agitated, I am guessing she has realised she has not enough money to pay for the food she has just ordered."

Jack leaned slightly to one side to get a better view of the counter. He then checked behind him for mirrors and quickly counted up the number of people in the cafe. Jack looked confused.

"How did you...?"

"Magic!" grinned Sabir, then he sighed.

"It is what positive energy allows me to do, sense things in space, anywhere up to one hundred yards maybe, depending on conditions. I have also become good at going unnoticed by those around me, helpful when you are famous. Which is why that fan over there has not spotted me yet."

Jack turned to see a man sitting at a table nearby wearing an Arsenal jacket. He hadn't noticed the logo during his brief count up, he wondered whether this was poor observation on his part or a side effect of Sabir's ability.

"Hang on, is this space perception thing why you're so good at football?"

Sabir chuckled.

"No, I have always been good at football, but it does help me understand the flow of the game. And make good long range passes. And avoid bad tackles. Actually yes Jack, it is quite helpful in my profession I suppose."

"And what's your 'special power' Rebecca?"

"Please don't trivialise this Jack."

"Sorry, it's just a little hard to take it all in."

"I understand. For my part I can channel positive energy to counter negativity that has taken hold of people or places. It's mostly a sort of emotional healing but it's sometimes possible to help with physical ailments too."

"That must keep you busy with so much pain and suffering around."

"Not really, it's extremely draining so I don't do it directly very often. Though I have learned through pastoral work how to use very small amounts in conjunction with good old fashioned empathy and listening."

Jack puffed his cheeks out and blew a long sigh.

"Well, I guess I'll discover my talents soon enough. Now maybe I should have raised this earlier, but about Professor Linthorp's death."

He recalled his encounter with the mysterious figure, and of the subsequent police investigation. Rebecca sought clarification.

"And you say the CCTV didn't pick up this guy at all?"

"Nope, not a thing. I wish I'd kept quiet about him now, everyone at the department thinks I'm going crazy."

Rebecca and Sabir exchanged glances.

"This does not sound good."

"Agreed," said Rebecca, "we should go to Aaron straight away."

"Aaron?"

"Aaron Ascarelli, he's the other Awakened I mentioned. The one who'll answer your questions, and hopefully shed some light on what you saw."

"I am starting to get a bad feeling about this," Sabir concluded.

The house was in Henrietta Street, Covent Garden, and they stood patiently outside its large black front door. Sabir had chosen to press the discreet button at the side rather than use the big brass door knocker. It was fashioned in the shape of a lion's head and all three could see the bright aura it gave off. Although the mist that rolled off it was violet, there was something else mixed in, not an obvious strand of red but something not entirely positive either. They had waited over a minute.

"Rebecca, are you sure he said he would be in?"

"Of course, I spoke to him whilst you were flagging down the cab."

Sabir sighed.

"I just know I am going to regret this."

He grasped the thick ring in the lion's mouth and rapped it hard against the door three times. Its energy flowed over Sabir's hand and up to his elbow until his whole lower arm glowed significantly more brightly. The intensity peaked and then the energy rushed back into the knocker like a wave breaking on a beach. Sabir withdrew his hand, he wasn't hurt but he had a strange sensation of having just been examined.

Moments later the door swung open and a serious looking man in his sixties stood to one side and ushered them in, Rebecca indicated for Jack to go first. The large ornate hallway was surprisingly dark and it took their eyes a moment to adjust from the sunshine outside.

"Mr Ascarelli, I'm pleased to meet you," Jack offered his hand. The old man looked down at it in silence, as if he'd never seen one before.

"Did I say something wrong?" Jack asked the others.

"Look closer at his aura," suggested Rebecca.

The man had a strong positive aura, but nothing like as strong as Rebecca or Sabir, it also consisted of a more normal set of obedient swirls.

"Ah, sorry about that. I guess I'm a bit nervous. And your name is sir?"

"Wilkinson, and that's quite alright Mr Eastwood. Just go straight up, he's on the second floor at the back." The old man grinned as he grabbed Jack's still proffered hand and shook it.

Sabir led the way and after two flights of thickly carpeted stairs they entered what looked like a very comfortable library. Save for a couple of leaded windows on the back wall, every other vertical surface was lined with antiquated books. A circular card table sat at one end of the room, with four well-padded leather chairs surrounding it. A man got up from one of these and walked over, his frame looming over them as he approached. He had the build of a professional rugby player and Jack estimated him to be at least six foot four inches tall. The man had shoulder length greying hair that framed a strong angular face. He smiled at them and held out his hand to Jack and Sabir before affectionately kissing Rebecca's cheek.

"Well met, Mr Eastwood, please call me Aaron." His voice was rich and deep, with a heavy Brooklyn accent.

He sat them round the table and used an intercom to call down to Wilkinson for tea.

"At the risk of boring these two, would you mind telling me your story from the beginning? Just the main points mind, I'll get the detail from you later."

For the second time that day Jack recounted his recent weeks, though this time more succinctly. He finished his description of the elusive Mediterranean man before the teapot cooled. Aaron sat back in his chair and looked at each of them carefully before he spoke in a measured tone.

"I'm not certain of what you saw Jack, we'll need to do a little more digging on that. What I do know is that I have seen auras similar to yours before." He paused as Jack shifted a little further forward on his seat.

"I've been awakened for over forty years now and in that

time I've done a lot of travelling. I've looked for more of our kind all over the globe and occasionally I've found them. Three times I've come across people with auras like yours."

"Forgive me for interrupting," said Jack, "but what does my aura look like? I can't really see much of it and mirrors are no use."

"Of course. Take my hand and relax."

The huge man put his hand palm up on the table. Jack leaned forward, grasped it gently and closed his eyes, letting his mind go clear. He was aware of a tugging sensation, as if his body were being yanked by a rope. A second quick jerk and then on the third he felt his consciousness slam forwards and across the table. He opened his eyes and found himself staring back at Jack Eastwood. He kept very still indeed. He could hear Aaron's voice as if off in the distance.

"Look Jack, focus in on the components."

He concentrated in the same manner he had become accustomed to and saw the bright hazy aura resolve into discrete strands. They were whipping out and around his body in just the same way as those of the others sat at the table. He continued to focus and started to notice something different about the swirls around his body. When he concentrated hard enough, he saw that each one was actually composed of a number of smaller swirls. When he focused on one of the smaller ones it then appeared to consist of even tinier ones. Jack kept focusing on increasingly smaller component strands until he'd lost count of the number of layers he'd gone down through. He heard Aaron's voice again.

"It goes on like that forever Jack, but you can return now."

Jack rushed his consciousness back to observing the whole of him and then braced himself. After a short pause he felt himself fly back into his own body, as if a rope under tension had been cut. He was back in the chair and breathing hard.

"That was, different."

Aaron smiled at him.

"One of the things I've picked up over the years. The first time I moved my own consciousness I ended up in a dog. I don't recommend it."

"So what does my aura mean? It looked fractal to me, self-similar across scales."

"That's a fair if rather technical description, but what it means will take time to find out. The three people I've met like you were all very different and of greatly varying accomplishment. What they all had in common though was the ability to manipulate the fabric of space-time. Creating, changing and destroying matter, manipulating forces. They were also able to interact at a fundamental level with the veils and the planes of energy beyond. Even the weakest of them could draw significant amounts of power."

"That sounds like a big responsibility," Jack said warily.

"It is. Especially as two of the three died using their abilities and the third vanished without a trace."

"Right. OK." He looked at Rebecca and Sabir, both of whom made sympathetic faces back at him.

"But enough of that," Aaron's smile had returned and Jack felt noticeably calmer for it, "we'll have plenty of opportunity to help you safely explore your powers later. For now, I suggest we take a closer look at that mysterious figure you saw. If you'll all hold hands this time. Jack, just relax again and concentrate on what you saw, I'll help you bring some of the detail back. You two just observe and please stay quiet, we don't want a repeat of last time." He looked pointedly at Rebecca.

They linked hands around the table and very quickly Jack felt himself inside a lucid dream. He was back on the stairs in the department, walking upwards though more slowly than when it actually happened. He felt like he had control over the pace he was going, but could only continue on the course he'd trod previously. He looked behind and saw the other three a few steps down watching him. He decided to continue upwards. Again his head dropped as he rounded the corner and he was aware of something in front of him.

He chose to slow things down and take a good look this time, but as before he felt an intense unease when looking at the man's volcanic aura. He pushed on past and wound through the rest of the recollection at half speed. Just as he got to the part where the picture fell from the wall, he heard a yelp from behind him and turned to see Rebecca with her hands to her mouth. He felt the floor underneath him wobble and throw him off balance. Before he hit the ground he woke up to sounds of confusion.

Aaron was groaning and clutching the front of his head, Rebecca was apologising, and Sabir was speaking to Wilkinson over the intercom and requesting an ice pack. Jack sat quietly and ate the last biscuit from the tray whilst things settled down.

"I'm so sorry, I can't believe I did that again," said Rebecca.

"Actually I can," Aaron said in a generous manner, "that took me by surprise too. I might not have kept it together even if you hadn't squealed."

"Sorry, am I missing something?" asked Jack.

"We saw why the picture fell," said Sabir, "part of your aura shot out and ripped it from the wall, like a striking cobra. It was very fast and happened out of your line of sight, but we all saw it."

"I have no idea, before you ask," said Aaron, he held the ice pack to his head as he continued.

"I do however have a theory on the being you encountered. I'm not certain but it might be a construct from the negative plane, a physical manifestation of some kind. Rebecca's colleagues would probably call it a demon, though maybe that's not vanilla enough for most C of E folk. Sorry Rebecca, no offence intended, this headache's making me crabby and the ice isn't helping any," he paused briefly, "actually, that's a damn good idea."

Aaron got up and opened a drinks cabinet that was disguised as a couple of rows of books. He swung the front open, the false spines revealing a fine array of spirits. He split the ice pack open and cubes clinked into glasses. Aaron brought four cut crystal tumblers to the table, together with a bottle of Gentlemen Jack. He splashed a generous measure of Tennessee whiskey into each glass and took a healthy swig from his own.

Sabir took a more cautious sip from his drink and addressed the others.

"I do not know if this will help, but I did pick up something from your recollection Jack. I saw the label in the coat he was carrying. It was a Higgins and Hall."

The others looked blank.

"Probably the oldest bespoke tailors in the City and known for their blend of traditional and contemporary styles."

Jack and Aaron raised their eyebrows.

"He likes his clothes," Rebecca apologised.

"It was a nice coat," protested Sabir. "Anyway, it may be worthwhile if I take a look around the area, to see if I can find any trace of him, or it." Sabir looked to Aaron for confirmation.

"Good idea, though take Rebecca with you, we don't know what he is or what he's doing here. It'll be safer with two of you. I'll start looking into what our visitor might be and help Jack with attuning to the positive veil. Keep in touch and we'll meet again when we know more. Sound like a plan?"

They all nodded and got up to leave. Jack called Mandy to let her know he'd be late and stayed behind to have a chat with Aaron. The other two left the house and headed off to find a taxi. Sabir stopped halfway down the street and turned to Rebecca, taking her in his arms he hugged her close for a long few moments.

"What was that for?" she asked.

He kissed her tenderly on the forehead.

"Because I love you, and I always will."

Chapter Ten

"We need to reclaim our national identity. In an increasingly confused global society, we all need to know what Britain is, what it stands for and what it means to be British. A clear identity for all."

Hetty watched as John Tavens strutted about the podium, enthusiastically pointing at members of the audience, drawing them into his vision for the future of the country. The leader of the Albion Patriotic Alliance was a charismatic man, of that there was no doubt. His working class roots and military background gave him a lot of credibility with his followers, but it was his personal presence that drew people to him. Hetty examined his strongly negative aura, a few weak purple strands dominated by thick red bands of smoke. It was a powerful aura, that of a natural leader, and not one she wanted to have to go up against if she could avoid it.

She didn't really listen to his words, her mind wandered and only brief snippets of Tavens' principal address to the national meeting of the APA registered with her. She didn't need to hear the details to understand the impact he was having. Large billows of negative energy rolled off the platform and infused the assembled crowd. Many were regional leaders and officers of the party, but a large contingent came from the general public, some of them getting their first taste of the Tavens effect.

Tom sat next to her, hand clasped about hers and listened with rapt attention, an inspired look on his face. Hetty wondered how long the speech would go on for. There was a bar at the back of the large, drab hall and she was really in need of a drink. Unfortunately Tavens seemed to be just warming up, so she shifted in her seat and tried to get comfortable.

"Every country must look after its own, it makes no sense at all for us to be footing the bill for people to come and live here. I don't blame them for wanting a better life, but they should stay and fight for it in their own land, not try and steal it from you and me."

Hetty stifled a yawn and tried to keep awake. She had fed hungrily on the abundance of negativity in the room, but having absorbed more than her fill now felt sleepy. It was too much of a good thing. She looked around the hall and burned some of her excess energy by skimming the thoughts of those sitting nearby. She was intrigued to find a couple of teachers who were both trying to work out how they could include more of Tavens' ideology in their lessons. Next to them was a human resources director for a major corporation, he emanated a conflicted blend of great excitement and intense discomfort. He loved being there but was scared of being recognised. He needn't have worried as no one had a clue who he was, but his sense of self-importance left him convinced that discovery was imminent.

The audience as a whole looked like a reasonable cross-section of society. There was a slight emphasis on the stereotypes that had become associated with groups such as the APA, with a greater than average concentration of pseudo-military clothing and aggressive haircuts. The balance however was more mainstream in appearance. Hetty could see all types, from bankers and businessmen to pensioners and housewives. She sensed there were quite a few current or ex-military, and the number of civil servants pleased her. The Government's new legislative plans were having the desired effect and had galvanised responses to the prospect of more positive discrimination in the workplace. She was glad that her efforts hadn't been in vain.

"There are those who criticise us, who would label us racist. They are wrong. We are patriots. I have no problems with someone's skin colour or their religion, but I do have a problem with them imposing their way of life upon you and me. On them insisting we conform to their image of society."

As much as Hetty's plans were working, she couldn't help but be jealous of her brother and his success. Since Ferren had established links with journalists from two national tabloids, the media coverage of the killings had exploded. Every paper was now vying for their moniker to become the de facto name for the twisted perpetrator. 'The Oyster Catcher' and the 'Tube line Torturer' were the front runners, but headline writers came up with new ideas on a daily basis. She sensed the increased anxiety of travellers on the Underground and hoped her own journalists would prove as useful in fuelling the public's emotions.

"And another thing, and let me spell this out clearly. If you live here, speak the fucking language. Excuse my French ladies and gentlemen."

The audience roared with approval and Hetty forced herself to clap enthusiastically, her thoughts still elsewhere. She mulled over the latest scheme Ferren had taken to Avaro, and wondered how she might best use it to her advantage as well. He'd been lucky enough to recruit his killer from the Security Service, an experienced member of "K-section", and had hatched a plan using some of the man's inside knowledge. She wasn't convinced Ferren was smart enough to pull it off though. He'd actually tried to get into a mosque of all places! She chuckled to herself at the thought of him squirming as he neared the door, completely unable to force himself inside such a sacred area. Idiot.

He'd nearly blown it a second time by looking for targets on an Internet chat room. If she hadn't pointed out that they'd all be monitored, he might have drawn some very time and energy consuming attention from the authorities. Hetty shook her head as she remembered the look of disappointment on his face – you'll have to be smarter than that little brother.

"But my friends, to an extent we get what we deserve. This country voted in a government that thinks immigrants are better than hard-working British people, that they should be placed above you and me. I say to you that this is wrong and we must make them hear us loud and clear."

Despite his level of incompetence Ferren was clearly a long way in front and Hetty was keen to catch up. She had been concerned her plans were not direct enough, but Avaro seemed to think that subtle was better in the long run. Ferren might generate a lot of energy by playing on people's primal anxieties, but that could easily fade if the source was neutralised. If the killer was caught then the backwash of relief would undo most of his good work.

Avaro reasoned it was better to go for the more insidious approach, corrupting people at a more fundamental level, twisting their very nature to one of greater negativity. Like his smartphone game, she'd thought it a stupid idea when she first heard what he'd been up to. Since then, he had attracted over one hundred thousand users, each of whose life was turned a bit further every day towards selfishness and rapacity.

"We have a long and glorious history in this fair country of ours, and it's being whittled away by the very people who should be protecting it. I'm proud of who we are and I'm not going to apologise to anyone for that."

She knew that if she was going to catch up with Ferren, not only would Tavens have to play his part, but that her other schemes would need to come to fruition too. She was grateful that the time she'd spent at Stiletto trying to track down the right member of 'the in crowd' looked like it was finally going to pay off. The target she'd selected for her trap would be back next week with his friends, and she was pretty confident he could be made into the focal point she needed.

"So my friends, let us all devote ourselves to making Britain for the British!"

As Tavens' concluded with his trademark slogan, Hetty jumped to her feet and joined the rest of the crowd in rapturous applause. The standing ovation lasted for several minutes before he finally left the platform and the meeting broke for the interval. Hetty stayed close to Tom and kept to her role as his dutiful girlfriend 'Samantha', there was no shortage of regional officers who introduced themselves, all keen to get on the right side of the Alliance's money man.

During the second half Hetty all but fell asleep, the other speakers not having a fraction of the charisma of their leader. The questions from the floor were a little more interesting, especially when the subject of direct action came up. Although the responses from the leadership were somewhat cagey there was a clear groundswell of support for the APA to fight its cause using a more public approach.

Tavens spoke again briefly at the end before bringing the assembly to a close. The crowd dissipated quickly onto the streets of east London whilst Tom ushered Hetty towards a nearby private members club, where a handful of the Executive Committee had planned to meet for a quiet drink and debriefing. During the short walk to the Duke's Rooms, Tom was more assertive than he had been on their date two nights previously. Hetty was amused by the empowerment he now displayed, buoyed by the fervour of the meeting.

On arriving they took seats in the busy main bar, the walls tarred a dull yellow with the accumulated grime from decades of patrons' tobacco smoke. They were joined by Tavens, his rather glamorous wife Sylvia, and three other members of the committee. Hetty didn't listen to the conversation, it centred on the success of the evening and was more self-congratulatory than analytical. She concentrated instead on the auras of her companions. Tavens she'd already assessed in the hall, and Sylvia's was also quite strong and of similar composition. The bond between them was clearly based on a shared ideology. Two of the others, one man and one woman, were both above average strength and also intensely negative, yet nothing unusual. The curiosity was the man introduced to her as Dave Tyrell, for his aura was much stranger indeed.

Overall he appeared quite strong to Hetty, the various wreaths of smoke encircling him were thick and bright. There was however a definite pattern to the way that the negative aspects were all on the surface, with the positive elements of his personality obscured beneath them. There was also a much higher proportion of purple in his aura than she would have expected. So what was he hiding?

Hetty took several deep breaths and relaxed in her seat. She had recharged with plenty of energy during the meeting so had no difficulty in reaching into the man's mind, forcing her way in quite bluntly past the blocks in his subconscious. His voice faltered slightly as she rummaged around, but he continued as soon as she withdrew, shocked by what she had found. His name was not Dave Tyrell, and he most certainly was not a loyal member of the cause. She refocused and went back in to get specifics. A minute later she took a large swig from her glass, finishing her vodka and tonic in one. It had taken a little more energy than she had anticipated, but she had what she wanted. The question was, how best to use it?

She stopped a man who walked past their table and asked him to take a picture of their group with her phone, her attitude and tone of voice deliberately light and infatuated. He obliged and she then excused herself to go to the toilet. She waited for several minutes in a cubicle, doing nothing other than scribble a few lines on a scrap of paper from her handbag.

She returned just in time for Tavens to be going to the bar for a second round.

"Oh, hey John, let me help you with that."

She playfully put her arm in his and almost skipped to the bar with him. After he'd ordered she turned to face him, careful to keep her face away from their table.

"So Samantha, what line of work are you in, you're not an accountant too I hope?"

"Oh no, not at all. I work for the family business, if you know what I mean." Hetty let forth an impulse of suggestion pointing him towards connections with organised crime. She couldn't be sure whether it had taken effect so she carried straight on.

"And in my line of work it pays to know who you're getting involved with. So I've had my contacts do some checking."

She smiled sweetly, her lips laden with false innocence.

"And what did your contacts say about me?"

"About you? Nothing, I checked you out ages ago. You're cool John, but Dave isn't."

Her smile faded to seriousness, Tavens' cheery glow was replaced by calm professionalism.

"The photograph?"

She nodded.

"Go on."

"He's Special Branch."

"Don't mess with me girl," there was ice in his reply.

"Real name, address and badge number." She tapped a finger on a piece of paper that sat folded on the bar between them. He stared at it for several seconds. She broke the silence.

"Do you want me to take care of him for you?"

He looked at her, trying to take her measure. She risked sending another wave at him, this time of sincerity and trust. She really couldn't tell whether she'd got him on board. She desperately wanted to avoid having to force or thrall him directly. Apart from the huge amount of energy it would cost her, it just wouldn't be as effective as good honest trickery. Tavens made up his mind.

"No, thank you. I'll deal with the filth myself."

He slipped the paper into his pocket and took out cash to pay for the drinks that had arrived. He reverted back to joviality as they returned to the table, though Hetty noticed him skilfully steer the conversation away from details of future plans. Tavens drew the night to a close after they'd finished their second drinks and clapped Tom on the shoulder as they left the pub.

"You've got a top girl there lad, make sure you be nice to her."

The younger man smirked back and missed the look that was exchanged between Tavens and Hetty.

Chapter Eleven

Twilight descends, announcing the approach of the true darkness yet to come. The few people who still make their way through the grounds of Hyde Park and Kensington Gardens pull their coats a little tighter, the relative warmth of the day diminishing rapidly. In the gloom, an army of giant sentinels stand guard, their leaves rustling in the light breeze. Set back some fifteen paces from one of the pathways linking the Broadwalk to the Small Pond, a mature common lime tree soars upwards, thick foliage sprouting along the length of its truck. Amongst the dense profusion of low growing branches clustered around its base, an amorphous form lies heaving on the hard earth.

On closer inspection the anonymous shape resolves into that of a young man lying on his side, hogtied awkwardly to the base of the tree. His wrists are secured behind his back with a single large black cable tie, his ankles bound similarly, with a third tie attaching them to the one about his wrists. A fourth binds the knot of limbs around a two inch thick branch growing near to the floor. Electrical tape wraps several times around his head securing a balled sock in his mouth.

He is clothed in black shorts, striped sports socks that have settled around his ankles and a pair of battered old trainers. His top is a blue rugby shirt with a small heraldic logo on it, spattered with flecks of mud and streaks of grass stains. The front is black with blood flowing from a deep wound to his belly. The thick liquid oozes through the fabric and drips steadily onto the parched earth beneath. With his well muscled arms and legs pinned tightly behind him, his abdomen is stretched taught and the gash bleeds freely, weakening him further with every passing second.

He wears a livid bruise on the front of his neck and his nose is smashed, though it produces only a trickle in comparison to his belly. His right arm angles back unnaturally, either broken or dislocated from the shoulder joint.

Lying nearby is an open sports bag with its contents spilling onto the ground. A dirty white towel bears the same logo as the shirt – a quartered crest with lions and a harp, an open book at its base. Imperial College's motto is stitched in tiny letters beneath it, SCIENTIA IMPERII DECUS ET TUTAMEN.[1] The rest of the roll of electrical tape lies next to a few scattered books, the only one face up gives its title as Kumar & Clark's Clinical Medicine. A smartphone sits a few inches away from the young man's face, a tiny symbol indicating its status as set to silent.

The man breathes hard, in short rapid intakes that he struggles to get through the remains of his nose. His eyes are wide open, the white of the left one tinged pink with the blood dribbling down his face. He looks at the phone so close by and strains his body in an attempt to move nearer. The effort puts him into a consuming spasm, the fit of coughing just a dull thudding through the gag. When he settles again he finds himself with his chin on the screen of the phone. He tries to drag it across the touch screen to unlock it, but two days of stubble thwarts the contact. He tries again and succeeds only in pushing the phone beyond reach entirely, the thrashing of his head unable to retrieve it. He looks at it one last time before momentarily screwing up his eyes in frustration and abandoning it.

---

1 Knowledge is the glory and the protection of the Empire.

He looks down at the blood pumping freely from his torso and starts rocking on his side, his left arm underneath him acting as a pivot. He manages to manoeuvre himself onto his back, which causes the cable ties to slice viciously into his limbs, his hands and feet crushed beneath him.

A flicker of triumph enters his eyes as he sees the new position force his knees slightly forwards and the tension ease a little on his abdomen. The rate of blood loss appears to slow, but now it trickles back down his chest and separates into two streams as it hits his chin, one going down either side of his neck.

The dark liquid is a stark contrast to the parts of his face that are not covered with tape or blood. Even in the failing light they are extremely pale, his features tired and haunted.

The minutes pass and his breathing gets slower and more shallow, his eyelids beginning to droop. He blinks them open several times in a desperate bid to stay awake and alive for a while longer. His tenacity is rewarded by rustling near his head followed by the appearance of a small Smooth Fox Terrier. The young man rotates his head to look at the little animal, which proceeds to sniff around his face, the thin black cord leading away from the collar and back through the leaves.

"Lucas! Lucas!"

An artificially shrill female voice pierces the quiet of the evening. The dog ignores its owner and carries on sniffing.

"Lucas! Come here boy."

This time the voice is more insistent and is followed by a gentle tug on the cord. The dog's head jerks to one side, but he plants his feet and stands his ground.

"Lucas! Lucas! Come here!"

The terrier looks the young man in the eyes and they hold a stare for several painful heartbeats, the man's eyebrows arched in urgent supplication. Twice more the cord is yanked, but this time with much greater force. The dog strains at the collar, refusing to be dislodged from his place beneath the tree. He starts to bark. First a single yelp, then follows a torrent of yaps that only stop when someone pushes their way through the branches. An ear splitting scream echoes across that part of the park as a well dressed middle aged woman stumbles upon what Lucas has found.

The young man's head hangs limp to one side, his eyes staring blankly at her feet, the crest upon his shirt perfectly still.

Chapter Twelve

Jack and Aaron walked up Long Acre, crossed over Drury Lane and found themselves standing by the imposing metal doors on the corner of Freemasons' Hall.

"Aren't we going in here?" asked Jack.

"No, these doors are only used on ceremonial occasions, we want the main entrance down there."

They carried on a little further and entered through more approachable glass doors into the United Grand Lodge of England, one of the great world centres of Freemasonry. The porters recognised Aaron but checked his ID all the same before setting about issuing Jack with a temporary pass. Slightly in awe of the place, the younger man kept his voice low and discreet.

"So how long have you been a Freemason then?"

"I'm not," replied Aaron in equally hushed tones, "but there are some here who're aware of the wider reality and very much support our efforts. The Freemasons have spent centuries guarding against the agents of the negative plane, indeed throughout history a number of Awakened have been in the Masonic Orders."

"Like who?"

Aaron chuckled.

"All in good time, the important thing for now is that they

hold and protect the single best source of information on our powers that I know of."

Jack gave him a questioning look, but got nothing more from his companion than "come and see."

They headed off into a maze of corridors and stairwells, with Aaron pointing out the wealth of symbolism incorporated into the magnificent art deco building. Almost everything seemed to tell a story or be part of some bigger scheme. Jack was surprised by the energy that had soaked into the walls around him and asked his guide about it.

"Well, the whole place was built as a memorial to those who fell in the Great War and I dare say a few architectural secrets have been employed to good effect. If anyone knows them it would be the Masons after all."

Some minutes later they reached what at first looked like a dead end in the depths of the basement, until Aaron opened a small wooden box on the wall. He put his face up to the retinal scanner inside and a concealed door swung open to reveal a short corridor. It was filled with a strong aura generated by numerous constructions of energy on the floor, walls and ceiling – complicated lines and shapes that pulsed with duty and purpose. Jack hesitated.

"They're protective wards," explained Aaron, "just walk through and ignore any sensations you feel. You'll be fine."

Jack did as he was told and tried to blot out the realisation that he was being examined. He opened another door and entered a small oak panelled room lit by a single bulb hanging from the ceiling. It was furnished with only a modest table and two wooden chairs. Sitting comfortably on the table was a huge book, its thick age-warped pages trapped between covers made from heavy sheets of lead. On its front was a simple inscription in a language that Jack didn't understand, though he thought the characters might be a stylised form of Greek.

"What does this mean?" he asked, as he traced his fingers over the engraved surface of the metal.

"According to a good friend of mine, it most probably translates in modern terms to *The Book of Ways*."

"Which means what?"

"As best I can tell it's a sort of scrapbook of powers of the Awakened. Over the centuries various people have made entries where they've recorded things they learned how to do, or just described some aspect of interacting with energy or the positive veil."

Aaron opened the book and started leafing through the pages, all of which were blank.

"This section deals with wards and shielding effects, these are about influencing the mind and body, and the ones later on I can't understand. I suspect they're meant for someone of your talents."

"But there's nothing there!"

"Look closely, at the energy contained within. Just relax and let your senses expand into it, like we practised the other day."

Jack breathed slowly and concentrated on the aura of the book. After a few seconds he saw the page in front of him resolve into a mass of fine lines of positive energy. Elaborate symbols and patterns of astonishing intricacy filled the sheet of vellum, writhing and dancing in desperation to share their knowledge.

He let his consciousness sink into the calf skin page and at first all he could sense was confusion and his own ignorance. He had no idea how much time passed, but gradually became aware of aligning himself with the periphery of the pattern, a creeping understanding of its essential form and what it might represent. He knew he had barely scratched the surface of what it contained but already he was tired and so brought his mind back out from the book.

"Well?" Aaron asked.

"You're right. This pattern has a connection with the fundamental laws of nature. It's something to do with physical forces, about how to generate and manipulate them I think."

"Excellent, sounds like it is the right part of the book for you then. Now you just need to start experimenting."

Jack grinned.

"That I can do."

Sabir stood doubled over, his hands resting on his knees whilst he breathed hard. He gulped down welcome lungful after lungful as he recovered from the punishment of the switching drill. It required the player to dodge and weave around a pattern of cones laid out on the grass, the constant changes of direction utilising nearly every muscle in the body and testing balance and coordination to their limits.

He looked at the next of his teammates to be put through the exercise. From The Gambia, Baboucar Mboge was the leading Premiership goal scorer the two previous seasons and was about to secure a third crown. He was tall and powerfully built, yet the speed and dexterity with which he navigated the exercise astonished Sabir. He drew in the focus of his vision until he could see the big man's aura clearly, great billows of positive energy rolled off the Gambian as he attuned his body perfectly to the task before him. As Mboge cleared the last of the cones he looked hopefully at the coaching assistant.

"That's forty-three seconds dead, sir."

The man holding the stopwatch then coughed politely before announcing the rest of the result.

"Half a second clear of Mr Chadili."

The big man let out a howl of delight before playfully slapping Sabir on the back.

"I got you this time my friend."

Sabir chuckled at the innocent pleasure the larger man derived from the small victory.

"Well done Baba, it had to happen sooner or later."

The pair of them made their way over to a different practice pitch, one of ten on the site that sat north of the capital, tucked just inside the M25. The Arsenal coaching staff divided the players into teams of seven and set them off on a series of small, fast-paced games. The format encouraged close control and rapid movement; it also tended to get competitive very quickly.

Kick-off was followed by a sequence of intricate passes, the last of which came to Sabir at pace. He controlled it on the top of his right boot, bringing it instantly to a complete stop. As the defender stepped in closer to him, he flicked the ball past his man and dodged around him. Sabir caught up to the ball and hit it first time with the outside of his boot. An inch perfect pass curved its way over to a man free in front of goal, who slotted home to open the scoring. The defender who'd failed to stop Sabir leant in with his shoulder as he ran past, bumping him purposefully. Sabir ignored both him and the slight puff of aggression that hung as red mist in the air.

The game flowed back and forth, the auras of the honed athletes generating much positive energy as they went about their work. The occasional bad tackle contributed the odd splash of negativity to proceedings.

As the score tightened up, both sides took matters increasingly seriously and the pace quickened until everyone was flat out. Again Sabir controlled a fast pass and this time spun his defender, accelerating like a greyhound as he moved towards the goal. He could sense a tackle approaching so tapped the ball further forwards, out of reach of the incoming player. It was too late that he realised the ball wasn't the target for the tackle, his legs disappearing from under him as the defender he'd angered earlier in the game took his retribution. Sabir spun through the air and instinctively forced energy through his body, heightening his senses and reactions. He saw the ground rising towards him and twisted his torso in time to escape landing head first. What he couldn't avoid was his left leg getting caught under him and the knee twisting on impact.

As he came to rest he bit his lip in frustration, he knew from experience that the sharp pain was not a trivial injury. As the other players gathered round, Mboge pushed the defender who'd made the challenge and demanded to know what he thought he was doing. The man protested his innocence but stormed off before he could be held to account.

Sabir was helped to the medical rooms and examined by the chief athletic therapist. It took nearly an hour before he got the verdict, by which time he had also showered and changed.

"We won't know for certain until after the swelling has gone down and we've done the scan. Right now I'd estimate at anywhere from three to nine weeks."

"Nine weeks? You are serious?"

"Maybe longer if the damage is more substantial than simple straining of the ligaments. You should be able to walk well enough by tomorrow, but keep the brace on and be careful to avoid torsion of the joint."

"Is three weeks definitely the minimum?"

"Until you can resume training with contact, yes. Though given we're so late in the season I've recommended shutting you down, and the boss agrees. No sense in rushing you back at this stage."

"So I miss the derby then?"

"I'm afraid so."

Sabir breathed a long sigh as he took in the news. It wasn't the first time he'd been injured and he knew not to think too far ahead.

"Well thank you anyway Doc. I will phone you tomorrow to organise the follow-ups."

He hopped gingerly off the treatment table, threw his jacket over one shoulder and hobbled out of the room with the aid of a walking stick. As he got outside he spotted one of the youngsters hanging around waiting for him.

"How is it sir?"

"I've had worse," he lied, "did you draw the short straw then?"

"Driving you home ain't no problem sir, not when you've

come in the Jag. I volunteered."

The eighteen year old was grinning from one ear to the other as Sabir threw him the keys to his showroom condition Jaguar E-Type.

Sabir and Rebecca walked hand-in-hand down Cheapside, the City thoroughfare busy with lunchtime traffic. Rebecca wore a respectable skirt and jacket outfit rather than her clerical garb, acutely aware that drawing attention to herself needed to be kept to a minimum. Sabir had forgotten his sunglasses and was squinting a little against the glare from the modern light stone buildings that lined the road.

"How's it holding up?" asked Rebecca, conscious of the way her partner favoured his right leg.

"Much better thanks to you," he squeezed her hand in gratitude, "but I will still need to take things a little slowly."

The previous evening Rebecca had helped the healing process by focusing positive energy onto the damaged knee. It had only been a small contribution, enough to get him a touch more mobile without drastically reducing his recovery time. They'd both agreed that remaining on the injured list gave him the perfect excuse to stay away from training, he could then devote more time to the problem of the mysterious entity without his absence raising questions. Despite its modest nature the process had still cost Rebecca a significant amount of personal energy, she felt the effects a bit like a hangover or the start of a cold.

"I still can't believe Gary went in like that, you've always said he's a reasonable kind of guy."

"He is, and although I am sure he intended to go in hard, I do not think he actually meant to hurt me. His aura did not look malicious, aggressive perhaps. He apologised after he had calmed down."

They walked on slowly until they got to Wood Street, where the long established premises of Higgins and Hall clung to its spot on the corner. The narrow two storey affair was dwarfed by the gleaming corporate buildings surrounding it and the huge London plane tree that stood behind, the branches overhanging the small flat roof of the tailors. The large windows proudly displayed hints of the exquisitely cut clothes to be found inside.

Sabir held the door for Rebecca, and it took both of them a few moments to adjust to the relative darkness of the shop's interior. Rich wood panelling on the walls gave the impression of tradition and quality, while the clean lines of the furniture spoke of modernity and contemporary fashion. An older man stepped forward, leaving a younger colleague hovering by the counter.

"Mr Chadili, how nice to see you again."

The man fawned professionally as he sensed a sale in the offing. Rebecca took a seat while Sabir set about ordering a brace of lightweight jackets for the forthcoming summer. He was deliberately indecisive about the cut and material type so as to give them plenty of time in the shop.

Both he and Rebecca sensed straight away that something unusual afflicted both the men, though it took some time for their auras to reveal the few fine strands of red energy that trailed from their heads. The gossamer threads protruded at random points from their skulls and blew around in the wake of the much larger wisps of energy that encircled them. Rebecca studied them whilst Sabir played for time. Eventually the clothes were agreed upon and the pair of them left the shop and headed back out into the bright daylight.

"So what on earth was going on there?" asked Sabir.

"I don't know for sure, but it looked to me like something had gone into their minds, those threadlike things being the after effects of the intrusion."

"Could that thing Jack saw have altered their memories perhaps? Or controlled them in some way?"

"I would have thought so. If it can avoid being picked up in plain sight by security cameras, not to mention killing Arthur Linthorp, then I'd think mind control would be well within its capabilities. I'm sure Aaron will have a theory anyway, I'll call him tonight."

"Very good. Now, on to more important matters. What do you want for lunch, I am thinking steak."

Rebecca laughed at Sabir's mock serious tone and they agreed upon the Smithfield Bar and Grill. They carried on along Cheapside and then went north along Foster Lane, where they had to cross the road to avoid a large pile of masonry blocks that sat messily on the pavement. An old building was being torn down and its more historic components were presumably going to be recycled elsewhere. They turned left onto Gresham Street and right onto St Martin's le Grand. Not long afterwards Rebecca caught Sabir wincing with pain and insisted he rest his leg. They took a seat in the high walled churchyard of St Botolph's quietly beneath the trees, the placidity of the headstones contrasting with the traffic on the nearby road. After several minutes of contemplation, Sabir broke the comfortable silence.

"Rebecca?"

"Hmm?"

"What do you think about marriage?"

"What, as an institution?"

"No, as in us. The idea of us getting married."

"Are you proposing to me? In a graveyard?"

She couldn't help but laugh.

"I am just saying." Sabir shrugged.

"Saying what?"

She turned to look affectionately at his face, and waited for him to continue.

"We have been together for over two years now, we love each other and we are not getting any younger."

"But we're not old now, are we?"

"No, but why wait?"

"Wow, you're serious aren't you?"

"I guess so."

"What's brought this on Sab? You've always laughed whenever someone mentioned marriage."

"I just want ... I just know that ..." he paused in frustration, unable to find or say the words. He tried again, speaking slower to encourage his thoughts out.

"I want to spend the rest of my life with you, and I just want to make the most of our time together."

Rebecca put her arms around his neck and hugged him.

"And I want to be with you, but give me a little time with this, OK?"

Sabir nodded his acceptance and Rebecca broke into a grin.

"I also might need a while to get my head round the idea of moving from 'and girlfriend' to 'wife'."

Sabir chuckled.

"My darling, you are not now and will never be, a WAG."

They resumed their journey towards Smithfield and it wasn't until they walked alongside the grand new building of St Bartholomew's hospital that Rebecca spoke.

"So if we did get married, would that mean children too?"

"Hundreds."

"Hundreds?"

"Well, two at least," Sabir qualified.

"Boy and girl?"

"If you like, as long as they both play football."

Rebecca looked down at her feet.

"I wonder if they'd be awakened too?"

"Would that worry you?"

"No, I don't think so, but it would be a tremendous responsibility."

"How do you mean?" asked Sabir.

"Well, who knows what sort of power they might develop with us as their parents. And what if they turned out bad?"

"Have you ever seen a bad one of our kind?"

"You know I haven't, but then I've only met the people Aaron has introduced us to, and Jack of course. That doesn't mean they don't exist."

"That is true, and for what it is worth I think they probably do. However, I know for a fact that our children will turn out just fine."

"How can you possibly know that?"

Sabir put his arms around Rebecca's waist and pulled her to him, a mischievous smile on his face.

"Because they will have the most beautiful, enchanting and loving mother in all the world."

She groaned and playfully pushed him away. They linked arms as they walked on, Rebecca smiling contentedly, Sabir's expression more sombre. Once past the alleyway at the back of the hospital they arrived at West Smithfield, the cavernous entrance to one of Europe's largest wholesale meat markets just ahead. The grandeur of the building belied the tens of thousands of carcasses that would hang within of a morning.

Sabir's knee twinged again so they stopped and took a seat at the tree covered gardens outside the market.

"This thing, this being we are looking for, what do you think it is really?" Sabir asked.

"I don't know. I've been thinking about what Aaron said and if it is some form of construct born of the negative veil, that'd explain why so many religions have stories of demons and evil spirits."

"I am beginning to think that since awakening, we should have got more involved in asking the kind of questions that Aaron has spent so much time on."

"How do you mean?"

"Well you said it yourself. This gift of ours is special and therefore also a great responsibility. And yet what have I done to make good use of it, to understand it?"

"Hey now, you lead a good life. You bring joy and inspiration to tens of thousands every week, maybe millions if you include the television audience. Through they you get to experience beauty and artistry they wouldn't otherwise see. Your gift is just an extension of what is already within you."

"That sounds very much like what Aaron would say," retorted Sabir.

"And he'd be right. I'm a priest for goodness sakes; don't you think I worry that I should be helping people more? Using my gift in some grand fashion to bring more people closer to the greater truth?"

Sabir sat in silence, not sure how to respond. Rebecca tried to reassure him.

"Look, we each use our gift to help us be better at what we do, which in turn benefits others. That is right and as it should be. Now that we're faced with something different, something bigger, we can play our part in tackling that too."

She squeezed his hand and stood up.

"Come on, let's eat. I thought you wanted that steak?"

"So yes, the tailors had definitely been manipulated in some way, but I didn't want to risk looking further into it without a definite plan. We also couldn't see anything else particularly obvious in the area nearby."

Rebecca concluded the account of her and Sabir's visit to Cheapside. She sat back in her chair in the library of the old house in Henrietta Street and sipped from the glass of water in front of her. Aaron sat pensively, his fingers steepled together beneath his chin. The others looked at him expectantly for some moments before he obliged.

"Well I've not come across anything exactly like that before, but there are many ways to interact with someone's aura and I very much doubt I've seen them all. It could be a result of the type of manipulation used, removing memories for example, which is something I've never done. Or maybe a kind of signature left behind by the individual, and in this case I think it's safe to assume that it's Jack's entity doing the manipulation."

"Hey, why does he get to be mine all of a sudden?"

"Figure of speech Jack, sorry. Let's just call him the entity from now on shall we?"

"Thanks."

"Leave me to do some thinking about what you two saw. It may be we want to go back and see what we can get out of their auras or memories, but I think your instinct to leave them be was correct. If that thing is nearby then we don't want to alert it that we're closing in. Now, let's move onto Mr Eastwood's update."

Aaron shifted in his seat, trying to get comfortable as if settling down to listen to a long story. For Jack's part he also fidgeted in his chair, but in his case due to unease. Besides their host, Rebecca and Sabir, a fifth person now sat around the table, someone who Jack had a nagging feeling he'd seen before but couldn't place him.

He'd been introduced at the start of the evening as Reggie Wiseman, the remaining Awakened known to reside in London. His dark skin and mass of dreadlocked hair suggested a Caribbean origin, something confirmed by his rich lilting accent. He was tall and fairly slender, but carried himself with quiet strength and dignity. He looked to be in his forties, but Jack had been assured by Sabir he was significantly older than this, though how much so hadn't been elaborated upon.

It wasn't just the feeling of déjà vu that bothered Jack. Reggie had two other traits that drew his attention. The first was the way in which his somewhat manic gaze roamed constantly about the room, only resting upon a person or object for a brief moment before moving on again.

The second was significantly more unsettling. Reggie's aura was strongly positive and very bright, possibly of an even greater intensity than Aaron's. Its swirls reached out lazily to indicate his awakened status. However, all the component strands of energy, including the few weak red ones, seemed in places to phase in and out, disappearing momentarily before reappearing as if nothing were wrong. Jack couldn't help feel that the man was literally not all there, his entire essence never always present. Jack shifted again in his seat and did his best to ignore the distraction.

"OK. Well as Aaron said earlier, I've been making some good progress. I can see the veils pretty clearly now when I want to, and bring auras in and out of focus quickly. I won't bore you with all the details but I've also started to figure out how to do other stuff."

Jack reached forward and took a glass off the table, leaving the round wooden coaster behind. He'd no sooner started to look at the small piece of wood than it flipped onto its edge and started spinning. Its rotation accelerated rapidly until it was humming away like a child's toy. Rebecca and Sabir sat open mouthed, Aaron had a look of mild amusement and Reggie paid no attention.

"I can't really explain it," Jack began, "but basically all you have to do is feel the beauty of the fundamental laws behind whatever it is you're trying to achieve. The energy involved then flows from that appreciation or understanding."

"You mean you are bending reality to your will?" asked Sabir.

"No, I don't think so. It's more like the possibility that the coaster could spin already exists. All I'm doing is encouraging the universe to choose that possibility over all the others by my visualising the forces in action. The universe then realises its own beauty."

Sabir's weren't the only eyebrows that were raised.

"I'm not making much sense, am I?" Jack apologised.

"That is alright, I do not think you need to explain yourself or your gift to us."

"Agreed," said Aaron. "Anyway Jack, enough of the parlour tricks, tell them what you found out about Professor Linthorp."

"Oh yeah, right. The other thing I've been doing is looking into possible motives for the murder, and I think I've found something. You may or may not be aware that Professor Linthorp was a notable figure in the graphene community. He ..."

"Graphene?"

"A form of planar carbon pioneered by Geim & Novoselov at Manchester University, for which they won a Nobel prize. In its basic form it has some pretty strange properties, but when doped with other elements it gets really interesting. It's sparked a whole new field of material science that has the potential to revolutionise entire branches of modern technology."

"Like what sort of thing?" asked Rebecca.

"Well, in Professor Linthorp's case he was working on applications in high temperature superconductivity, so things that have no electrical resistance at say room temperature. The uses for viable materials are many and lucrative – ultra efficient power transmission, super fast transport systems, it might even give a fast-track to cold fusion."

He reached down for his glass and drank before continuing.

"The technical details aren't really important, suffice to say that the commercial opportunities are enormous, simply staggering. Assuming that products can actually be brought to market of course."

"So the Professor was close to some kind of breakthrough?"

"No, that's the first interesting thing. He'd already made the breakthrough. He was the joint patent holder on a range of compounds that as far as I can tell have the best chance of leading the field for the next five, ten, maybe twenty years."

"So he was due to become rich?"

"As Croesus. And so was another of the patent holders, a Dr Abutsworth who was the owner of a technology transfer company based in Cambridge."

"Hang on, you said *was* the owner?"

"That's the second interesting point. He also died a few weeks ago, reportedly of a heart attack. He was in his fifties but apparently in excellent health, a keen sportsman according to his website."

All except Reggie exchanged glances.

"And there's more," said Jack with a grin.

"The third and final patent holder is a company that is wholly owned by a financial powerhouse here in London. *Avar Investments* is located in Gresham Street, which is conveniently just down the road from your tailors."

"So how does killing the two men behind these wonder materials help the remaining patent holder? Surely the scientists would be needed to help make the most of the inventions wouldn't they?" asked Rebecca.

"Not necessarily. With the patents published there'll be no end of companies seeking to exploit the technology and develop applications. The value in the intellectual property will be through licensing it to others, not through its sole use by the holders."

"But wouldn't the rights usually pass to the beneficiaries rather than co-holders?"

"I guess so, but then I have no idea of the arrangements in this case. At the very least I would suspect that the financiers now have complete control over what directions the patents are taken in."

"So how much are we talking about, what are these patents worth?"

"Impossible to say. They could be sold on quickly to someone else, or used to draw in royalties until they expire. Either way I'd guess at billions in the long run."

"Well that's motive enough," said Rebecca, "whatever its plans are it's a safe bet the entity will need money."

"Call a spade a spade, it's a demon, Becky."

The others turned to Reggie, the first time he'd spoken since sitting down at the table. He still glanced around the room, not concentrating on the others.

"Well whatever it is, it looks like we've got a better fix on its location," said Aaron, "the question is what to do next?"

With that he got up from the table and went over to the drinks cabinet for something stronger than the water the glasses had been used for so far. He phoned down to Wilkinson for tea for Rebecca and the others took the opportunity to get up and stretch their legs. There was much discussion over how to approach the situation and the debate lasted for nearly an hour. Eventually Aaron called it to a close.

"So, we're all agreed then? Reggie and I will take a look at the Gresham Street site first, then we'll let the rest of you know if it looks safe to come down. Assuming it is then we'll take it in turns to keep an eye on it. We'll keep the rota so that either myself, Reggie or Sabir are there," he looked at the north African, "are you confident you'll be able to hide yourself and whoever else is with you?"

"I am. It might be draining, but I am sure I can do it."

"Good, that's the spirit."

As the meeting broke up, Jack made a concerted effort to speak to Reggie before he left.

"Excuse me sir, I might be completely wrong but haven't I met you somewhere before?"

The older man smiled and for the first time looked straight at Jack, steadily holding his gaze.

"They said someone would come, but not on which side. So I keep an eye out for you, and sure enough they were right. That day in the Square I was watchin' which way you'd go. And you turned out OK, didn't you boy?"

Jack suddenly remembered the man emptying the bins in Russell Square Gardens. He opened his mouth to respond but Reggie had already turned and was heading down the stairs. Sabir slapped Jack on the shoulder.

"So that is Reggie."

"Yeah, not sure what to think yet."

"Well, whilst you are making up your mind, why not join Rebecca and me for dinner. We have a table at The Ivy, it is not far."

"I'd love to, but I'm seeing Mandy tonight."

"Bring her along, we still have not met this woman of yours."

"OK, thanks. Actually, she's been really keen to meet you

guys ever since I told her I'd found some friends of Professor Linthorp who also think he was murdered. I reckon she was quite relieved at that, though I haven't told her much else yet. Anyway, let me call her."

Rebecca joined them and they headed out into Covent Garden as Jack rearranged his evening. He put his phone away as they set off towards Shaftsbury Avenue.

"Mandy'll meet us there. So what's the deal with Reggie then? He said someone told him about me, what did he mean?"

Rebecca sighed.

"For want of a better description, he was referring to ghosts."

"Seriously?"

"Afraid so. They're real, or at least they are to Reggie, it's one of his powers that he can see and hear them."

"All the time in fact. It must be maddening," added Sabir.

"You saw how his aura fades in and out?" Rebecca continued.

"Yep."

"Well that's because he's in constant contact with both the planes, part of his aura is always connected to each one. Ghosts are souls that are trapped in both the planes at once, rather than having passed through to one side or the other, which is why Reggie can see and hear their presence. He can even communicate with them after a fashion, but whatever they say is always obscure and unreliable."

"Why's that?"

"I think it is because they are confused," suggested Sabir, "their existence being an unresolved struggle between the two energies. Rebecca puts it down to their negative element being inherently devious, is that not so?

"It's only a theory on my part, but yes, that's how it seems to me. Which is also why I don't trust Reggie. How can anyone be in constant contact with the negative plane and not be influenced by it?"

"It is more than just that though, is it not my love?"

"What do you mean?" asked Jack.

Rebecca was clearly reluctant to answer so Sabir continued.

"Soon after we first met Reggie, Rebecca offered to try and help him, to see if she could ease the constant suffering caused by the intrusions of these restless spirits. He accepted and opened his mind up to her."

"And?"

"And what I saw horrified me," said Rebecca, "it was like being on a battlefield, surrounded by bloody combat, except those fighting were all part of the same army, tearing itself to pieces. The confusion, the pain, the conflict, it was so disturbing. I couldn't even begin to understand it, let alone help him cope with it."

"Yet despite all that, his aura has only the smallest of negative components, no bigger than Rebecca's and certainly smaller than mine or yours. No offence Jack."

"None taken, I don't pretend to be a saint. But surely then Reggie must have incredible willpower to suffer from this constant barrage from the negative plane and yet remain relatively normal? If you see what I mean."

"I completely agree," said Sabir. It took some seconds for Rebecca to comment.

"Maybe, I don't know. I just can't get that horrible sensation of tortured discord out of my head."

They had reached the sharp corner of West Street and Litchfield Street where the latticed stained glass frontage of one of London's most popular restaurants stood. They entered the Ivy and whilst Sabir negotiated a larger table, Rebecca collared a waiter and ordered a large gin and tonic.

Chapter Thirteen

As the ordinary looking man inspected himself in the hall mirror, he ignored the muffled noises coming from the open doorway nearby. With his shirt sleeves rolled up the fine leather gloves he wore looked out of place. It didn't seem to bother him. He turned his arms to get a better view in the reflection and spotted some blood on his elbow, so he walked calmly to the small bathroom and carefully washed the offending mark from his skin. The water was shaken off rather than towel dried, and the shirt sleeves then rolled down and fastened.

He stood again in front of the mirror, satisfied this time that he was clean and ready to go. He put his large raincoat on, pulled the collar up high and made towards the door. Just as his hand got to the handle he stopped in his tracks and turned to walk back across the hall. He was in the lounge for no more than ten seconds before he came back into the hallway, slipping an Oyster card into his pocket in the process. On the second attempt he left the apartment, the door closing gratefully behind him.

Not yet summer, the late evening air was cold and made chillier still by the strong breeze that whipped around him. He stood on one of the upper balcony levels of the Barbican residential estate, the wind having a clear run at him, not at all slowed by the surrounding blocks of accommodation housed in their concrete shells.

He walked briskly down the steps and through the warren of brick paved alleys and walkways that interlaced the 1960s complex. It wasn't long before he arrived at Moorgate station and descended into the warmth of the Northern line. He waited quietly the five minutes it took for his southbound train to arrive, and then sat down unobtrusively amidst those already huddled in the carriage. Most were workers travelling back after clocking up unpaid overtime in their offices, though some had clearly been putting their hours into drinking rather than selfless effort for their employer.

At London Bridge, three lively young women got on and made their way to spaces not far from the man. They all still wore their workplace ID badges, which proudly announced the large financial services firm they belonged to. Their faces were flush with alcohol and one of them carried a half finished box of fried chicken, which another of the girls helped her to consume. The grease laden smell hung heavy in the air to the obvious disgust of the other passengers aboard, something picked up on by the girl who wasn't eating.

"How can you eat that shit, Kate? It smells revolting."

"But it tastes *so* good."

She waved the box closer to her friend and small pieces of batter fell through the cracks in its side. The third girl laughed and was soon joined by her companions as they broke into drunken conversation. They talked loudly and animatedly, oblivious to the presence of others in the carriage. Those passengers that got off at Elephant and Castle were grateful to do so. The conversation continued as the train moved on.

"You know, it's so cool we all ended up working for the same firm after all this time."

"Oh my God, it was like six years ago we were all sixteen. Can you believe it?"

"I know, I just hope I die before I get old, like thirty-five or something. My boss just had her birthday and she looks all worn out, like wrinkles and everything. No way I'm ending up like that."

The man's eyes narrowed as they fixed upon the owner of the now empty box of chicken. He sat and studied her as the other two girls said their goodbyes and got off at Kennington. By the time the train approached Oval he was still looking at her, her slightly bloodshot eyes staring straight ahead, oblivious to her observer. She stood up as the carriage slowed and hung on to a metal upright for support.

The man checked his watch and looked at the dial for some seconds. The train stopped and he glanced up at the girl as she started to move, and then back at his watch. He sighed and crossed his arms, sitting back in his seat. The girl got off the train and it carried on its journey southwards.

He alighted a couple of minutes later at Stockwell and set off down the main road, large redbrick blocks of flats on either side. It wasn't long before he turned down a road lined with smart and expensive looking townhouses. He retrieved a bunch of keys from a pocket as he walked past the last of these bigger properties, then turned up a path towards another block of flats. A main entrance led to a small lobby, and two flights of stairs later he used the key to open the door to a modest apartment. He balanced on each foot in turn in the cramped hallway as he took off his shoes and added them to the other three pairs sitting neatly on the floor.

His coat was hung in a fitted cupboard, and he leaned forward past the other garments to access a small safe set at the back. Into it he placed a gun he drew from a concealed holster, a lock-knife from an inside pocket and an Oyster card. The latter joined the six others that sat in a neat pile on top of a small leather medal case. He shut the safe and then the cupboard, and headed towards a closed door. As he opened it, the nightlight in the hall shed a dim but warm glow onto him as he crept quietly into the room. He bent down next to a small bed and tenderly kissed the forehead of a sleeping boy, perhaps ten years of age. He walked further into the room and repeated the process with a second smaller child. He paused to look at the two young forms so peaceful in their rest, before closing the door softly behind him.

He went to the tiny kitchen and took a bottle of cheap Russian vodka from the freezer, almost emptying it as he poured himself half a large tumbler full. He walked the few paces to the lounge and sat down wearily on the inoffensive Ikea sofa where a small red light at the bottom of the television set shone in the darkness. He got up to switch it off completely, using the button at the side and then sat back down as heavily as before.

A swig was taken from the glass every few minutes but it was still half an hour before the drink was finished. He got up and went to the bathroom, the light that came on shone underneath the door, adding to the glow in the hallway.

He came out and went to the only other door in the flat, which he opened with exaggerated care. The soft illumination of the nightlight shone through and onto the face of a sleeping woman. The small hairs on her arms stood to attention as they lay outside the duvet, hugging it tightly to her chest. The man slipped quietly into the room and closed the door.

Hetty stood in the middle of her room holding the skimpy black dress against her naked body, she couldn't decide whether she liked what she saw. She turned to the side, momentarily ignoring the dress in order to concentrate on the shape of her thigh. She nodded in approval.

The dress hit the bed and another one took its place, a dark blue strapless that had an even tighter cut. She pursed her lower lip in indecision and went back to the black dress.

"Ferren!"

Her summons was loud and assured, with enough easy command to suggest it was accustomed to being answered promptly. She turned round, holding the dress against her back and looking over her shoulder, trying to see what it might look like from behind.

"Ferren!"

This time her voice was more demanding, the note of righteous impatience rewarded moments later when the door opened and her brother walked in. Hetty smiled to see the bright flush rush up his neck as she turned to face him. The black dress was brought slowly round to the front, eventually covering the object of Ferren's gaze.

"I can't decide what to wear little brother. There's this," she pulled the dress taught around her chest, and then causally swapped it for the blue one, "or this. Which one do you like me better in?"

He stood with his mouth open, unable to respond.

"I quite like this," she picked up the black dress again, "but I wasn't sure whether I look slutty or not."

Ferren was trembling ever so slightly as he managed to force out a reply.

"No sis, you look fine in that."

She dropped her hands and let the dress hang down by her side as she stepped closer to her brother. Her breasts touched his chest and she shuffled a little further, pressing against him and pushing her left thigh forwards into his crotch until she could feel him. Ferren was breathing harder, intoxicated further by the sensuous aroma of her body lotion. She moved her head slowly, her lips just a tantalising inch from his. As he leaned nervously forwards to meet her she shifted gently to the side, letting their cheeks brush until she could whisper in his ear.

"I want to look slutty, you pathetic little fuck."

He stepped back in horror and fumbled the door open, then fled down the corridor chased by her laughter.

With a huge smile on her face she put the black dress back in a wardrobe where she also chose some shoes to go with the blue number. Her knicker drawer took longer to sort through, the various sets of lingerie each getting careful consideration. She had to move the thank you present from John Tavens to one side in order to get all the parts of the black silk combination she had decided upon, the dark shape of the Browning 9mm pistol nestled comfortably amongst the lighter shades of the garments left behind.

Once her choices were assembled she dressed quickly and put the finishing touches to her makeup. She threw a few items into a small designer handbag and sauntered down the stairs, calling behind her as she confidently planted one high heel after the other.

"Don't wait up for me darling!"

They swayed in time to the beat of the music, the DJ at Stilleto having just started a Paloma Faith medley with *Broken Doll*. Hetty slipped her arms around the waist of the attractive girl she'd been dancing with and stared into her eyes to reinforce the control she'd placed on her aura. It had been built up over a couple of weeks and now held the girl completely enthralled, her pupils heavily dilated. The positivity generated by the music was quickly subsumed by the thick red band that wrapped around her, stopping her component swirls from moving freely.

Hetty looked over the edge of the balcony to the boisterous group in the middle of the main floor of the club. They'd been there nearly an hour and few of them had left the confines of the collection of sofas they lounged upon. The core of the Tottenham Hotspur team were celebrating a convincing win over Chelsea and alcohol was being consumed in quantity. There were approximately as many women again in the group though clearly not one to each man, some were wives, some girlfriends and others rather less permanent fixtures.

Hetty focused on one player in particular and sent an impulse towards him. Steve Marshall was one of the most famous men in the country, not just the captain of his club but also of an England team that had finally started to live up to its potential. His fame was compounded by his marriage a few years earlier to the talk show host and national favourite, Michelle Kalendar. She was so smitten that despite her career she had even discarded her own surname in favour of his. She was not amongst the women in the group that evening.

Marshall shifted in his seat and gazed up at Hetty. She held his stare and then leaned forward and kissed the girl, long and passionately, turning so that she maintained eye contact with Marshall below. She noted the throbbing of his aura, the bright bands of energy pulsating as they swirled around him. He was strong and a complicated mixture of positive and negative influences struggled for control.

He said something to the man sitting next to him and left the group, making his way up the stairs to the dance floor. Most of the squad then started to follow, several being led by the women they were with.

The music had changed to *Do you want the truth or something beautiful* by the time Marshall walked over to Hetty and started to dance close to her. She avoided making eye contact with him and continued to focus on the girl a pace in front of her. Step by step he manoeuvred himself between the two women, but Hetty turned her back on him and carried on dancing. His teammates and their various partners were now on the dance floor too, some of whom egged him on, others looked on in disgust. One of the women urged her partner to intervene, but he shook his head and distracted her by dancing closer.

Intent burned on Marshall's face as he grabbed Hetty's arm and turned her to face him, pulling her body next to his. She glared defiance back at him and sent an impulse at point blank range. He lunged forward to embrace her, the kiss aggressive and hard. Hetty returned in kind, almost biting his tongue in the process. Then she pushed him away to arms' length to make room for the other girl to slip in between them, over her shoulder Hetty mouthed at the footballer,

"We come together."

Marshall grinned, his aura pulsating strongly as the negative started to dominate the positive. He grabbed the girl and forced his tongue into her mouth. She put up no resistance and only meekly participated. Hetty joined the embrace and the three of them stood holding and kissing each other for a couple of minutes, lost in the energy of the moment. When she sensed the time was right, Hetty put her lips to Marshall's ear.

"I know somewhere we can party properly."

He nodded and turned to say something to one of the other players nearby, but Hetty put a hand on his arm to stop him.

"No, just the three of us."

"Sure, OK. My driver's out the back."

Marshall led the way holding Hetty's hand, while she in turn held the other girl's. The three of them left the dance floor to a mixed chorus of cheers and disapproval from the other dancers.

Hetty stood in her stockings, suspenders and bra, her neck flushed and her inner thighs aching. She leant on the dressing table for support, trying to catch her breath and focus on her plan. Soon after they'd arrived at the exclusive London hotel she had discovered just how voracious the footballer's sexual appetite was. She hadn't particularly enjoyed his crude approach but she had gratefully soaked up the waves of aggression he gave off.

She put the energy to use straight away and threw up a simple shield around her as Avaro had taught her to do. A shroud of red mist surrounded her almost naked form that made the two figures on the bed oblivious to her presence, though by the looks of things they wouldn't be noticing much anyway. Marshall was already at work again, thrusting forcefully into the girl from behind. She held onto the headboard as she was rocked violently back and forth.

Hetty took the smartphone from her bag and switched it to video mode, using the screen to sight the action on the bed. Marshall grabbed the girl's hair and jerked her head back towards him as he let forth a stream of expletives in her ear. Eyeing past the camera Hetty could see his aura take on a new level of intensity, the negativity now swirled in coruscating waves that consumed his personality.

With his other hand he slapped the girl with all his strength on the buttock and thigh until her skin was as bright and inflamed as the aura her tormentor now possessed. Hetty moved slowly round towards the head of the bed, careful to keep them both in frame until she had clear pictures of their faces. His a vicious grin, hers sobbing and bobbing with each thrust. Her tears sparkled in high definition as they dropped down onto the bed sheet and disappeared.

Hetty finished her filming and gathered her dress, shoes and knickers from the floor, taking them with her handbag to the bathroom. She sent a brief text message and then hurriedly put her clothes on, taking a few moments to adjust her hair and redo her makeup. By the time she rejoined the main room, Marshall was close to climax. Seconds later he shouted as he thrust a few last times into the girl and then collapsed on the bed, momentarily exhausted. The girl slowly unclenched her hands from the bed frame and lay down, curled up in a ball.

Hetty dropped the shield and leaned over Marshall to use the last of her reserves and wave another impulse at him.

"Don't forget to leave via the side exit, and take her with you, see she gets back safely."

"Hey, where are you going?"

"Home, which is where you should be."

Hetty slipped out the room and took the lift to the main entrance where she climbed into a waiting taxi.

Some half hour later the discreet black side door opened and Marshall stepped through, he held out a hand to help the girl down the single step and into the street. Two seconds passed.

"Oi, Steve!"

The footballer turned to face the noise and a volley of flash photography went off, forcing him to blink and then shade his eyes from the lightning of the paparazzi.

*

Ferren bent down and scratched the back of his leg, the third time he'd done so since putting the trousers on. In the end he'd gone to a charity shop to find the clothes he needed, something cheaper and more worn than anything he had in his wardrobe. He was sure they were supposed to have washed the jeans thoroughly before selling them, but he couldn't get rid of the nagging feeling that maybe the itch was a result of the previous owner's personal hygiene standards. What could it be, a flea or mite perhaps? He forced himself to stop scratching and tried to ignore the irritation.

He stood near a street corner on Holloway Road, the north London part of the A1 that ran southeast from Archway to Highbury & Islington. It wasn't just vehicles this major arterial route carried, but also culture and lifestyle. The largely Victorian area had long been a melting pot for the wide array of people who gravitated there, from immigrants and students to trendsetters and media types. A lively blend of sights and smells overlaid the fumes and noise of the heavy traffic.

Ferren took a packet of cigarettes from his pocket and lit up. He was careful to avoid inhaling as even the low tar brands made him cough, but he found them to be a great device for looking inconspicuous while hanging around without actually doing anything. Despite Avaro's coaching he couldn't get the knack of blending in or shielding himself in the way that Hetty could, so he had to rely primarily on more mundane methods. Five times in the last few weeks though he'd resorted to direct manipulation of individuals who had been suspicious of him, but the instances were rarer since he'd started dressing more casually.

He leaned on a lamppost and watched a group of young men sitting on plastic chairs outside a street cafe, where they chatted jovially and laughed at each other's jokes. The Islamic taqiyah that each of them wore on their heads was the only thing that distinguished them from any other bunch of well-to-do friends.

The strongest and strangest of the auras was the final target that Ferren had identified, the last one he had yet to work on. While the rest of those in the conversation were brightly positive, the largest purple strand in this man's personality appeared stretched until it was almost flat. It kinked and twisted in places which prevented it from swirling smoothly around him and instead moved in a jerking and laboured fashion. Where it had folded upon itself the strand had grown strongly negative and dark red filaments now sprouted from these sites and wrapped themselves around the other parts of his aura. Ferren marvelled at the complex and profound warping of the young man's once pure ideology and knew he had little left to do.

It wasn't necessary for Ferren to interfere with the man's current philosophy, it already pointed in the direction he needed and, in any event, to do so would be a complicated and fiddly task. All he focused on was implanting a memory of the man having met him before, and an accompanying sense of complete trust. Although Ferren was skilled in such manipulation, it was still a taxing exercise and he reeled slightly as he sent the last piece of the implant towards the man. It took him a few minutes to recover enough energy to perform a final scan and check everything was in place.

Ferren threw the butt of the cigarette into the gutter and smiled at a job well done as he turned to leave. The weeks of searching and chasing leads had finally secured him all the component parts of the teams he needed, now he had to worry about moulding their ambition to his design.

The late evening air had a slight chill to it as Ferren strolled past the comfortable town houses. There were quite a few people out and about, some coming back from work, the balance heading towards the various entertainments North London had to offer, many of them students and young professionals. Ferren stopped outside a house where a bright light shone in the front room, its occupants silhouetted against a net curtain. The different shapes and activity suggested a family sitting at a table, perhaps eating dinner. He paused to get his thoughts in order and then rang the doorbell. After ten seconds he started to fret as to whether he should ring again and realised he needed to calm down. He used a small amount of energy to lower his pulse and proceeded to wait patiently. The door eventually opened.

It revealed a small, amiable old man dressed in loose fitting clothes and a taqiyah. The gentle kindliness of his aura made Ferren's skin crawl. He muttered something Ferren didn't understand and looked back expectantly.

"Khadim?" tried Ferren, suddenly nervous he'd got the wrong address.

The old man nodded, turned slowly and then beckoned over his shoulder as he shuffled off towards the back of the house. He rounded the corner and waved a hand to indicate the white door close to the bottom of the stairs. He smiled at Ferren and then ambled back to the front room, from where the noise of happy children escaped briefly until the door closed behind him.

Ferren glanced around unsure how to proceed. He decided to knock on the door and wasn't reassured by the two deadened taps he managed to produce. Forcing himself into his role he followed them with a pair of more confident and assertive knocks. The door opened only a crack at first, but after a couple of seconds the gap grew wider and a hand encouraged him into the darkness.

Whilst it took some moments for his eyesight to adjust from the bright corridor, the auras of those present were beacons that filled the small room. Three men sat on the floor and a fourth stood next to him having just closed the door. All of them displayed the characteristic thinning and folding of warped convictions, of sensibilities corrupted to malign purposes. A level of synchronisation had built up amongst them and each of the twisted strands pulsed to the same stilted rhythm.

Ferren felt the heat of the accumulated negative energy and breathed it in gratefully, intoxicated by its complicated flavour.

The man next to him clapped a hand on his shoulder and addressed the others who looked up at them.

"My friends, let us welcome Casimir, who will help us on our most blessed path to Paradise."

Chapter Fourteen

Jack closed the door behind him and went through to the living room where he dropped two bags of shopping onto the coffee table. Sabir stood by one of the windows looking out and down at an angle into the street, a pair of field glasses held steadily to his face. Jack took place beside him and followed the other man's gaze towards the London office of Avar Investments.

"He still in there?" Jack asked.

"If he did not sneak out when I was going for a pee, then yes, he is there."

"You still up for this? I mean, we don't have to go in tonight, we could always wait for the others."

"Jack, back home we have a saying. *Unless you poke the camel, it will never move.*"

Jack frowned at his friend, who continued to look out through the binoculars.

"Yeah, well I'm not sure I like the sound of poking the camel, but on the other hand it has to beat sitting here all night. Oh, and I brought some food too."

They had been on their shift since lunchtime, when they'd relieved Reggie of lookout duties. Renting the flat had been Sabir's idea, and he'd paid the extortionate deposit and first month of rent in cash. The small apartment was on the top floor of a building across the street from Avar Investments and some fifty yards further down. The viewing angle was acute but it also meant they weren't so close as to feel exposed should their target glance in their direction.

In the ten days they had been taking it in turns to monitor the entity's activities, they had observed it to be keeping standard if somewhat lengthy office hours. It had only turned up three times, but when it did it arrived early morning, and always departed mid evening.

Jack shared out the contents of one of the shopping bags and they chatted quietly as they ate, alternating watches on the building across the street.

"So what disguises did you choose?" asked Sabir.

"Well, you said you wanted normal faces rather than monsters or anything too outlandish, so how about these?"

Jack took two large latex masks from the other shopping bag and held them up proudly.

"Bush and Obama? I should be grateful it is not Clinton and Lewinski I suppose."

Jack kept the rubberised George W and threw the other to Sabir. They pulled them over their heads and looked back at each other.

"Is this a change we can believe in?" asked Barack Obama.

"Don't misunderestimate it," retorted a strangely camp George W Bush.

"OK, so I think we can drop the accents," said Jack as he turned to peer out the window, "but hang on a minute, what's this?"

The two presidents looked out together and saw the unmistakable aura of the entity as he left the building, rounded the corner and headed away towards Cheapside.

"Seven-forty," Sabir checked his watch, "let us wait thirty minutes, just to be on the safe side. Then we go in."

The pair of them finished their food and Jack stayed observing as Sabir took a call from Aaron. Despite the roof of the Avar building being several stories higher than their position, Jack noticed there was something on top of it that appeared to have an aura of sorts. He stood on a chair to get a better view and couldn't make out what it was, it looked vaguely like someone crouching though its red aura was static, not dynamic like a human's. He checked the publically available satellite images on the Internet and could see a number of indistinct shapes forming a circle on the roof of the building. He added it to his list for investigation.

"Aaron is sending over an email," Sabir put his phone away, "but the summary of what can be found, is that the few records there are say it is on the site of what in Roman times was a large villa. There is nothing further until the Great Fire of 1666, at which time whatever was there burned to the ground with everything else in the surrounding area."

"Where did Aaron dig that up? He doesn't really strike me as a history buff."

"He is not, but his *good friend* Sophia is, she is an archaeologist at the British Museum."

"Good friend? You mean as in ...?"

Sabir nodded.

Jack smirked, but he let the subject drop.

"Well it doesn't sound like there's much to go on does it?"

"I agree. However, he did say the current building was most certainly constructed in the early 1920s, with the frontage an addition of the early 1970s."

"Which is strange, as all that limestone we can see is pretty classical in design don't you think? Not exactly what I'd call modern architecture."

They went over their plan one final time before leaving the apartment, the masks in a small backpack. They walked to an alley nearby where Sabir stopped and took several deep breaths, focusing his concentration on making the pair of them as unobtrusive as possible. When he was satisfied that he'd achieved as powerful a shield as he could comfortably maintain, he handed George W to Jack.

"Now we will see if this works."

They donned the masks and walked round the corner to the Avar building, passing a commuter on the way who ignored them completely.

"So far, so good," ventured Jack.

Having already observed that the main doors wouldn't be locked until much later – one of the traits of a hardworking investment firm – they pushed them open and walked straight in. The guard at the desk was engrossed in the sports section of a newspaper and didn't even look up, so they crept past him and glanced up at the CCTV camera covering the lobby.

"Check the panel," hissed Sabir.

Jack tiptoed back and looked over the guard's shoulder, there was a small black and white monitor that was displaying the view of the lobby. The overlaid text identified it as 1 of 26 in the building, though as far as Jack could tell the view had been left on that one and it wasn't cycling through the others. He rejoined Sabir and whispered his findings.

"We should be OK, he's not paying any attention. Let's not hang about though."

They went through the doors and into an open plan office that took up the majority of the ground floor, two people worked quietly at computers on the far side.

"Can you feel that?" asked Jack.

"I know, it is ..." Sabir swayed a little and grabbed hold of Jack for support. One of the workers looked towards Bush and Obama, but after a couple of seconds shrugged and went back to his computer.

"It is OK, do not worry, the shield is still up. Whatever is down there is strong. Very strong."

They could both sense a huge concentration of negative energy below, it produced a tingling sensation akin to being charged with static electricity.

"Look, I think we both know where this is heading, but why

don't we start at the top. I want to see what's on the roof if we can, and at least check to see what else is here."

Sabir agreed and they made their way up the nearby stairwell. They went past the seventh and final office floor and got to the roof exit. Jack reached out with his aura and checked the door and its surround for alarms. He found no trace so pulled back the large two bolts, and reached again with his thoughts to the lock. It took a few seconds for him to feel the alignment of the pins inside, nudge them into position and then rotate the whole mechanism until it clicked open.

"Nice work Mr President," complimented Sabir as he pushed the door open and they stepped out onto the large flat roof. Arranged in a circle about two thirds the width of the building was a collection of seven statues, each of which was set on top of a plinth about a metre tall and faced roughly clockwise around the circle. The figures were a collection of monstrous humanoids and mythological creatures each with pained and distorted features. They all crouched down in some fashion, and none were more than a metre high. The figures and their plinths were all made of a dark grey stone that looked black in the failing light. As they got closer Jack and Sabir could see the stone surfaces had once been polished to a fine sheen, though all were now dull and stained with the best that London's smog and pigeons could throw at them.

The intricate carving was both gruesome to behold and exquisitely executed, with curled lips, bared teeth and penetrating eyes all threatening to come to life in but a heartbeat.

Jack could now make out the aura that he had seen from below. Each of the statues glowed an intense red but it wasn't quite as static as he'd first thought. The negative power they contained actually pulsed very slightly, as if they were alive somehow. He could sense the movement of energy in the space before him but it was slow, so slow and subtle that it wasn't easily perceptible. He walked into the middle of the circle and stood there, trying to attune himself to the energies around him.

Sabir was still inspecting a statue of a vicious ogre-like creature when he heard the dull thud of Jack falling to the ground. He rushed over and found him blinking and shaking his head.

"The bastards, it's just like my experiment! Well, I reckon I know what this thing is now. Would you mind helping me up please?"

Jack went and sat by the door whilst he waited for his head to clear before explaining.

"You see how each statue is pointing two statues to the left? Well there is some kind of weak negative energy field that each is sending in the direction it's looking. It's not like aura energy, it's more a slight crease in the negative veil itself. The shape the creases transcribe is a heptagram, a seven-sided star, and the overall field it's producing is creating a rotating flow of negative energy that it's sucking in from the atmosphere around us, just like the top of a whirlpool."

"So where is the energy going? I do not see much up here."

"Exactly, just like a whirlpool the flow is going off along the axis of rotation, in this case downwards. I'm willing to bet the point it's focusing on is somewhere in the basement, where we sensed that strong presence coming from."

"So this is all some type of negative energy generator?"

"More of an accumulator, I don't think it generates anything, just concentrates what's already floating around the City."

"That does not sound very good, my friend."

"Nice understatement. Come on, let's see what else there is to find."

They agreed to have a quick look round the rest of the building before venturing towards the basement. As they descended the floors they passed only a few people working late, none of which paid them the slightest attention. Some doors to small private offices were locked, but much of the building had been altered to accommodate slightly larger open plan working spaces. The interior was a strange contrast of muted modern furnishing in the office areas and art deco styling in the corridors. Large metal lattice decorations ran along the walls in places, their design characteristic of the 1920s. Jack stopped frequently to inspect them more closely.

"This must be how the energy is transported downwards. There's a weak flow inside the metalwork, it's acting like a conductor."

Sabir focused in as hard as he dare, conscious that he didn't want to let the shield he still maintained slip.

"But that is so very weak, I can hardly detect it at all."

"Sure, but this stuff is all over the building, I think there's more inside the walls too, not just what we see on the surface. Add it all up and that's quite a lot it's siphoning from up above."

They carried on making their way downwards until they arrived back at the ground floor. Jack checked on the security guard and found that he appeared not to have moved, the CCTV image on his monitor still showed the same picture covering the main entrance.

They spent ten minutes searching for routes downwards and eventually concluded that the only possibility inside the building was the unlabelled door in the lobby. The lock was more complicated than the one on the roof and it took Jack several attempts before he could get it open. They looked around the small office space inside and were about to start leafing through the drawers and paperwork.

"Hang on a moment, I don't think we should touch this stuff," said Jack.

"Because?"

"Well, we're bound to leave some trace of our aura and we've no idea how easily that thing will be able to detect it. The last thing we want to do is alert it, right? I'm already thinking I shouldn't have messed with the lock."

"OK, we leave this lot until we come back with the others. What about that though?" Sabir indicated the more substantial inner door on the far side of the office, where an aura surrounded the lock.

"Whatever kind of manipulation has been done to it already, there's no way I can open it subtly, if I can open it at all."

"So this is as far as we go this evening. A shame, I had really wanted to find out what was down there."

"Me too, but we can't risk it. Whatever it is, it's probably better faced with all of us anyway."

They looked round the room again and couldn't see any obvious trace of their presence in terms of things out of place or lingering energy, so they retreated and let the door lock behind them. Two minutes later they were back in the alley where they removed George W and Obama to reveal two quite sweaty but real faces. Jack grinned, he had enjoyed the thrill of their foray, his confidence buoyed by his increasingly adept abilities.

"So do you want to tell the others or shall I?"

Rebecca paced around the Gresham Street apartment, the impatient movement helping to ward off the anxiety she felt as midnight approached.

"I still think we should keep someone as a lookout, what happens if it comes back whilst we're in there?" she said.

Aaron leaned back in the sofa and clasped his hands behind his head.

"Then we'll deal with it together, better that than leave one or two behind to risk facing it alone. Besides, from what the boys said it sounds like we're better off staying as a group."

Reggie muttered something from his place at the window that neither of the other two could hear, then returned to gazing out through the gap in the blinds. Rebecca glanced at him before changing the subject.

"Maybe you're right, we'll see. Did you manage to find anything else out from Sophia?"

"No, not really. She just confirmed that there are distinctly fewer records concerning that site than others nearby. Certainly the museum doesn't have anything more on it."

They lapsed into silence for several minutes until Sabir and Jack came in, each carrying a sledgehammer.

"What on earth have you got those for?" asked Rebecca.

"Well, we probably only get one shot at this, so I want to make sure we get those grotesques up on the roof. If we can't figure out a smarter way to disable them, then ..." Jack hesitated, "better the hammer than the camel?"

He looked to Sabir for confirmation, who chuckled at the other's attempt.

"Jack my friend, we will make a Berber of you yet."

"Have you two been drinking?" enquired Rebecca.

"No my love, but our apologies for being late. We are here now."

The five of them readied themselves and then left the flat for their assault on Avar Investments. Sabir maintained a shield on them as they congregated in the nearby alley, whilst Aaron donned the Bush mask and set off for the main entrance. He reached the big glass doors and knocked twice, a few seconds later it was opened by the security guard.

"Evening Sir Lyell, what brings you in this late?"

The portly watchman ushered Aaron into the lobby.

"Just preparing for a big meeting tomorrow. Anyone else in the building?"

"No Sir, last one left at 22:45."

"Good. You can return to your desk and rest now. Write your password down too would you."

"Right you are, Sir."

Aaron sent the last of a series of strong impulses towards the man, who scribbled a few characters on a pad on the desk, then sat back in his chair and promptly fell into a deep sleep. Within seconds he was snoring comfortably, so Aaron stepped back outside and signalled to the alley. Obama jogged up and went straight to the guard's desk, after logging into the system he started shutting down the twenty-six CCTV cameras in the building.

"All clear."

Jack took off his mask and by the time he'd stowed it in a backpack, the others had joined him in the lobby. They used the lift to get to the seventh floor, then walked to the stairwell to access the roof. With improved fluency, Jack opened the lock before they even reached the door.

They stepped outside and were greeted by a gentle breeze that made the air seem chillier than on the sheltered street below. They gathered round the nearest of the statues, a deformed fox-like creature sitting on its haunches. Reggie ran a hand over its smooth surface.

"This stone's some kind of diorite, like the Egyptians use for the top of their pyramids. It's also bloody hard stuff."

He climbed up onto the plinth and grasped the statue underneath its snout. He calmly and slowly lifted the front end a few inches and then toppled it sideways onto the roof. It fell with a dull and heavy thud as it bit into the roofing felt.

"Aaron, if you please, this might get noisy man."

The American reached forth with his aura and set up a shield around them, one that wouldn't let any sounds they made travel very far. Reggie jumped down, took a sledgehammer from Sabir and swung at the grotesque lying on the floor.

Jack was amazed at the strength of the wiry Caribbean, he handled the fourteen pound hammer as if it were nothing at all. For all the force he deployed though, little more than a chip came off the figure. He carried on swinging, but each time nothing larger than a small lump or flake would come loose. He stopped and leaned on the handle.

"I can keep goin', but we'll be here quite some time. Anyone got a bright idea?"

"Well, potentially we don't need to break all of them," offered Jack, "even one should help a lot."

"How do you figure that?" asked Rebecca.

"It's all to do with symmetry. The reason this thing works so well is that it's based on a prime number, with seven statues there's no line of symmetry. I reckon it's why triangles and pentagrams are traditionally associated with the occult. If you have lines of symmetry then you need to accurately balance everything either side of them or it won't work. With no symmetry, everything just contributes its maximum to the whole."

"You didn't mention this before."

"Sorry, it's only just occurred to me," Jack shrugged apologetically.

"It makes sense," said Aaron, "in most of the stories I've come across about the Awakened working together, they're usually in threes or fives. But this is the first explanation I've heard."

"With all respect, can we leave the study group until later?" asked Reggie.

"Sure. Actually I might have an idea, give me a moment," said Jack.

He inhaled deeply and as he breathed out let his consciousness relax and extend to the statue. He attuned himself to its form until he felt the imperfections in its structure, the natural fault lines within the stone. He spotted what he was looking for.

"There," he said, pointing to a spot just above the figure's shoulder, "hit it there, in this direction."

He waved his hand to indicate the line of motion.

Reggie planted his feet, hefted the sledgehammer and swung with all his strength. The hardened steel head drove straight through the statue, shattering it on impact into hundreds of smaller pieces. Reggie looked down appreciatively at the sledgehammer in his hands, and then grinned at Jack.

"Good work my boy, what about the next?"

One-by-one Jack sought the weakest point in each statue and instructed Reggie where to strike. Despite two of them requiring several attempts, it took barely ten minutes for the whole collection to be reduced to rubble. The stone chunks that littered the roof still glowed with residual negative energy, but the directed whirlpool effect had vanished. Aaron slipped a small stone shard into a pocket for later examination.

"That's a good start guys, shall we see what's downstairs?"

They set off for the lobby, the mood amongst them one of cautious determination. Once there, Jack dealt swiftly with the first lock and looked to the others before he attempted the second one in the former broom cupboard.

"Look, I can't tell for sure what it is that's been done to this one. It could be an alarm but my gut feeling is that it's a secondary lock. I'm just going to try and rip it apart, so let's move quickly once it's down, OK?"

They all nodded their agreement and he turned back to face the door. Jack concentrated on the complicated knot of energy that sat around the mechanism and sensed the different strands used in its construction. He reached out with his aura and took hold of the three component filaments. Once he felt his grip secure he tugged at all of them simultaneously. The strands smoothly unravelled from the complex seal, and vanished into red vapour as soon as they were free. The door now appeared entirely mundane, so Jack reached in again and manipulated the mechanical parts of the lock until it clicked open.

They descended the rough stone corridor and felt the energy build as the passageway curled downwards. Body hair stood on end and they could see the weak negative elements in each other's auras pulse brighter as they fed hungrily on the thick atmosphere.

When they reached the bottom they could see an intense red aura shining through the gaps around the solid oak door, the wood itself looking hot to the touch. They all inspected the door carefully but the energy it radiated seemed uniform, with no evidence of a ward or seal on it. Aaron grasped the metal ring and turned it easily, the door swinging wide open.

The negative aura within hit them like a blast furnace, its intensity was so great that it had even started to manifest itself as a visible red glow in the middle of the room.

The heat washed over them and the worst of their personal traits immediately swelled as the energy attempted to undermine them. Jack reeled as he felt his insecurities rise to the surface, his heart thumping as he realised that Mandy didn't love him after all, he'd just been deluding himself all along. In which case, what was the point, why did anything else matter? His head swam with the crushing inevitability that he was, in fact, truly alone.

Then he felt a hand on his shoulder and a steadying, calming influence settle upon him. He glanced back to see Reggie standing peacefully, the swirls of his aura lapping out and tenderly reassuring each of theirs. His core glowed with resilient positivity as he passed some of his strength onto the other four.

"We're all strong, we're all good in our purpose. Let's enter this place, it holds nothin' over us."

They walked into the burning dryness of the room, its oppressiveness a heavy weight pressing down on their shoulders. Although every step was difficult to take, none of them buckled as they struggled forwards. As they neared the centre, half-way between floor and ceiling, they saw the single point that was the focus for all the energy. The negative veil itself had started to unravel. Tiny sparks played around fine threads that hung in the air, the fabric of the barrier between the real world and the negative plane seemingly worn and frayed. They could all sense the enormity of what lay beyond the veil bulging against the weak point, threatening to burst through.

"What the ...?" Sabir left the question hanging, unable to work out what to ask.

"It's a rift," said Jack, "a partial tear in the negative veil. The energy in here is eating away at it."

"Why would negative energy attack the negative veil, that doesn't make sense?" asked Rebecca.

"Strange as it may seem, I think each of the veils is actually constructed from some form of the opposing energy type.

So when you draw from across the positive veil, it takes your innate positivity to temporarily suppress the negative energy it's made of. In the same way, all the negativity gathered here is slowly dissolving the positive energy that the negative veil is made of, resulting in a very weak point, or rift. Sounds screwy I know."

"Do you see the area surrounding the tear? Where it looks like it has re-grown? I think the hole used to be bigger, I'll bet that's how the entity got through," suggested Aaron.

"Maybe," Jack replied. "Perhaps it partially closed up afterwards, a kind of reflex reaction. Whatever the case, with this whole building set up as an accumulator – even with the stuff on the roof destroyed – I can't see it being too much longer before the rift is fully open again. And if that happens, who knows what else might come through."

"So the real question is what do we do now?"

They all looked hopefully at each other.

"Whatever we do, we'd better do it quickly," warned Reggie, "we can't stay here much longer."

Jack bit his lip as he pondered, his aura prodding the tear in the veil, testing it, understanding it. He made up his mind.

"I can repair it. I think."

"Are you sure?"

Aaron was unable to keep the scepticism out of his voice.

"No, but I reckon it's worth a try. I can feel what needs to be done I'm just not sure if I have enough strength. This place is making me weaker with every minute we spend here."

"The rest of us can help with that. We'll channel what energy we can to you, maybe combined it'll be enough."

Aaron arranged them in a circle around the rift and each then focused intently on their role. Reggie kept on watching over their auras and sent the remainder of his strength around the circle towards Jack. Sabir lent what he could, as did Rebecca. She also tried to draw directly from the positive veil, but in that place it seemed so far away she wasn't able to gather any more than she already had. Aaron collected the positive energy from the others and passed it smoothly to Jack, who stood next to him. By the time the American had contributed his own reserves as well, there was a steady and substantial flow for Jack to use. He forced himself to relax and began to attune to the rift in front of him.

Jack had no idea how long he stood there, time failed to register with him. As he delved deeper and deeper he ceased to be aware of himself and his consciousness merged with the fabric of the veil. He was its structure; he was the layer upon layer of complexity. He was every single thread, composed of ever smaller ones. He felt himself exist at lower and more profound levels until there was nothing except him/the veil and a single infinitesimally small point where he/it no longer existed. He willed the gap to close, he believed with every fibre of his being that it would.

Nothing happened.

At first.

And then, the tiniest of gaps was gone, filled by the threads of the veil around it. They started interlacing, one wriggling its way into a tight weave with those nearest it, then another and another. As Jack felt his consciousness retreat he could sense the veil repairing itself, reordering back to its most fundamental pattern, whole and strong again.

Suddenly he was back in his body, staring at the smooth sheen of an intact negative veil. Then he realised he was on his knees, panting hard to get his breath back, sweat dripping down his face. He looked up at the others, they now stood close around him, strong arms helped raise him to his feet.

"My boy, you're a marvel!"

Reggie slapped him on the back as Rebecca and Sabir both hugged him. Aaron looked on, gently shaking his head in disbelief, amidst the celebrations the others didn't hear his question.

"My God Jack, just how powerful are you?"

They wasted little time in getting away from the terrible presence the room still held, though they were confident the energy would start leaking away now that both the accumulator and the rift had been dealt with.

Aaron stopped briefly to implant a final instruction in the security guard. The next day he would call in sick and then catch a flight to Spain to stay with relatives, he might even consider starting a new life there. The group regretted his involvement and hoped his absence would save him from any immediate retribution.

Maybe it was the influence of the basement room giving them each a heightened sense of danger, but in their haste to leave the building they completely forgot about searching the office for further clues as to the entity's intentions. Something they wouldn't realise until they met safely back in Henrietta Street the next afternoon.

Chapter Fifteen

Ferren and his sister walked briskly down Queen Street heading for The Copper Pot, one of London's most antiquated coffee houses.

"So he was in a strop?" asked Hetty.

"More like incandescent, it was all I could do to get him to meet somewhere vaguely public, I thought it might be a little safer."

"Why take it out on us? It's not our fault the rift's been closed, it's always been his thing. He's never let us near it, not since the day we arrived anyway."

"I know, but he didn't sound exactly rational on the phone. I hope he's calmed down a bit by now, please try not to piss him off."

They arrived at the dark frontage of the shop, its black paint flaking in places, the small grimy windows in serious need of a clean. They went in and made their way between cramped chairs to the counter to place their order, nodding an unreturned greeting to Avaro on the way. He sat with his back to a wall and looked straight down at his cup, no hint of the usual easy smile on his face. Sweat began to prick Ferren's brow as he hissed to his sister.

"Look at him Het, when was the last time you saw that much

energy?"

The older man's aura was glowing so brightly that it seemed almost white to the twins in the dark confines of the coffee shop. Only a couple of tiny patches on the surface were dulled, he looked not so much like lava as pure molten core.

They sat down with their drinks and sipped them quietly, waiting for their summoner to speak. After an exaggerated delay he obliged, his tone flat and dangerous.

"You took your time."

"Sorry about that, the Tube was running slow, passenger action I believe," apologised Ferren.

Avaro looked back at his drink and fell silent again. After a couple of minutes Hetty was bored of sipping her latte.

"So what happened?"

Avaro looked up, his expression still dull.

"Two nights ago a group of guardians broke in and closed the rift, they also destroyed the intensifier."

"A group?" Hetty exclaimed. "I thought you said there was only one."

"One that I knew of for certain, the warlock that I ran into at the university. It was always likely there would be more, the other place was not going to suffer such an imbalance without some form of reaction."

"Some form of reaction? Our plan is screwed! Well it looks like you underestimated that bloody warlock doesn't it?"

The malice in Avaro's eyes burned into Hetty as he unleashed the full weight of his aura. A bolt of red hot energy hit her in the face and enveloped her head. To most patrons in the coffee shop the pair of them sat glaring at each other. Ferren flinched at the ferocity of the mental strangle hold placed upon his sister.

"Do not presume to question me, whelp."

Avaro tightened his grip and Hetty whimpered involuntarily at the pain.

"I am the eldest. I am the one entrusted with this task. I will see it done," he squeezed the grip tighter still.

"Av, she didn't mean to ..." Ferren was cut off as a second bolt struck him and added his suffering to that of his twin.

"I will have your silence too."

Both Hetty and Ferren were held motionless, the rest of the shop oblivious to the torment being exacted upon them. For several long breaths Avaro kept them there while he savoured the temptation to crush them. Then he sighed and dropped the holds, the vicious brilliance of his aura subsiding a little as he did so. The other two sat cowed, their senses reeling from the attack.

"It is of little consequence, there are other ways to achieve our objective. You two must focus on your own projects. With the intensifier gone we will need to inspire even greater levels of energy within the population. You should stop by the chamber on your way home and stock up before what has accumulated ebbs away."

"Yes sir," Ferren managed meekly, while Hetty just nodded.

"Good. Now, here is what we do next ..."

The fat strip of pavement was crowded with commuters as they waited in frustration for the arrival of the next bus. Two had already passed with little room for people to cram onto them, and most at the stop were determined not to let a third go by. Some had even resorted to walking to the stop back up the road in an effort to secure their place. A collective feeling of righteous indignation rippled amongst those left behind.

The morning rush had become like an arms race for bus travellers, with people starting their journeys earlier and earlier to beat the queues. With so many moving off the Tube, London's above ground network was at bursting point despite the extra services laid on.

On this morning a rather thin man in his twenties was oblivious to the tensions around him as he focused intently on the smartphone in his hands. He was lost deep in an alternate reality where the streets of London were somewhat more sinister than those actually around him, the artwork chosen by the game's developers being more reminiscent of Gotham than Hackney. In this world he wasn't Gary Hawkins the secondary school geography teacher, but Gaz_the_Gr8 the muscled enforcer who bowed to no-one and roamed the capital taking whatever he wanted.

As his avatar entered the glowing door of a nearby building, he failed to spot the hazy shape that followed him into the unique instance, its form made all but invisible by the special stealth ability the character employed. Once inside, Gaz_the_ Gr8 quickly started searching the halls for monsters to beat up and loot, the ultimate prize being to find one of the more valuable pieces of treasure in the game, the American Espresso Black card. This was only ever dropped by the Chief Executive Officer whose chance of appearing was a mere 13%, and then only if the player had entered the instance from the proximity of its real world equivalent location. Having tried the same quest every day for the past two weeks, he had mapped out a route that would get him to the boardroom and give him a shot at the top prize before he reached his place of work.

Gaz_the_Gr8 stood motionless for a while on the fourth floor whilst Mr Hawkins pushed his way onto a bus, and then resumed his trail of slaughter towards the top floor.

He vanquished countless low level office workers, a posse of cleaners who wielded mops as deadly weapons, several zombie security guards and a particularly nasty vampiric secretarial pool.

His gym bag was bulging with cheap loot by the time he reached the ante-chamber, which was guarded by a very prim looking executive PA. Having faced her before, Gaz_the_Gr8 knew she was one of the toughest monsters in the game and had to be killed before trying to attack her boss, otherwise she became nigh on invincible in his defence. Eager to try out the solution he'd read about online the night before, Gaz_the_Gr8 grabbed the PA's stapler from her desk, used it to pin her to the wall and then proceeded to beat her to death with the Handbag of Envy he'd looted from the HR manager on the sixth floor.

"Yes!"

Several heads turned to look at Mr Hawkins as Gaz_the_ Gr8 kicked in the doors to the boardroom to reveal the CEO cowering at the far end of a huge marble table. He'd finally got lucky and this time the prize was within reach. As he marched forwards a group of five sharp suited figures materialised in front of him, each holding copies of Hostile Takeovers – Lessons in Company Combat, with which they started to attack. The fight was brutal and fast, the corporate lawyers taking a lot out of Gaz_the_Gr8 and forcing him to use all his medpacks to survive the combat. Soaked in blood he turned to the CEO, who promptly dropped his wallet and dived through a secret door behind him, which slammed shut before Gaz_the_Gr8 could respond.

He reached down and looted the wallet, the much sought after charge card appearing as a special icon in the corner of the screen. He started to make his way towards the express elevator which would take him straight back to the lobby, when all of sudden the icon disappeared and a blurred motion rushed past him.

You've just been pickpocketed!

The phrase flashed up in bright yellow and Mr Hawkins let out a howl of rage, which drew more raised eyebrows from those on the bus. He knew straight away that the card was lost to him, whoever had stolen it must be a thief of at least the same level as his enforcer to have piggybacked his instance. He charged in vain towards the elevator, only to find it already going down. There would be no way of catching up to them now, they'd be long gone by the time he got to the lobby.

Mr Hawkins sat and seethed, muttering expletives under his breath until a thought struck which prompted him into action. Gaz_the_Gr8 equipped his Hudson's Heroic Motion Tracker and set it for all players in the same instance. He got only one ping on the display and it was right on top of him. They must be extremely close, they must be on the bus with him.

Mr Hawkins got up and walked back down the aisle, looking for signs of anyone else logged into Streets of Gold. Seeing nothing upstairs, he went to the lower level to continue his search where he found one man absorbed in his smartphone. The guy was in his mid-twenties but quite overweight, the cheap suit he wore bulged about his doughy physique. Mr Hawkins peered at the screen and recognised the stolen icon in its corner. His face red and the thin veins of his temples pulsing visibly he clenched his fist, the other hand holding onto an upright near the door for support as the bus swayed its way along the road.

He wanted to say something, he wanted to hit the bastard, he wanted to make him pay, but he knew he wouldn't. He'd always been too timid, allowing himself to be pushed around by others. He was wrestling with his timidity when the other man got up, slipped the phone into his pocket and took a place by the door next to Mr Hawkins. The man's grin went from one side of his face to the other, and as the bus slowed he muttered quietly to himself.

"Gaz the great fucking noob more like."

Before he realised what he was doing, Mr Hawkins stuck out his foot just enough to catch the other man's trailing leg as he went to jump off the bus. Missing his step, the man fell forwards and headlong into the gutter where his face smashed against the concrete kerb. Passengers getting off at the stop crowded round to help as the bus started to pull away. Mr Hawkins remained on the bus, exhilarated by the triumph he felt as he looked out the window at the receding scene.

"Who's the fucking noob now, arsehole?"

It was late evening and the southbound Victoria line platform at Oxford Circus station was still fairly busy. A few were on their own, but most people sought the safety of two or more as they chatted nervously in their eagerness to have their journeys completed without incident. Ferren and Hetty also waited for a train back home, their mood somewhat more relaxed than their fellow travellers.

"Blimey, had it really been around for that long?" asked Hetty.

"Oh for sure, three millennia at least, and properly open several times."

"Wow, no wonder he was upset. That must be kind of embarrassing, to have a bunch of lowly guardians destroy such a venerable rift."

"Not so lowly, after all they did manage to close it."

"True, but it's still a huge mistake."

"Absolutely, the irony of course is that Av almost certainly led them to it as a result of killing those scientists, all for a bit of extra coin. It's priceless really."

The twins' laughter was a little hollow, it not being so easy to enjoy the misfortune of another when it affected them too. Hetty stopped chuckling when she spotted something a little further down the platform, which she pointed out to Ferren so they could watch together.

A woman on her own had been rummaging in a rather large handbag and unwittingly dropped her purse on the floor. A man had seen her do this and approached to point it out. He said a few words and crouched down to retrieve it for her, but as he stood up the woman became agitated. The purse was proffered only for her to pull a small canister of pepper spray from her bag and proceed to cover the man's face with the liquid.

He screamed and staggered backwards into his group of friends, two of whom started shouting at the woman, who also shouted back. The commotion soon escalated and platform staff arrived to try and calm the situation. Within minutes a uniformed officer was also on scene and arbitrating between the parties involved.

Hetty shook her head and smiled.

"I've got to hand it to you little brother, that killer of yours has really got people spooked."

"Why thank you Het, that means a lot to me."

They boarded their train and a little while later were walking back from Pimlico station to their house, grateful for a stroll in the cooler evening air after the heat of the Victoria line.

"You know," said Hetty, "I still think we should just kill the warlock, and the other guardians for that matter, assuming we could find them. Why risk leaving them at large?"

"Come on sis, Av's right, much better to have him on our side than dead."

"I suppose, but what if it doesn't work?"

"Yeah well, it had better. I wouldn't want to face the boss if there's a second screw-up."

"No way, me neither."

Their walk continued in silence as each contemplated their part in the new plan.

Steve Marshall stepped out through the front door of his mansion in that most exclusive of London's streets The Bishops Avenue, and had the uneasy feeling he was being watched. He got swiftly into the back seat of the Bentley Mulsanne that had pulled up outside, letting his new driver know that he was running late and that they should hurry.

Marshall sighed. Yes, he probably was being watched – on-line by a million perverts and hypocrites. The video had spread all over the world and although reputable sites had removed it fairly promptly, it was still available on countless thousands of others.

Michelle had moved out and was staying at Claridges, the high profile haunt no doubt recommended by her publicity expert. She had retained the best in the business to help guide her through the minefield of what was left of their marriage.

As the car sped away from Hampstead Garden Suburb and towards central London, he recalled the events of that evening and still couldn't work out exactly what had happened. He knew he'd been set up alright, but how could he have been filmed so blatantly without him realising it?

Fortunately Marshall wasn't the type to brood. What was done was done, he'd screwed things up good and proper and he'd just have to make the best of it. Much better to focus on the forthcoming derby, the points were critical if Tottenham were to pip both United and Chelsea to the title.

After he'd gone over in his mind that month's set plays from the training ground, he realised they weren't far off arriving at the awards ceremony he was about to attend. Yet another evening of media types fawning over each other and pretending not to be jealous of their colleagues' success. Still, his own PR guy had said an appearance would be helpful. Michelle was sure to be there and it would give him a chance to show the public that he wasn't hiding anymore. No smiling, just be respectable and professional. And stick to soft drinks.

He smoothed his dinner suit as the car pulled up at the red carpet outside the Grosvenor House Hotel on Park Lane, and stepped out into the ever present wall of flash photography. Despite the loathing he felt for the vermin, he nodded politely at them and gave a small wave to the huge crowd lining the walkway ahead. Many rows deep they surged forward against the barriers, the vast majority of them booing and hissing as loudly as they could. The taunts from some of the women were particularly vicious, as bad as anything that could be found on the terraces.

Marshall had come to expect the abuse and had all but stopped hearing it. It had the same venomous ring to it as many away games and his skin was thick enough to block it out. As he neared the end of the carpet, a teenage girl with a serious face stepped out in front of him as two security guards tried desperately to push their way through the barriers to get at her. She took a couple of paces towards Marshall until she was little more than arm's length away and swung a hand up from her side.

An arc of thick red paint flew through the air, spattering up his dinner suit and over his neck and face. Instinctively he'd stayed his ground, never one to back down, so her protest had landed almost entirely on him, only a few drops losing themselves amongst the lush pile below.

Marshall opened his eyes, two bright white circles amidst the crimson mask, and held her triumphant glare until she was tackled by the belated security guards and led away. He turned slowly on the spot, for the first time properly aware of the hoots and screams of derision that came from the crowd and walked back towards the traffic line where a limousine was pulling up. The onlookers went deathly silent as Michelle Kalendar, for she had resumed her maiden name, stepped from the car and stood face to face with her husband for the first time since she'd moved out.

"Hello Steve, red faced again?"

The crowd erupted in cheers and applause as she swept straight past him and into the hotel. She didn't look back.

While he waited for his car to be brought round, he took off his jacket and used it to wipe as much of the paint off as he could. The jacket was then handed to one of the event staff who, as it turned out, would later sell it via an online auction site for quite a lot of money.

Eventually he was able to retreat to the backseat of the Bentley, where he sat stunned and wondered just how his PR man was going to try spinning the evening's events.

Avaro stood on the corner of Goodmans Yard and sighted down the Minories. He had been trekking about the eastern edge of the City of London for most of the day, trying to make sense of the modern road alignment and judging where places of old might now lie hidden beneath the tarmac. He set off for what he believed should be his destination and enjoyed the feeling of closing in on his target.

He knew that he could have started his search online and no

doubt located what he wanted in a fraction of the time, but he'd felt strangely nostalgic the last few days and doing things the hard way seemed like suitable penance for the recent mistakes.

In a previous incarnation he'd known the area extremely well, but his memories of the early days of Londinium had been difficult to recall. He remembered the smells and sounds as if they were yesterday, the stench of the tanner's yard, the metallic ringing coming from the blacksmith's. The feel of the ancient city he recalled perfectly. The exact details of place and direction less so.

He got half way down Haydon Street, turned down an alley beside a lengthy residential block and into the parking area behind. He shook his head at the inappropriateness of such a blandly utilitarian structure as a car park covering as significant a site as this. Admittedly not all grave yards were places of great power, but then that rather depended on who was buried there.

Avaro stood to one side to let a driver pass by and spread his arms wide. For several minutes he concentrated, sending his aura deep into the ground as it searched for the traces he was interested in. Three times he moved to other parts of the car park and focused upon different areas until he was satisfied he'd found the cemetery's boundaries and inspected all of its domain.

He frowned.

He wasn't surprised not to find much, but he was a little disappointed. There was a small residue under the mirrored glass office block that bit into the north-west corner of the car park, but what he sought was certainly long gone. He sat down on a low wall nearby and took out his smartphone. Time to resort to the Internet.

He browsed for nearly an hour as the evening started to draw in, making deft use of the tiny display to conduct his research. Just as the battery warning alarm started to flash, he got the answer he'd been looking for, and it made him smile. He had been meaning to go to the British Museum and see what gems they had unwittingly recovered from around the world. Now he would show them just what the relentless progress of modern life had unearthed in the violated ground below a simple car park. Some things were never again meant to see the light of day, including one of Londinium's greatest legacies.

Chapter Sixteen

Jack gratefully slurped the top half-inch off his pint of John Smith's to avoid spilling it as he retreated back through the throng in the hospitality suite of the Director's Box. On reaching some space at the rear of the room he raised his beer to Sabir's orange juice.

"Cheers!"

The Moroccan smiled at his friend's excitement, but the disappointment in his eyes said he'd much rather be playing in the north London derby than watching from the stands. Although his leg wasn't troubling him too much, he was still quite a few weeks from being able to train, let alone re-join the squad. His season really was over.

"Come on Jack, let us take our seats."

They made their way outside and into the swell of energy that filled the Emirates Stadium, sixty thousand excited auras contributing to the miasmic haze. As they reached their seats, Jack stood for a few seconds before he sat down, to breathe in the atmosphere and marvel at the rippling currents of energy sweeping the stands. Vociferous knots of supporters started chants and songs, some of which died out quickly, others spreading until they were the refrain of thousands.

The vast majority of those present were Arsenal fans and it

wasn't long before most had put voice to a sustained chorus of *Stand up if you hate Tottenham*. The hairs on the back of Jack's head bristled as the electricity of the collective chanting flowed over him. He wasn't an Arsenal fan, and he didn't dislike Spurs, but he found it impossible not to be drawn by the power of such unity amongst the army that surrounded him.

The two teams lined up and went through the perfunctory ritual of shaking hands with each other, before letting a coin choose the direction of engagement. The accompanying music and announcements went unheard, drowned out by the torrent of abuse crashing down upon the cohort of supporters at the away end. With both sides primed and ready, the referee raised an arm and blew to start the match.

The first passage of play was lightning fast as each team sought to stamp their authority on the game. Tackles flew in and possession changed frequently, until after a short while the pattern of the game started to emerge. Tottenham were overwhelmed in midfield, the centre of their formation critically weakened with Steve Marshall sitting on the bench, unable to exert his influence. Arsenal pushed forwards repeatedly in swift, elegant attacks that carved easily through Spurs' defensive ranks.

As fascinated as Jack was by the skill and artistry being exhibited by the players, he was more intrigued still by the intensity of the energy being generated on and off the pitch. It fed back and forth between players and supporters with a bewildering complexity.

"Hey Sab, I knew people got pretty passionate about their football, but this is insane."

Sabir turned to him and grinned.

"Well, this is one of the more energetic games of the year."

"But it's all so confused. There's inspiration and loathing, sincere fervour and vitriol – all in the same person! Multiply that by tens of thousands ..."

Jack swept his hand out in front of him, indicating the massed hoards crammed within the stadium. Sabir had to lean closer to make himself heard above the chanting of the fans.

"Football is just giving them the opportunity to express themselves. I genuinely believe that for most here it is a harmless release. They can satisfy their tribal instincts and let out some of their negativity in a harmless manner, or relatively harmless anyway. Hopefully they go home a little better than when they arrived, more so if I and my colleagues play well and show them how beautiful the game can be."

"But what about all the problems that football's had with violence and hooliganism?"

"Thankfully it is not so common these days, but if someone has that intent then they will always find a way. Whether through football, or in a nightclub, or just randomly on the street. People bring free will into the stadium with them Jack. If they want to be inspired they will be, if they want to be aggressive then that is their choice too."

Jack looked at some of the people nearby and studied their auras closely. He could see that despite their manner and the words they used, for the most part they were gently venting the negativity within themselves, not generating significant amounts more of it. There were some sections of the stands that glowed bright red with a more sinister sense of purpose, but these were a small minority.

He sat back and let his concentration de-focus so that he could get a broad impression of the stadium as a whole. The mood ebbed and flowed like a rolling tide as the spectators reacted to the events on the pitch. The average colour of the energy in a given area fluctuated depending on the allegiance of its inhabitants and their team's momentum within the game.

The home crowd enjoyed the first half. Arsenal's strength in midfield held Tottenham to a few poor quality chances and provided many better ones for themselves. Despite their superiority the match remained scoreless, the tension heightened by anticipation of the all important first goal.

Jack and Sabir went for more drinks at half-time, the latter exchanging greetings with numerous people in the hospitality suite. One particularly beautiful young woman embraced him warmly and enquired after his injury.

"It is coming along very well thank you," he replied, "I have the summer to get back into shape and I hope to be ready in time for the pre-season tour. But where are my manners? Mel, this is Jack Eastwood, a good friend of mine. Jack, this is Melanie Pomaynay, songstress and fashion icon."

She raised her eyebrows at Sabir's description but demurely proffered her hand to Jack, who wasn't sure whether to kiss or shake it. He chose the former.

"Delighted to meet you Miss Pomaynay. My girlfriend loves your music, and your line of clothing," he frowned good naturedly, "actually, I rather think she wants to be you."

Melanie laughed at the compliment before taking on an affectedly coy demeanour.

"Ah, but if she were me then she wouldn't get to go out with you, would she ..."

As Jack started to blush, the girl winked at him and disappeared into the crowd. Sabir tried hard to stifle his laughter.

"Sab, was she just flirting with me?"

"I believe she was, but do not take it personally, she does that with everyone she is attracted to. It annoys her boyfriend – our left winger – most intensely."

"Seriously, Mandy is never going to believe this."

They finished their drinks in the company of some of the other luminaries watching the game, Jack somewhat relieved that Melanie didn't reappear. The second half had just started by the time they hurriedly resumed their seats.

After fidgeting for several minutes Jack apologised for not going at half-time and made his way up the concrete steps towards one of the many blocks of toilets. Twenty seconds later he was back next to Sabir.

"That was quick."

"No, I haven't been yet. But I've seen something really strange."

"Such as?" Sabir asked absentmindedly, his focus on the corner about to be taken by Arsenal.

"I don't know exactly, but I think it's another entity."

It took several seconds to register with Sabir, but when it did Jack had his full attention.

"I am sorry, say that again."

"Over there." Jack turned to his right and pointed down towards the rows of seating nearer the touchline, some forty metres away. Following his line-of-sight, amongst the inflamed auras of the other spectators, Sabir could see a woman who appeared both powerful and peculiar. The weak positive and negative strands of a normal human were each enwrapped by thick, strong cords of red smoke, so dense and coherent that they looked more like steel cables than ethereal vapour. They coiled so tightly around their underlying filaments that it was difficult to make out the colour of the strand underneath. In many places the tight outer coils frayed and the tendrils that had come loose lapped out at the surrounding air in the same manner as did the auras of Jack and Sabir.

The woman was young and, though very attractive, her face was hard and unforgiving. Sabir shook his head in disbelief.

"Another one? It cannot be."

"What else then? If she were just awakened surely the aura would look more like ours. But that? It doesn't look very natural to me."

"Agreed. I will call the others and give them the good news," Sabir said ruefully.

"And I'm going for that pee. For some reason the need just got a little worse."

By the time Jack returned to his seat Sabir had got through to Rebecca and made arrangements, which he filled Jack in on.

"We watch and wait for now, and try to follow it when it leaves. The others will meet up in town and be ready for our call. We will coordinate with them as we go."

"Fair enough, but how do we stop it spotting us? We might be alright in this crowd but what about when we leave?"

"Ah, well I might have a solution to that. You know the concealment shield I can do? Well Aaron has been teaching me a version that masks the aura of an Awakened. I think I should be able to keep our nature fairly well concealed, but we should be careful all the same. Also, I can sense her presence from at least this distance so we need not get too close, though it is quite hard in this crowd."

They settled down to keep their vigil, with only half an eye for the action on the pitch. With nothing on the scoreboard a quarter of an hour into the second half, both managers tried substitutions to break the deadlock. Amongst those entering the fray was Steve Marshall, whose reception from both sets of fans was deafening and almost universally hostile.

Despite the crowd booing every time he touched the ball, his impact was immediate. His strength and skill brought the middle of the field under Spurs' control and very quickly the tide turned in Tottenham's favour. They forced several decent chances during the next ten minutes before it became obvious to Jack and Sabir what the woman's real interest in the game was.

As the play neared the edge of the pitch closest to where she sat, they saw her stand up and a bright bolt of crimson energy shoot from her to Marshall. It fizzed sparks like a firework before striking his aura and causing it to pulse dangerously. Within seconds he had lunged into a tackle that he was never going to win cleanly, and brought the other player painfully to the ground. As a cluster of opposition surrounded him he squared off with Danny Jacobs, another mainstay of the England squad and in other circumstances a good friend of his.

They were toe-to-toe when suddenly Marshall head-butted Jacobs, the smaller man crashing to the floor with blood streaming down his face. Pandemonium broke out amongst the players and it took the match officials more than five minutes to restore order, by which time Marshall had been escorted forcefully from the pitch by security staff.

For a few moments the crowd put their differences aside and joined together to hurl abuse at the perpetrator as he was led away. Vast plumes of negativity rolled down the stands and pooled on the pitch, where a thick fog had started to gather. Jack and Sabir saw the woman draw from the energy and her aura strengthened considerably as mist flowed into her, a beacon amongst the flames of the angered crowd.

The match eventually restarted with Tottenham down to ten men and their handicap was soon exploited by Arsenal. The home team took the lead through a stunning finish from Mboge and, having scented blood, added another a few minutes later. The bulk of the fans were elated and gave voice to a variety of deafening choruses, though the chanting was aimed more to taunt their unfortunate opponents than express happiness at their own good fortune.

The accumulated negativity weighed heavily on Jack as he saw the atmosphere in the stadium for what it was, the underlying menace making his scalp tingle as it would on an unpleasantly humid day.

"Well I guess we know what she wanted then. This feels really bad to me."

"Most certainly it is not pleasant, but it is also transient, it will dissipate quickly enough once the crowd disperses."

"But the ramifications won't Sab, this will cause a national outcry. Marshall was already being vilified by the press, this'll raise the hysteria to epic proportions – he'll be loathed by most of the population."

"Do you think that thing is behind the rest of his troubles?"

"I don't know, maybe. Everyone thought he was crazy about Kalendar, but then it wouldn't be the first time a footballer with a fantastic wife's been that stupid."

"Indeed. Look, it is on the move."

The woman left her seat and made her way up the steps to an exit. Sabir and Jack grabbed their coats and headed up and out through the Director's box, then down to the concourse that ran round the outside of the stadium.

"We will have to catch up before we lose it in the crowd, hurry Jack."

They had to dodge their way through a flood of away fans, many had seen enough and were heading off in disgust. Sabir had guessed correctly about the direction the woman had taken and he put a hand on Jack's arm to slow him to a less conspicuous walk.

"I have located it now my friend, it will not escape us."

Jack saw the strain on Sabir's face as he concentrated on maintaining a shield around them at the same time as keeping track of the woman. The shield not only subdued their auras but also kept the throng of fans from noticing them, despite Sabir's fame.

Jack tried desperately to keep his aura steady to make it easier for Sabir to maintain the shield, but he couldn't hold back the flush of adrenaline that coursed through him. The chase was well and truly on and he felt exhilarated.

They followed their quarry across the Ken Friar Bridge and down the steps to street level. They had to keep the pace brisk to maintain their position with the woman, who they could see in the distance casually burning energy as she willed people out of her way.

A couple of minutes later she descended into the confines of Arsenal station and her pursuers had to push their way to the front of the queue to make it to the platform in time.

The woman had got onto a westbound Piccadilly line service, which Jack and Sabir just managed to slip onto some two carriages back from her. They had to limit their conversation for the first three stops as the crowding on the train gave them no chance of privacy. Sabir just shook his head at each station to indicate their target had not left the train.

The crush eased at Kings Cross St Pancras and Sabir relaxed a little as he whispered to Jack.

"It is easier to locate the aura with fewer people around. I think it is sitting down now."

The train carried on through the depths beneath London and, as the adrenaline wore off, Jack started to feel tired. He was yawning widely when Sabir nudged him.

"It has stood up, get ready."

The doors opened at Green Park and Sabir paused for two seconds to be sure his shield was as strong as he could make it, then he stepped off the carriage with Jack close behind. The woman walked to the end of the platform and then disappeared up an escalator. They set off in pursuit, purposefully trying to avoid hurrying lest they get too close.

By the time they reached the surface, she had already walked along Piccadilly and was turning into Berkeley Street. With no sight line, Sabir and Jack were less cautious and hustled up the road, stopping at the corner she had just rounded.

"Wait a moment," said Sabir, "I think it has stopped."

He popped his head round the corner and although he couldn't see her directly, he could tell where her aura was.

"It is in that shop with the blue frontage, on the first floor."

"The Promethean Spa? Are you saying having caused an incident that will enrage the nation, she's having her nails done?"

They decided to wait in the pub a bit further down the road, so doubled back and went round via Stratton Street to avoid the beauty salon. The Green Keeper was traditionally styled and Jack's eyes lit up when he saw the range of ales to choose from. He considered ordering a pint of his favourite Seafarers but, conscious of the situation, opted for a fruit juice instead, while Sabir phoned Rebecca with an update. He put his phone away after several minutes of discussion.

"She will be here in twenty minutes, Reggie too. They could not get hold of Aaron."

"Hmm, that's a shame. I'd have felt better with him around, but with four of us we should be OK. If she is having some kind of treatment in the spa ..."

"It," Sabir interrupted.

"Sorry?"

"You said *she* Jack, that thing is an it."

Jack raised his eyebrows at the correction but let it pass.

"OK, if it is having some kind of treatment, it's likely to be in there a while so why don't we have something to eat. You look knackered and it'd help to keep your strength up. Maintaining that shield is pretty draining, isn't it?"

"A little, yes. I am not as practised as Aaron so it still requires a lot of concentration. It feels good to use my powers though, make more of the gifts we have been given."

"I'll drink to that."

They ordered food, which arrived shortly before Reggie and Rebecca, the latter hugging Sabir close. They settled down to discuss the situation, with Sabir quieter than usual due to maintaining a watch on the woman's location.

"OK, so we follow it, find out what it's up to and hopefully where its lair is. If it is linked to the one from Avar Investments, maybe we'll get a location on that too," said Rebecca.

"What I don't get is why we've come across two in such a short space of time. I know I'm new to all this, but you guys have been awakened for a while and this is the first you've seen of these entities, right?" asked Jack.

"It's a sign of the times my boy."

The others waited for Reggie to elaborate further but he didn't seem inclined to and just carried on letting his gaze shift around the pub.

"Well, whatever the reason they're cropping up now, we dealt with the last one and we've got the jump on this one too. From what you've said it doesn't sound as strong either, so we should be able to cope with it."

They went on to discuss their plans for following the woman

and had come up with a range of strategies by the time Sabir announced they should get ready to move.

His shield back in place, he looked out the window and saw the woman stroll smartly down Berkeley Street towards Green Park station. She paused long enough to take a phone call, the content of which clearly annoyed her as she argued vociferously with the caller. She put her phone away in anger and carried on towards the Tube. As soon as she was onto Piccadilly the group of four had set off after her, and got as far as the ticket hall before splitting up as per their plan.

Sabir and Jack continued to track the woman, confident that their auras could be masked whereas they had been worried that the strength of Reggie's might prove too much to conceal. They jumped onto an eastbound Jubilee line train while the other two hung back for the next one.

When the woman got out at London Bridge, Sabir followed her while Jack remained on the platform. Four minutes later Reggie stepped tentatively off the next train, and on seeing Jack he signalled to Rebecca to alight also.

As soon as they were above ground Jack took his phone out and started leading them west along the bank of the River Thames. He used an application that he'd downloaded on his and Sabir's smartphones back at the pub. It automatically sent the GPS location of one to the other at thirty second intervals, the receiving phone then displayed a map with walking directions to the other.

They crossed over Borough High Street and skirted past Southwark Cathedral which loomed on their right hand side. Its rich combination of architectural styles gave notice of the thousand years the building had spent growing to match the swelling population south of the river.

The old and narrow streets were busy with early evening revellers whose excitement fed the spirits of the three pursuers. As they approached the Clink Street arch they were aware of the dim red aura of the former prison, its inglorious history still resonating several hundred years later. On the other side they passed the spectacular modern temple of wine that was Vinopolis, before going along Bankside towards the modern replica of Shakespeare's Globe. Jack's phone rang to reveal Sabir's urgent voice.

"Left, go left now."

Jack instinctively looked around but couldn't see anything so he led them down New Globe Walk as requested. They'd just passed a coffee shop on their left when Sabir's voice called from their right. At first the alley behind the Globe looked deserted, but on doing a cartoon style double take Jack noticed Sabir was there after all, his shield now gone.

"It went into the bar in The Globe, so I stayed out here. It is too crowded inside for me to identify the aura, too much energy. But I will know as soon as it leaves."

"Are you sure it's still in there?"

"It has not left, I am certain. It will be easy to sense once it leaves the bar."

Sabir sat down on a nearby set of steps and concentrated on trying to pick up the woman's aura, Rebecca sat with him companionably. Jack looked at the way Reggie's gaze constantly shifted around the street and realised that he no longer felt unnerved by the older man's strange behaviour. He wondered whether it was the excitement and agitation he felt himself that made Reggie seem less weird, or just that he'd grown accustomed to him in the weeks since they'd first met.

"What are they saying Reggie?" Jack asked quietly.

The Caribbean fixed his eyes upon Jack, complete lucidity beaming forth for a short period of time.

"They're really not happy, somethin' has them scared good and proper, but I can't make out what."

"Are they scared of something right here, or are they just generally upset?"

"Here. It might be that demon lady, I don't know. The past, present and future are all so confused to them, it's hard to tell."

Jack was about to ask further of Reggie's constant companions when his eye was caught by a man who walked past the end of the alley, away from the theatre. He was very tall, at least six and a half feet, and so lean that the skin drawn tight across his face made him look cadaverous. However it wasn't his unusual height or build that drew Jack's attention, so much as his peculiar aura.

It was quite bright but, without exception, all the outer components were red and all those nearest to his core were purple. The contrast was absolute and very distinctive. As the man continued to walk down the street, Jack gathered the others to take a look at him, they moved out of the alley to get a clear view.

"Have you ever seen anything like that before? It's like he's ..."

It was mid-sentence that Jack felt the ripple of energy from behind him, the prickly warmth of concentrated negativity. He was the first to turn and see the very slight shimmering of the space, like a heat haze on a scorching summer's day. Instinctively he reached forwards with his aura and straight away sensed the shield in front of him. Without thinking about it he seized hold of all parts of it at once and pulled in every direction, the concealment effect evaporating in an instant.

Standing ten metres from the group was the woman, her arm extended as she levelled a hand gun at them. Next to her was a man of similar age, his angular features reminiscent of hers though without the steel that lay behind her expression.

Before any of them could react, the gun barked twice and the retorts echoed around the tight confines of the street. Jack's aura was already extended towards the woman so he shifted it to the gun and in a fraction of a second had understood its workings. He willed the firing mechanism to fuse itself with the body of the weapon just in time to be hit by a bolt of energy from the woman. The crimson lance skewered him as she sought to wrestle control of his mind.

His legs almost buckled underneath him as he marshalled all his reserves to fend off the attack. He could feel her will burrowing into the edges of his consciousness and his mind squirmed as he tried to push back at each of the intrusions. He felt himself weaken in a couple of places, his defences almost breached, so he retreated from those areas of his mind and instead shored up those he still held.

He felt her fiery presence close in as she burned her way through the last of his resistance. Just as she was about to have access to the core of his being, she let out a shriek both mental and physical, her presence abruptly disappearing from his mind. His senses reeling, Jack looked around and tried to work out what was happening.

He saw the woman recoil from Reggie, who had stepped forwards with his arms raised and was crushing her will with the full strength of his aura.

"You shall not have him demon. Flee I tell you, flee!"

The woman grabbed the arm of the man, who was cowering off to one side, and pulled him away and off down the street. As Jack turned to watch them go his heart missed a beat when he saw Sabir lying on the tarmac, blood pooling underneath him from wounds to his head and chest. His aura was extremely faint, the strands thin and weak, their pulsing erratic and feeble. Rebecca sat on the floor cradling him tenderly in her lap, whispering to him between desperate sobs.

With calmness and clarity Jack took out his phone and called for an ambulance, then left a voicemail for Aaron with the basic details of what had occurred. By the time he turned his attention back to his injured friend it took him a few moments to realise what was happening.

He could see Rebecca's aura swirling rapidly in a highly coherent, rhythmic pattern. With each cycle it throbbed and a portion of it separated off and flowed into Sabir. She was pouring her essence into him at a perilous rate, her own strength diminishing rapidly. Jack crouched down and spoke steadily.

"Rebecca, please let me help. I beg you, take energy from me, I still have plenty to spare."

Without looking up she shook her head, and continued to rock gently back and forth as she tried to save her lover. Reggie placed a hand on Jack's shoulder.

"I'm afraid you can't help, my boy. The healin' can only come from within, lest very bad things happen. It's not like patchin' up rifts in the veil. It's her love that'll save him, or nothin' at all."

Jack stood up and walked a pace away before urgently whispering his reply.

"But she might kill herself at this rate, and he's still fading."

"It's her choice boy, not yours."

"No it's not, but it wouldn't be his either."

Jack crouched down again and put an arm around Rebecca, gently squeezing her shoulder to gain her attention.

"Rebecca, listen to me. Sabir loves you more than life itself, and there is no way he would want you to sacrifice yourself for him. You must stop this. Now."

She turned to face Jack and his heart ached to see the pain written in her eyes.

"But I love him Jack, I can't lose him."

"I know, but if you honour his love for you, then you must not trade yourself for him. He would never forgive you for that."

She looked back at the broken figure in her arms whose aura barely pulsed and hugged him tighter as tears flowed down her cheeks and onto his head, the drops washing tiny paths through the blood that covered his face. Jack saw the flow of energy stop and Rebecca's aura stabilise, almost immediately what remained of Sabir's started to ebb away. As the sounds of multiple sirens wafted over the rooftops, their tones awkwardly out of phase, the last of Sabir's essence evaporated and his aura disappeared completely.

Chapter Seventeen

In the dim hallway of the Henrietta Street house, two suitcases sat patiently against one wall. Through a nearby doorway came the sound of crockery and cutlery being arranged, accompanied by the warm glow of bright sunshine.

Cascading down the stairwell was the sound of a piano being played, the busy rush of notes a playful torrent of harmonies. Three floors higher up Jack stepped out of one of the guest bedrooms, fresh faced after having showered and shaved. As the music washed over him he had the sensation of standing in a mountain brook, the cool water flowing past his ankles and chilling his feet. Intrigued, he shivered and went up a flight to find the source of the playing.

The top floor of the house was an open plan loft space with a worn parquet floor and rich yellow paper on the sloping walls between the windows. At the far end sat Aaron at a huge Bösendorfer Imperial Grand, his fingers flying over the keys with effortless dexterity, hands crossing each other in rapid succession.

Modest wooden chairs were stacked at the back of the room and Jack took one to sit on. He stared in wonder as he felt the last few rivulets fall around him and settle in a pool about his feet.

Aaron kept his hands poised above the keyboard and Jack leaned forward in anticipation. The hair on the back of his neck stood on end and he could smell the electric tang of ozone. The sky outside had filled with dense black clouds and as Aaron brought his hands down in a thunderous entry the room exploded in a flash of lightning. As the notes flew from the piano, Jack felt the wind swirl around him and a howling gale rise up that threatened to knock him off his chair. Bright light strobed the room and thunderclaps shook the floor beneath him. The storm raged back and forth, the elemental force that had been unleashed was determined to defeat him. A brief respite in the tumult proved false, as the storm gathered for a final assault. It grew in speed and intensity until a devastating volley of thunder and flashes surrounded him, at which point he suddenly found himself back in the room, the final chord still hanging on the air.

He stared at his dry clothes, hardly able to believe that the images and sensations weren't absolutely real. Aaron began to play again.

This time a haunting theme escaped from the piano, one that spoke of loss and pain. Jack felt it keenly, his heart aching at the sound until he became aware that he stood in a field, a high pasture land with snow-capped mountains in the distance. An older couple were standing before him, a farmer and his wife, the intense sadness coming from them. A child had gone to off to war and not returned, the hurt was a searing hollow inside each of them, yet also in the music was the love that they felt for him and the joy he'd brought them.

Then a gentle refrain in high register, an angelic voice was talking to the parents, telling them of the child's enduring love and reassuring them that all was well even though he could no longer be with them.

Then the voice was speaking of the confusion and pointlessness of war, of anger and conflict, of rage in battle and of his loss at leaving loved ones behind.

The tone changed again as the child reflected upon his

life. What was I? Did I give all I could? Should I have lived differently?

A melody then grew that carried the final thoughts of the child back to his parents. I can see everything in creation now and it is truly magnificent. All around me is awe and wonder, and I understand what it all means. Do not grieve for me for I am now part of the glory.

The parents stood with heads bowed, holding hands, *but yet you are still dead my son.*

Jack awoke to find tears streaming down his face, sadness and compassion for the parents' loss, and joy for the child finding his place in the universe. He quickly wiped them away on his sleeve.

It was some seconds after the last of the notes had faded to nothing that Aaron raised his head and took his hands from the keyboard.

"Good morning Jack."

"Morning. That was astonishing, and beautiful. What was it?"

Jack got up and went to sit on the deep window sill nearest the piano, Aaron turned to face him.

"Franz Liszt, *Switzerland,* the first of his *Years of Pilgrimage.* There's more, but I sense you've had enough for now."

"The images and emotions were so clear, so vivid. The others had said you were a great pianist, but I'd never have thought music could do that."

Aaron chuckled.

"Being an Awakened does allow me some advantages of expression, but you would get something not too dissimilar from any good player who really feels the music, their own interpretation of course."

"I'll confess I did look you up on the Internet. You were a concert pianist, some critics even said the artist of your generation, but yet you gave it all up. What happened?"

"I saw things that changed me, experiences that redefined

who I was. Plus I awoke, which gave me other things to concentrate on."

Jack could sense the other man's discomfort and didn't know how far to push it.

"You changed how exactly?"

He could see from the expression on Aaron's face that it was a subject he didn't find easy to think about, let alone talk of.

"I'm sorry, I've no right to pry, forgive me."

"No, it's alright Jack, I'm fine."

The older man took a deep breath and exhaled slowly as he brought many long years back into focus.

"Well, right from an early age all I really knew about was music. To get as good as I did you have to dedicate yourself to it, the piano was everything to me. I'd just turned twenty and started what everyone said would be a glittering career, yet within weeks of playing to a packed Carnegie Hall the Vietnam War escalated and I signed up."

"You chose to go?"

"Sure did. At the time I thought it was the right thing to do. 3rd Battalion, 4th Marines, the Thundering Third."

Aaron smiled briefly in remembrance of those he'd fought alongside, before his expression changed to reflect what he'd gone through.

"It was over there that ... I saw things, saw people do things that should just not happen. Unspeakable things – on both sides. And in the midst of the horror of war, I awoke."

His eyes drifted into a thousand yard stare as unspoken memories played themselves out. Jack felt a chill descend, and needed to end the silence.

"Blimey, that must have been something to deal with. I've found it bewildering and I'm safely here in London with you guys to support me through it. I can't imagine what it must have been like for you."

Aaron broke his stare and grinned slightly at Jack.

"A walk on the dark side for sure. Anyway, by the time I got back I was a changed man, quite literally. I tried to resume my career and for a while it went OK – great reviews, critically acclaimed recordings and so on. But pretty soon I realised my heart wasn't in it anymore. Since awakening nothing really challenged me technically, the piano had become easy, and what I'd witnessed in Vietnam was colouring everything I played. I didn't want that to be the basis of what I was communicating to audiences, so I stepped away from it all and concentrated on exploring my gifts. That and searching for others like us. I still play of course, just not in public."

"You should do. I mean, I don't know anything about music but your playing sounded sublime to me. More people should get to hear that."

"Kind of you to say so Jack."

Aaron closed the lid of the piano to signal that this part of the conversation was most definitely over.

"Anyway, enough about me. I meant to warn you that the police were on the phone last night after you'd gone to bed. They want to speak to Rebecca again."

"I thought you'd helped point that Chief Inspector away from what really happened."

"I have, but I think they just want to go over it again, see if any other details come loose," said Aaron.

"Well I'm sticking to the same line. I'll tell the truth but leave out that we'd followed the woman, and why we were really there obviously."

"Good, it'll only make things worse if they actually find those two."

"They'll struggle to do that. When we were there I spotted that the CCTV camera in the street wasn't working."

"That's a result then. If they were caught they'd just manipulate the police and stir up trouble for us in the process.' He paused. 'Just so I know exactly what happened, would you mind taking me through it? I've already seen it from Reggie's viewpoint but yours would help fill in the gaps."

"Of course, I'm sort of interested to see what happened myself."

Jack lay his hands palms up in Aaron's and relaxed his mind as he let his consciousness drift back a couple of days. He established an image of the football game and relived the sounds and the feel of the surging crowd, breathing in the atmosphere until he knew he was back in the stadium, but this time only as an observer. He brought things rapidly forwards to when he spotted the woman and her encounter with Marshall, the extra detail provided by this lucid dream made the experience seem even more real than the first time around.

He skimmed through his and Sabir's pursuit of the woman and then played steadily through the fateful events behind the Globe theatre. As Aaron started to weave in Reggie's recollections, Jack was able to step away from his body and observe proceedings from a short distance. The dislocation helped depersonalise the memory and made it easier to witness again.

He saw the shots fired and the woman launch her attack on him, the pair of them locked in a ferocious battle of wills. At the same time the woman's companion tried to initiate an attack on Reggie. The negative energy he projected was weaker and less assured than the woman's and didn't even make it as far as Reggie's aura before it was swatted aside.

Jack saw the Caribbean man's willpower surge forward and batter the aura of the man, who stumbled sideways and brought his hands up to shield his face, crouched in defeat. Reggie then switched his focus to the woman, the tendrils of his aura reaching forth and ripping her grasp from Jack before pushing her backwards.

Despite not being in his own body in the dream, Jack recognised the feeling of relief as the woman was removed from his mind and his consciousness breathed freely once more.

Jack found the next few minutes very hard to relive and he constantly fought the desire to skip the passing of his friend.

He steeled himself and stayed the course to allow Aaron to complete his picture of events that evening.

When the recollection was over Jack let the contact break and stood up to walk around, the movement an attempt to shake the feelings and emotions he'd just recalled.

"I guess we just got unlucky," he said, "I'm pretty sure they weren't expecting to encounter us. That shield she had up was meant for the tall guy they were following, not us."

"Agreed. She must have put it up in the bar and it seemed to Sabir like he just lost her in the crowded atmosphere."

"I'm so sorry I let her into my head, I just wasn't prepared for it," said Jack.

"Don't blame yourself, it takes time to learn how to control your own mind, let alone defend it."

"I'll be stronger next time, I promise."

"I'm sure you will. However, it's likely they know who you and Rebecca are now, so you'll stay here until we've dealt with them. There's still a chance they don't know about me, and this place is better protected than most."

"I spotted the wards and alarms on the windows, very subtle, how did you create those?" asked Jack.

"Just manipulation of energy, I'll show you later how to construct them, it should be easy for you."

"Thanks, I'd appreciate that. Say, something I still don't get is why wouldn't Reggie let me help heal Sabir, he said something about bad things happening?"

"That's because it requires energy to be attuned very precisely to the person being healed. If someone uses their own, they can mould it exactly as needs be. If another provides it then they won't be able to attune it properly to the recipient, or at least not without having let it spend quite some time as part of their own aura first. I've seen what happens when un-attuned energy is used to heal and it's awful Jack, the recipient becomes less than themselves, their spirit diminished. At best they are a shadow of their former self, at worst they end up a sort of wraith-like figure, their will driven by the veils and currents of the planes rather than their own soul."

Jack shuddered, but as he thought more about the mechanics he just couldn't get his head around it.

"But manipulating the veils is easy, how can healing be so hard?"

Aaron laughed affectionately and tried to explain.

"Look Jack, the soul – the essence that inhabits and powers both mind and body – is the most complex thing in the universe, axiomatically more complex than can ever be comprehended. Heisenberg should have taught you that."

"Because we are human we can't perceive or know everything about being human?"

"Exactly. Healing involves dealing directly with someone's soul. It's an unbelievably complicated and very delicate process, one that has to be done through love and conviction as much as through understanding."

Jack puffed his cheeks out and sighed, his comprehension of the way things worked suddenly less sure than it had been. Aaron saw his confusion and tried to reassure him.

"For all that the laws of nature can be dissected and understood Jack – and make no mistake about it your talent for that is extraordinary – the expression of free will that is intelligent life is the greatest of wonders."

"So what happens next? Rebecca almost killed herself trying to save Sab, you've seen how weak she is."

"She needs time to let her soul heal. Sabir's loss has exhausted her. She needs to let her spirit re-grow."

"But she's in so much pain."

"I know, but grieving is natural Jack, she will build herself again, by remembering the good times with him, by embracing the love she felt and still feels. Grieving hurts, but it's not inherently bad, it can go either way. If someone lets their soul refill with negativity of course they'll become bitter and vengeful. Rebecca is afraid of life without Sabir, that is natural, yet it's only if she lets that in that she's in peril. She is the one who has to choose, it is her will that's being tested, but I have confidence she'll come through."

"So what, we just have to be there for her, stay strong ourselves and give her the time and space she needs?"

"Yes, that is precisely what we do."

Aaron checked his watch. "Now I believe breakfast should be ready."

They went downstairs and found Rebecca already at the dining room table, her eyes puffy and bloodshot from lack of sleep. Her aura was still pathetically weak, the dim swirling a much more even balance of colours than was normal for her.

They took their seats and tried to keep the conversation light as they enjoyed Wilkinson's cooking, while Rebecca kept quiet and had to be encouraged to eat more than a few mouthfuls. She took a cup of coffee back upstairs as she retreated to her room. Even breakfast seemed to tire her.

Jack looked at Aaron, his eyebrows raised. The American shrugged at the unspoken question.

"Just give it time."

Jack decided to enjoy the sunshine and set off for a walk around Covent Garden. He knew the area reasonably well having spent many an evening socialising there with friends, but was keen to discover the less obvious nooks and crannies it had to offer – perhaps an unusual restaurant he could surprise Mandy with the next time they were able to meet up. Despite their best efforts, each of their very different types of work had kept them mostly apart the last few weeks, and the loss of Sabir made Jack feel her absence all the more.

It was too early in the day for the usual plethora of street entertainers, he'd always found the mimes slightly creepy anyway, but the bustle of those on their way to work was infectious. He breathed in the life and sense of purpose of those scurrying across the Italianate piazza, the contrast with the atmosphere in the house was stark.

He spent a few minutes watching a woman start a chalk sketch on the pavement and was intrigued by her subject. She had drawn a large outline that looked like an ornate gold picture frame and was filling it with a caricatured reflection of what she saw in front of her. The Opera House was scarily gothic and gaudily dressed patrons strode arm-in-arm on its balconies, their expressions delightfully haughty. A throng of tourists started to take shape, their countries displayed through use of national dress, with space kept blank in which to depict whichever entertainers turned up later in the day.

Jack left the woman to her work and promised himself he would come back in the afternoon to see the finished piece. Rejuvenated by his walk he went back to Henrietta Street and knocked gently on Rebecca's door.

"Come in."

Her voice flat and listless, she lay on the bed and looked up at the ceiling, her eyes an unfocused stare. Jack sat on the end of the bed as the optimism from his walk quickly drained away, replaced by the heaviness that pervaded the room. He fought the change in his own emotions and tried to concentrate on more positive feelings, on memories of happier times. He sat quietly, his presence itself a gesture of the compassion he felt.

It was a few minutes before Rebecca broke the silence, and when she did there was a hint more life to her voice.

"You know Jack, I don't think I could have saved him anyway, even if I'd given everything. Thanks for stopping me."

"I thought you'd be mad at me?"

"Nope, you were right. He'd have wanted me to live, to carry on."

Jack was grateful for the absolution, and then felt guilty for his self-indulgence. After all that had happened surely his own worries were of the least importance. Rebecca interrupted the wrestling match with his conscience.

"You know, I felt him slip away, felt him pass over to the positive plane. I know he's somewhere better, I know he's surrounded by love and beauty, but I wanted more time with him. It's selfish of me but ..."

"No, it's absolutely not. We are creatures of the reality we see around us, we are meant to live our lives here. Wanting to experience that to the full is natural, it's what we're meant for," said Jack.

"Maybe. We had so many plans, you know he asked me to marry him? He was so funny, not the grand romantic gesture I would have expected, he just sort of blurted it out one day. I didn't even take him seriously at the time, I wish now I'd just said yes. But I did love him, I really did want us to spend our lives together, children, the works. I hope he knew that."

"I'm absolutely sure he did, he was devoted to you."

Jack was surprised to feel a little uncomfortable speaking for Sabir, it was almost as if he was betraying his friend's confidence. He changed the subject.

"Did you get any sleep last night?"

"Not really, I was up most of it still trying to get hold of his parents back in Morocco, but I couldn't reach them, I think they must be away. They'll have heard through the media by now I'm sure. That hurts, it should have been me who told them, told them that their son is dead."

She got up and fetched her mobile from the dressing table and sat next to Jack as she checked for messages and email. She sighed when she found nothing new and Jack put an arm round her shoulder for reassurance. She turned to look at him, the pain and hurt on her face echoed by the confusion in her weakened aura.

"He's gone Jack, they took him from me."

Tears welled up and she cried into his shoulder, the sobs fierce and raw as she gave voice to her grief. Jack held her tightly, desperately wanting to ease her pain but knowing full well that this was another type of healing he couldn't help with.

Chapter Eighteen

Hetty tapped her fingers on the kitchen table, the phone call had dragged on long enough and her patience was reaching its limit. She forced a smile and put a false touch of warmth into her voice, something that made both Avaro and Ferren wince.

"Uh huh, so it's definitely decided then? That's great news, tell John I'll be in touch. Oh yeah, you too Tom."

She ended the call and dropped the mobile onto the table, where it clinked against her coffee mug and caused a few drops to slosh over the rim. She rested her head on her hands and pouted.

"Blimey that guy's tedious. Tavens is the only one of them with any real spirit, I should have gone after him you know, he'd have been way more fun."

Ferren looked across at his sister and chose to be reassuring.

"Maybe, but the accountant was the right choice, the easy mark, you know that. Do I take it you've got the date settled for the big rally?"

"Eventually. It took them long enough to agree but it's going to be June 23rd. Every branch from across the country will be marching and they're roping in most of their affiliate groups too."

For the first time that morning Avaro looked up and showed

some interest in the twins.

"And the counter marches?"

"Now the date is fixed I'll leak it to the press and get them to push the angle that the APA needs to be resisted. I'll also make sure that Tavens instructs his people to go armed. One or two pushed in the right direction on the day to kick it off and we'll have a full scale riot."

"Perfect."

"But what about those guardians?" asked Ferren.

Avaro's nostrils flared briefly but his tone remained measured.

"What about them? One is dead, another distraught. She may even turn if we are lucky, grief has been known to do that."

"A fallen priest? How delightful," said Hetty.

"The warlock we need anyway, and the older one I will deal with if the time comes."

"Good," said Ferren, "I don't think I fancy going up against him again. And I don't know what you're laughing at Het, he smacked you around like a rag doll too."

"At least I put up a fight you coward."

"Yeah, well we'll see about that you ..."

"Enough! Stop your bickering and concentrate on the tasks at hand."

Avaro's command settled the twins down but they continued to glare at each other.

"June 23rd it is. I will have the *Streets* aligned towards that date. Those playing are now so addicted they will not be able to resist the lure of unique events and items placed near the rally."

"Are you really sure they'll come? Even with everything else that'll be going on?" queried Ferren.

"Of course. Do not underestimate the power of rapacity, it is capable of consuming a human's soul like few other base instincts. Now Hetty, you focus on isolating the warlock, we must get him away from the others."

"Already on it. I found out enough when I was in his mind to know what his weak points are. He won't be a problem."

"Good. Ferren, you will have my assistance with your cell, if this works then it will feed both your and Hetty's plans. I also have arrangements in place for the vessel. An acquisition for each of us and we will be ready."

Avaro approached the imposing facade of the British Museum as a hoard of tourists streamed past him. It was nearly closing time and the swarm of mostly foreign visitors parted to avoid him. They were ignorant of why they walked a longer way round the giant columns guarding the main entrance, before then setting off down the steps towards the less historical delights London had to offer.

Avaro distantly recognised the architecture of the building. It was Greek revivalist but still a fair facsimile of that it imitated, of which he held many memories from previous manifestations.

As he pressed on into the central Great Court of the building he looked up at the staggering modern roof conceived by Foster & Partners. Thousands of triangular panes of glass arced in graceful curves to link the rectangular outer walls with the circular inner structure. Such was the beauty of the design, and the level of inspiration it generated in those who saw it, that the whole courtyard was filled with excited positivity left behind by the day's attendance. Avaro sneered at the taste in the air and his aura pulsed all the stronger in defiance.

The strength of the shield he had cast about himself meant he could walk with total freedom about the building – people, cameras and alarms would not bother him. There was some time to go before he was due to meet the helpers he had arranged, so he set off through the building to satisfy his curiosity as to what else of interest the museum might hold.

The majority of exhibits had auras of sorts, reflecting their often singular nature or significant provenance. Most were quite weak and many conflicted due to the contention they had inspired since their creation. Much of the negativity was well attuned to Avaro and he breathed in the remains of the covetousness that surrounded many of the items on display.

Two gold crucifixes from medieval Spain caught his eye, the piety and devotion they stored was wrapped in a torrid blanket of red that promised a confused history. Precious metals tended to retain negative energy better than positive and it always amused him when gold or silver was chosen for religious artefacts. For all their beauty and the devotion lavished upon them they were still magnets for selfish desire. He certainly wasn't going to complain.

The famed Rosetta Stone elicited a wry chuckle from him, he could see from the fingerprints on its aura that there was no luck in it having been discovered in 1799. It was not so much a miracle of archaeology but rather the meddling of a guardian of substantial power. Still, for every step humanity took towards enlightenment, it always found a way to plumb new depths somewhere else. Again, something that he wasn't going to complain about.

Although the Egyptology section with its mummies and funereal items was dramatic to look at, he was disappointed in terms of its true content. The ancient corpses the museum had chosen to display held no real interest for him.

Twice he briefly paused to consider whether he should liberate objects he had spotted. The first was a seemingly innocuous decorated silver bowl from somewhere within the Roman Empire. It was presented as being a simple if rather high value drinking vessel, but he could tell it had been used many times to collect the blood of human sacrifices. A practice which historians seemed remarkably keen to deny had ever held much prevalence. The bright intensity of its crimson aura could be helpful in the days to come but it was a luxury not a necessity, so he let it be.

The second was a copper alloy figurine from the ancient Levant. It was one of a number on display and quite incorrectly labelled as a votive offering. It wasn't a gift from a worshipper in recognition of their deity, it was their deity. The energies and links to the veil that the diminutive statue contained were exceedingly strong. However, after careful consideration, Avaro judged that harnessing and taming the little bugger would be as much hassle as its usefulness, so he regretfully left it standing in its display case.

He had just finished walking the main galleries when the alarm on his phone went off. It woke him from the indulgent mood he had drifted into and he headed off towards the real purpose of his visit. It was now dark outside and the internal lighting had been turned down to a meagre background ambience that allowed for long and heavy shadows down the corridors. He passed through a room of treasures from Mexico and upon seeing the two museum employees waiting by a set of doors kept closed to the public, he extended his shield to include them. One of the men was a senior security guard and the other was a Deputy Curator for Romano-British Collections. Avaro was pleased to see the thralls he had placed on each of them were both still completely intact.

"Gentlemen, shall we?"

The door was opened and the curator led them down several flights of stairs to the basement levels. The museum only displayed a small percentage of the objects it owned and much of the huge reserve was stored in the vaults underneath the main building. It took several minutes to reach the storeroom they wanted, by which time they had passed well beyond the boundaries of the building above and were not far from New Oxford Street.

The curator swung back the heavy metal door and strip lights flickered on to reveal a large room painted institutional grey. Rows of tightly packed metal shelving were crammed with wooden containers of all sizes, from cigar boxes to packing crates. Even from the doorway Avaro could see instantly what they were looking for. A bright red glow emanated from a long box on a low shelf near the back of the room. He walked over and despite being able to sense the contents quite clearly he was eager to see it with his own eyes. Not wanting to interfere too closely with its aura at this early stage, he sent the security guard to fetch a pry bar rather than use energy with which to manipulate the lid. A few minutes later the top was teased off the 5' by 2' by 2' container and a brilliant aural glow emanated from within.

What the curator and guard saw was a child-size lead coffin, the lid of which was decorated with the images of three scallop shells set amidst a pattern of astragalus, as if garlands of the herb had been laid upon the box to settle that which lay within.

"Do you want to see the contents? It's all there as per the photographs I showed you," checked the curator.

"No, leave it intact for now. He has been disturbed by unknowing hands enough already. Seal it back up and let us be away."

The guard awkwardly forced the wooden lid back on and the three of them shifted the crate onto a trolley that the curator had left nearby. They walked back underneath the museum compound where they took a cargo lift up to an internal courtyard near the rear of the building. The consignment was loaded into an unmarked museum van and the three of them climbed into the cab as Avaro extended his shield to encompass the vehicle. The guard drove carefully through the narrow tunnel that lead onto Montague Place and turned to accelerate down the road and off into the night.

Mandy tapped away at her keyboard, desperately trying to get the ad proposal finished before the close of business. She'd been rushing around all day and was enjoying the opportunity to finally clear the task from her 'to do' list. If she could finish it quickly she'd still be able to make dinner with Jack, something she'd been very much looking forward to. She missed him and was anxious to see how he was coping with the death of his friend.

The keys were being attacked with rapidity when Linda

walked past her desk and whispered,

"Watch out, Tinkerbell's heading your way."

The moniker was their code for one of the senior partners, a petite and rather spiky woman in her early fifties that was known for being somewhat curt with the junior members of staff. Mandy could see the sternly dressed woman approaching from the other end of the office, strutting towards her with purpose, so she surreptitiously tilted the polished metal coaster on her desk to check her hair and makeup. Seeing everything in order she sat up a little straighter, her confidence buoyed for the forthcoming encounter.

"Good, Richardson, you're still here then," said the woman.

Silly bitch thought Mandy, it was only 4:30pm and she rarely left the office until closer to 7pm. Stay calm.

"Of course Ms Bishop, what can I do for you?"

"I need you to meet a client this evening, they're interested in starting a viral campaign and it seems they've been impressed with your work on the Craven Insurance rebranding."

"That's good to hear but ..."

"But what?" snapped Ms Bishop.

"But I'm not really available this evening, I'll happily book them in for first thing tomorrow though."

"No my dear, you'll see them tonight. They're one of our oldest accounts and they asked specifically for you. I wouldn't normally trust this to someone at your level but they were quite insistent. Check the details with Jill and report back to me tomorrow, OK?"

Mandy fought the urge to let her superior know just what she really thought and nodded her agreement instead.

"Certainly Ms Bishop."

She checked the details with the senior partner's assistant and was glad at least that the client wasn't due until 6:30pm. She was disappointed at having to cancel on Jack and felt horribly guilty when she left a voicemail for him.

Mandy put the remainder of the afternoon to good use by

finishing the proposal, and was a little cheered by a reassuring text back from Jack.

She spruced herself up and got to the lobby a few minutes early. The reception staff had finished for the day and she was keen not to have an important client kept waiting. Exactly on the half-hour a confident and attractive young woman swept into the lobby of Hamilton & Beach. Mandy could sense she was someone of import and took an educated guess.

"Miss Viha? I'm Mandy Richardson, very pleased to meet you."

"The pleasure's all mine, I assure you. Thank you so much for meeting me at such short notice, I hope you didn't have plans."

"Not at all, it's fine."

"Look, seeing as it's so late in the day, why don't we talk over dinner, I know a charming place where we won't be disturbed."

"Sure, that'd be great."

They headed out through the revolving doors and off down Berners Street towards Soho.

"So Miss Viha, how long have you been with Avar Investments?"

"Oh, not long, I'm a relatively new hire. And please, do call me Hetty."

Chapter Nineteen

David Walsingham looked at the steady drip of rainwater as it fell onto the dirt floor of the disused warehouse. It had started to pool and an oily film had spread across the surface, the rainbow of colours constantly disturbed by the ripples from each drop.

He caught himself staring and blinked a few times to get his concentration back. Today was a big day and he couldn't afford to be anything other than totally focused. He'd been with K-Section for three years and the Service for five in total, and all his training had led to this opportunity to take down Dragonovich, one of the most elusive arms dealers operating in Europe. Technically it was his operation but in reality it belonged to the strange looking deep cover agent who waited patiently a few paces away. Walsingham still only knew him by his codename of Lazarus and wouldn't have been surprised if even the man's handler wasn't aware of his true identity.

It amazed him how someone so distinctive could be successful as a spy. Lazarus was six foot seven, rake thin and possessed of an almost non-existent body fat percentage. He could never be mistaken in a crowd, save for a fancy dress party with a Grim Reaper theme, but clearly he was subtle enough to lure a shark like Dragonovich to a meet.

Not far from the silver BMW off-roader they were supposed

to have arrived in, a third MI5 officer stood dressed like the others in an expensive and sober dark suit. Lazarus had insisted the budget stretch to tailoring befitting the sort of clients Dragonovich was accustomed to dealing with, and getting that signed off had caused Walsingham no end of bureaucratic headaches. He'd been shocked his superiors were prepared to let cost cutting measures affect an operation as important as this one, but in the end common sense had thankfully prevailed.

He turned to his colleagues, who nodded their readiness, and then spoke aloud for the benefit of his in-ear micro-transceiver.

"Perimeter team, confirm status."

"In place and awaiting kick-off. Will confirm as soon as we have visual on the target."

"Roger that. Assault team, confirm status please."

"Weapons checked and ready."

Walsingham was pleased their comms were still loud and clear, despite his second team being hidden inside the battered metal cargo container off to his right.

"Roger that. Now remember everyone, no one moves until the merchandise is pronounced as *viable*. Got that? The go word is *viable*."

He was reassured by the quality of the two teams he'd managed to secure for this operation. He'd worked with some trigger happy people in the past, but both four-man units were experienced special forces and as professional as they came. It was critical that they didn't show their hand until after they had confirmed Dragonovich had brought the goods with him. If this turned out to be just a preliminary meet then they needed to maintain their cover and keep playing along.

Walsingham forced himself to stand calmly for a few minutes and not give sign of the excitement he felt by fidgeting or pacing about. He wasn't nervous, but he did want to get on with it. He was grateful when a squawk came over the comms channel, followed by the confirmation he'd been waiting for.

"This is Perimeter, we have visual on a Range Rover, IR

shows three occupants, with you in ten."

The three men standing in the warehouse could hear the thrumming of a supercharged engine getting louder as it approached, and the decibel level leaped as soon as the boxy vehicle sped through the open door. The exhaust noise reverberated off metal walls as the car slowed to a halt at a cautious distance from the MI5 officers, where water droplets sparkled on its polished black bodywork.

The engine was cut and the warehouse fell into silence for a few seconds before the doors clicked open and three men stepped out. They were also clad in sharp black suits and save for the surroundings the scene looked very much the business meeting it was meant to be. A well muscled bodyguard stood either side of Dragonovich, who in sizeable contrast to his opposite number was quite short. It was the first time Walsingham had ever seen the Russian's face clearly and the eyes were as cold and hard as glacial ice.

The two lines faced each other at twenty paces and it was Lazarus who chose to open proceedings.

"Good evening gentlemen, do you have my device?"

"Of course, do you have my money?"

Dragonovich spoke perfect received English with not even a hint of an accent. Lazarus signalled to Walsingham who walked across to the open boot of the BMW and brought back a laptop. He placed it on an empty chemical drum between the two sides, then flicked the touchpad to deactivate the screensaver and reveal the banking applications already running. He stepped back and opened a palm to indicate the others were welcome to approach.

One of Dragonovich's men came forward and spent nearly a minute checking the account status before he nodded approval to his boss. He then walked back to his Range Rover and took out a medium sized suitcase which he had to waddle with back to the laptop, its weight causing him some difficulty before he placed it carefully upon the ground.

Walsingham came walked forward and crouched down to inspect the contents of the suitcase. Upon opening it he knew instinctively that it was the genuine article, a GRU-54 tactical nuclear device. One kiloton equivalent yield, lethal radius of over a kilometre when deployed properly, pretty nasty for a good bit further than that.

Despite the speed with which his pulse raced, he forced himself to spend a few moments double checking that he was correct, including taking a handheld radiation meter from his pocket and measuring the leak rate of the fissile material.

He stood up calmly and nodded to Lazarus.

"The merchandise is viable."

"In which case gentlemen ..."

The remainder of the tall man's sentence was lost in the hail of gunfire that erupted within the warehouse. The noise was deafening and lasted for no more than a few seconds. Walsingham had managed to draw his concealed pistol but didn't have time to get off a shot before the engagement was over. The two Russian bodyguards had been killed but not before they'd shot the third MI5 officer in the leg. The four special forces soldiers stood with weapons aimed at Dragonovich, who had not moved an inch during the ambush. He glared at Lazarus and spoke with measured and total conviction.

"I will kill you. Slowly."

"Of course you will Drago, but not before we've had a long chat. The Americans and Israelis will be keen to talk with you as well, I should imagine. Best of luck with that old boy."

The soldiers stalked forward to restrain the Russian and Walsingham was about to call in a status report over the comm channel when he saw movement in the periphery of his vision.

Two small objects flew through the air from the direction of the entrance and at first he thought they were grenades, but by the time they clattered to the ground he saw they were small canisters about the size of drinks bottles.

Oh fuck! He thought, as he registered the sinister hissing sound that emanated from them, just in time to see the soldiers collapse to the ground. A fraction of a second later Dragonovich and Lazarus were also down, and then he felt his head swim, his legs give way and finally the sensation of falling.

Avaro stepped forward from just inside the entrance and cursed his miscalculation. The shield had kept him unseen but hadn't protected him from the stray bullet that was now lodged just under his ribcage. He'd not been in the line of fire so it must have been a ricochet. The pain didn't bother him, that was merely an electrical signal, but he'd already spent a lot of energy taking out the perimeter guards and even more on the group inside, so was loath to burn the amount required to rebuild his abdomen. Fortunately, he was a pure construct and so could manipulate his form much more easily than if he were using a human host, so doing a quick patch-job to at least stop himself bleeding was easy. He'd remove the bullet and repair himself properly later on.

His aura flared briefly as the wound closed over and he looked back up just in time to see a team of five figures run in through the doorway. The hazmat suits that Ferren and the others were dressed in were completely unnecessary as the canisters had issued nothing other than compressed air, but they made the deception more convincing for the wearers and more importantly for the hidden camera that the MI5 agents had placed to record proceedings inside the warehouse.

Avaro had to admit that he was quite impressed by the group of would-be terrorists from North London, and more surprised still that Ferren had actually planned and executed everything so well. Avaro had handed the serial killer to him on a plate, but in fairness this particular enterprise was almost all his own work. London was about to go into a frenzy and he was looking forward to the huge surge of terror-induced negative energy that was almost within grasp.

While the young extremists took photographs and videos of

the scene, Avaro went with Ferren for a chat by the van that waited outside.

"What do you think Av? Worked like a charm I reckon."

"Indeed, but the next step is critical. You must get that message filmed and online in time for the evening news and the morning papers. No delays you understand?"

"Sure, it's all ready, Ferren grinned, "set, script and everything. Then we sit back and wait for the explosion of hysteria."

"No," said Avaro sternly, "then you wipe their minds and bring the bomb back to the house. No subtlety required, just total erasure of the last couple of months. Make it complete, so that not even a guardian could drag anything from them. Understand?"

"Of course Av, you can count on me."

A few minutes later tyres squealed as the van sped off into the anonymity of the night, with bomb, terrorists and empty canisters on board. Avaro watched it go, then walked back inside to tie up a few loose ends, including waking the unconscious.

He was intrigued to find out what Dragonovich would do with the small head start he was about to give him – run or revenge? His money was on revenge.

In the early hours of the following morning Avaro arrived back at the Pimlico house and went straight downstairs to the basement. The lighting was meagre but he could clearly see the two items that lay side-by-side in the middle of the floor. He approached the grey metal coffin and basked in the heat of the negativity that radiated from it. The nature of the energy was so pure that it took only a few minutes' exposure to recharge himself enough to repair the abdominal wound, the bullet making a tiny dull thud as it squeezed out of his belly and onto the floor. He arched his back and stretched, checking the feeling of the new structure within himself. It was whole and strong again.

The energy level of the bomb was extremely low in comparison to its neighbour, but its value was more in its concept than its actual form. He could already feel the ambient levels of apprehension rising as news of its presence in London spread through the population.

Avaro looked at the pair of objects in front of him and smiled. Now in his possession were weapons of incredible power – ancient and modern – both of them born of the folly of man, folly he would exploit yet again.

Chapter Twenty

Aaron stared out at the changing skyline as the gondola rose slowly through the air. Reggie, Jack and he were the only occupants in the capsule as its slow and steady ascent chased the sunset, a race that was moments away from being lost. The London Eye dominated the South Bank area of the Thames, the giant Ferris wheel towering above the former County Hall building and providing spectacular views out across the city.

Jack turned away from the fiery pinks and yellows that spread across the horizon and faced the American.

"So why have you brought us up here?"

"Look outside, what do you see?"

"Well, over there are the Houses of Parliament, and running up that way is Whitehall with ..."

"No Jack," Aaron interrupted, "I mean look at the auras."

The younger man shifted his concentration and after scanning the horizon, took his time to observe several areas more closely. Eventually he hazarded a guess.

"You mean the colour? The way there's so much red out there?"

"Exactly. On average you'd expect the balance of the population to be positive overall, but I'd say that's mostly negative. I'll grant you Brits are pretty stoic, what with so many going about their business despite everything that's happening, but the level of trepidation out there is huge."

"I suppose, and look at the state of the ambient aura."

In addition to the myriad of tiny flames of energy that worked their way along the thoroughfares below, a collective aural fog hung above the city. The increased elevation meant it could be seen much more easily when viewed along its thickness.

"That really is a lot worse," said Aaron, "the last time I came up here it was distinctly mauve, now that's more the colour of blood."

"I'd always thought London was an awesome place to live, how did it get this bad?"

"Well in fairness that concentrator we destroyed was in the City, and can only have been gathering what negativity was already in the atmosphere. Unfortunately that was enough to allow those entities to manifest, and then spread their influence across the whole of London."

"Can we really be certain they're working together?"

"No, but surely it's too much of a coincidence for them not to be. Besides, it's the worst case scenario and that's what we need to be ready for."

Jack pondered for a moment exactly what might constitute a worst case and blinked away a vision of critical mass, it was all too easy to imagine a mushroom cloud rising high above the skyline of London.

"OK, but even then not everything bad that's going on can be a result of them. There are always plenty of terrible things happening in any big city."

"For sure, but look at the major ones. Take the video that hit the Internet of those terrorists, the news coverage says it's genuine. Are you seriously telling me a tin-pot group no one has ever heard of managed to pull off that caper on their own?"

"I'll grant you it certainly seems unlikely, and that would mean the entities have got access to a nuke. And then of course the police are tearing North London apart, which is just raising tensions even higher."

Aaron ignored the view outside as he paced uneasily around the capsule.

"In addition to the bomb, we know for definite that Steve Marshall's problems are down to them."

"Which has massively undermined the public's faith, not just in him, but in all their hero figures – *the idoloclasm of the cult of celebrity* – the Times called it. A bit pretentious, but they've got a point."

"And then there's the so-called Oyster Catcher, at thirteen victims and counting. The timing's too convenient for that not to be their doing. Putting a serial killer on the Underground was really quite clever," admitted Aaron.

"Clever? Damnably vicious more like."

"Well of course, but with so many cramming on to the Tube hoping to stay safe if the bomb goes off, they're then terrified of being the killer's next victim. There's nowhere to hide, people are scared all the time."

"And you know what? I reckon you can add that insidious smartphone game to the list."

"You really think so?"

"Come on – remember that guy last week who killed someone in the street over a dispute started in the game? And have you seen how addicted and inwardly focused those playing it have become? It's worse than social media."

"It does seem to have an unusual grip on people, but then I've never understood the appeal of video games," said Aaron.

"What's more, I heard someone on the bus talking about how there's going to be a huge event in central London on the 23rd, one that all the players will be turning up to."

"So?"

"So the 23rd is also the day the APA is holding its big march on Parliament. Again, it can't be coincidence, can it? They're obviously building towards something."

"But what? This really doesn't sound good."

"It's an apocalypse," said Reggie.

Jack and Aaron both turned to stare at the other man, who hadn't spoken a word since they'd stepped into the capsule.

"The Apocalypse?" Jack questioned, scepticism heavy in his voice.

"*An* apocalypse. It's Greek you know, means a sort of revelation."

Jack's tone edged towards exasperation.

"So it's a revelation. Of what? What's going to be revealed Reggie?"

"What do I look like to you boy, a magic eight ball?"

The silence that followed their exchange endured for a long moment, the accompanying friction palpable in the confines of the glass bubble in which they stood. Eventually the gondola jerked and started to swing, the gentle movement breaking the tension and softening the mood. Reggie spoke quietly.

"It'll be bad, proper bad."

"Is that what the spirits are saying?"

"The spirits are ... well, they say a lot of things, but that's the gist of it."

Aaron took a deep breath and sighed.

"Look, if whatever is going down will do so on June 23rd, that only gives us a couple of weeks, which isn't much time to prepare."

"OK, well I'll go back and see what else I can find in the Book of Ways, I've only really skimmed the surface so far," said Jack.

"Good, I'll get what I can from the other Awakened I'm in contact with, hopefully one of them will be able to shed some light on what the entities are. They're not easy to get hold of but someone must know something. What about you Reggie, can you try and make more sense of what the spirits are saying? Give us a better idea of what we're up against?"

The Caribbean was lucid and focused on the conversation, but yet he still shifted uneasily, as if the topic made him uncomfortable.

"Fair enough, I'll see what I can do," he conceded.

Despite the conciliatory tone, Jack couldn't shake a nagging feeling of suspicion that lingered long past the end of their trip on The Eye. He didn't know how to read Reggie's aura but something about it had betrayed an unspoken thought on the older man's part. What was it that he wasn't telling them? What was he keeping to himself?

The memorial service wasn't due to start for another ten minutes and the three men waited a little apart from the throng of sports stars and celebrities. Jack and Aaron wore sombre dark suits while Reggie's tweed jacket gave him a more paternal appearance, though he was fidgeting and clearly on edge.

Despite the private event being only for close colleagues and friends, there were over two hundred mourners gathered on the pitch at the Emirates Stadium. Jack took it as a sign of the affection and regard that Sabir had inspired, rather than the great and the good turning out in obligation. There were quite a few tears already and the service hadn't even started.

Having wanted to be sure that the entities hadn't decided to use the occasion to take another crack at them, Jack had just finished a thorough scan of the stadium. He turned to Aaron.

"All clear. You know what though, I still don't get how all this started in the first place."

"What do you mean?"

"Well, I understand how the concentrator worked, focusing ambient negative energy onto the rift in order to weaken the veil and allow the entities through from the negative plane."

"Uh-huh."

"What I don't get is how there was so much in the atmosphere for it to draw upon?"

"Come on Jack, don't be naive."

"What? London's a great place to live, it's vibrant and full of creativity. It has its problems, but what big city doesn't?"

"Sure, but where was the concentrator?"

"You mean literally? In the heart of the City of London."

"And there's your answer."

"You don't seriously mean that evil bankers caused all of this?"

"No, of course not. On an individual level bankers and financiers are no worse than anyone else. But their profession is based upon the wanton desire for profit and enrichment, often at the expense of others. It's one of the most powerful and fundamental of negative emotions."

"But they're just normal people. The friends of mine who've gone into banking are well-adjusted, honest and hardworking. And mostly they just manage other people's money anyway."

"And yet you've seen the results in the City for yourself. Look, for many years much of the rest of the population has been entirely complicit, just as eager for everything to carry on as it always had done. It's their pension funds and savings that the bankers have been playing with after all."

"But you are saying this mess all started back in the City?" asked Jack.

"Maybe not all, but it's certainly at the root of it. Technology has played its part as well, these days it's mostly electronic and abstract like some sort of game, it distances people from the consequences of their actions. Then you've got all the animosity directed back towards the City, everyone's blaming the bankers and business leaders – with much justification – but conveniently forgetting their own part in it all. Also, the economy being in such turmoil has made people scared stiff of what the future holds. Now of course, they've got worse things to worry about than the state of their finances."

Jack thought for a few moments, unsure that he agreed with his mentor's view of the situation. He was lifted from his introspection when he caught sight of Rebecca and gave a friendly wave. She returned him a flat smile and gestured she had people to attend to. He nodded and left her to do her rounds of the other attendees.

"OK, ignoring for a moment the exact cause of all this, where do we go from here?" he asked.

"Well I heard back from the guy in New York I'd been telling you about. He reckons that the two you encountered together are lesser manifestations, evils that have attached themselves to human hosts."

"You mean like as in demonic possession?"

"Sort of, though he was at pains to point out not to think of it in religious terms, there's too much superstition and dogma that's likely to be misleading," said Aaron.

"It makes sense though, judging from what their auras looked like. So what do we do?"

"The host is what allows the entity to anchor itself to our plane of existence, so you have to remove it before trying to tackle the entity itself."

"Which means what, killing the host?"

"Unfortunately, yes."

"Well I don't think I have a problem with that," admitted Jack.

"Neither do I. Even if we knew how to drive one out whilst leaving the host alive, I don't reckon there'd be much left of the original personality."

"That's what I'll tell myself anyway. What about the other one, any idea what it is?"

"Things get a little sketchier here, but as we thought, it's likely a pure construct of the negative plane, or greater manifestation. The best guess is that it can take whatever form it likes and rebuild itself at will."

"So what, it's invulnerable?"

"Maybe, we just don't know, there's very little in the way of records."

"That's weird, over the years you'd have thought that sort of thing would be at the top of the watch list for the Awakened."

"It may well have been, but the lack of an account of one

having been defeated, or even anyone surviving an attempt on one, ought to tell you something."

It took Jack a moment for the implication to sink in.

"Oh, I see what you mean. Marvellous."

One of Rebecca's colleagues from the Abbey called the crowd to order and they took their seats for the service. Jack and Aaron struggled to get Reggie settled, he'd been agitated ever since they'd arrived and his constant shifting and glancing drew unsympathetic stares from those closest to them. The ceremony got underway and for the most part he was content to mutter to himself. It was towards the end that he became more animated.

"No man, it can't be!" he blurted out with real panic in his voice.

Jack felt himself redden at the attention the outburst had drawn, and was instantly ashamed for feeling self-conscious while his friend was in obvious distress. He tried to pacify Reggie but it was Aaron's calm manner and soothing voice that did the trick. That and the strong impulse of positive energy he transferred to Reggie's fluctuating aura.

As the memorial drew to a close and the crowd started to disperse, Jack saw Rebecca look their way and choose not to approach them. He couldn't blame her given the circumstances, but he knew she was flying out to Morocco later that day to repatriate Sabir's body and he'd been hoping to speak with her before she went. He made a mental note to leave a voicemail instead.

He turned to Aaron but found him on his mobile, so spent a few minutes trying to distract Reggie by talking about what had happened in the stadium on that fateful day. The talk of Sabir only seemed to increase the older man's agitation so he dropped the subject as soon as Aaron finished his call.

"That looked important," said Jack.

"Maybe, I'm not sure yet. It was Sophia, she said there's been a really unusual theft from the museum, something we should take a look at."

"Do you want to go there now? It might help to calm Reggie down a bit, whatever I try isn't helping any."

"Yes, let's do that. There's something else we need to see her about as well, a suggestion from one of the other contacts I spoke to."

"Sounds interesting, tell me it's good news?"

"I hope so Jack, I really do."

The three of them waited in the hall at the top of the south stairs of the British Museum, where a large and bizarrely ornate monumental carillon clock from Strasbourg kept them company. To the relief of his companions, Reggie had calmed down on the journey there and now inspected the timepiece with interest. Jack was also intrigued, but not in a horological sense.

"So what's the deal with Sophia then? You said she's *not exactly* awakened, what does that mean?"

Aaron chose his words carefully.

"It means that she's not like us, but she is somewhat sensitive to auras. She can't see them but she can sense a bit of their nature, particularly with objects. I guess it's what drew her to archaeology."

"Does she know anything about us, as in what we are, about the wider reality?"

"Yes Jack, she knows pretty much everything about me."

"Ah. I see."

He had been curious for a while about the nature of their relationship, Aaron had mentioned her frequently and up until then Jack had been too respectful to ask outright.

"And she knows about you and the others," said Aaron, "and what's been happening. I trust her, so should you."

He turned to greet the late middle-aged woman who had approached them. They touched cheeks affectionately and Jack couldn't help but notice the way their auras recognised each other. He smiled inwardly, grateful that Aaron had someone in his life.

"Very pleased to meet you Jack, Aaron's told me so much about you."

"The pleasure's all mine, Miss Featherstone."

"Sophia, please. Reggie, good to see you again too."

She handed them each visitor badges that she'd already prepared.

"Now I bet you're all dying to know what's dragged you over here. Come this way."

While they walked, she explained that a deputy curator and a security guard had been found dead in a museum van, and it had taken a while to identify that a theft had occurred at the same time.

"It was only when the curator's computer log was checked that it was realised he had been accessing records on particular items. They were examined and one was missing."

They passed through rooms for Medieval Europe and Europe 300-1100 until they came to Roman Britain.

"Now what really caught my attention was this."

She indicated a modest stone sarcophagus sitting on a plinth towards one corner of the room. It was crudely decorated with images of foliage on its lid, baskets of fruit on its sides and a simple portrait of a youthful male on its front. The three men could see instantly that a strong negative aura emanated from it.

"Wow, that's had a pretty nasty past," commented Jack.

"That's what I felt, and the item stolen was a lead coffin that was found inside this sarcophagus."

She handed a photograph of the coffin to them before continuing.

"So I'm thinking that to leave a residual aura this strong, the coffin itself must have been very powerful indeed."

"You never handled it in person?" Aaron asked.

"Unfortunately no, it's not my department I'm afraid."

"Hang on a minute," said Jack, "from what I've seen lead is really good at blocking energy, so what on earth was in the coffin?"

"Records indicate it was the remains of a Roman boy, probably about ten years old, buried in the third or fourth century AD. The whole lot was excavated during redevelopment work in 1854, from Haydon Square on the very east side of the City of London, near where the wall used to be."

The four of them stared at the sarcophagus and then each other, as if saying aloud what they were thinking would make it worse. Jack took the plunge.

"So they've nicked the remains of an individual who presumably was possessed with immensely negative energy. But what can they use it for? A focus for some kind of ritual? A source of power from which to draw upon?"

The others shrugged.

"Can we be certain it was even them?" asked Sophia.

"It's a safe bet," Aaron replied, "but to be sure we'd better have a look at where it was taken from. There might be a lingering aura that would confirm it."

Sophia led them down to the basement of the museum where they found traces of negative energy that couldn't be accounted for by objects they saw. They concluded it was likely from coercion or obfuscation used during the theft, especially as nothing had turned up on any of the museum's CCTV cameras. Sophia took them back to her office where she put the kettle on for tea.

"On the other matter you asked me to look into Aaron, I may have better news for you."

"The Gorgoneion?"

"Indeed. Will any of these help at all?"

She retrieved a cardboard box from a drawer in her desk and carefully lifted the contents onto the table. Three discs of varying size, each of them clearly very old and bearing the image of a Gorgon's head.

Jack whistled upon seeing the positive auras that the discs projected, though one in particular caught his attention. It wasn't just its strength, but also its complexity. He could see it was not simply a reflection of the accumulated experiences of the object. Instead it was rather like one of the wards that Aaron had shown him how to construct, though more intricate and much stronger – a pattern of energy almost organic in its sophistication. Interweaved lines pulsed dutifully, as if driven by a hidden purpose.

"What are they?" he asked.

"A Gorgoneion, as you can just about see, is an image of a Gorgon, a snake haired figure from Greek antiquity. You have to use your imagination a little as some of the depictions aren't so obvious. Typically it would be used as an apotropaic symbol, that is to say, a device that repels evil."

Jack held the best of the amulets aloft.

"This is amazing, I don't know what it's meant to do, but the aura has got layer upon layer of crafting in it. Does anyone mind if I take a closer look?"

Aaron and Sophia shook their heads.

He extended his thoughts until his aura had met with that of the disc, and then started to work his mind around the many components of its construction. He'd felt his way towards the heart of it and was on the brink of understanding its form, when the disc writhed on the end of its chain. The female face sculpted on its front opened her eyes and stared right back at Jack. The snakes animated and started to bob and weave through her hair, flicking their delicate tongues out from the surface as they tasted the air in the room.

Sophia gasped and Aaron peered forward, even Reggie stopped glancing around and took notice.

"Erm, not sure what I did there guys," offered Jack.

Where previously the woman's face had been dull and worn from years of handling and use, it was now perfectly smooth skinned, and minutely detailed. The austerity of her high cheek bones and piercing blue eyes demanded respect as she glared at those who observed her.

She winked at Jack and then in an instant became still and

lifeless again, appearing just as mundane as a two-and-a-half thousand year old electrum medallion should do.

Silence descended on the group as they stared at the amulet, and then each other. Eventually Aaron spoke.

"Well, I think that deserves some further investigation, don't you Jack? See if you can work out what to do with it, but don't take too long, the 23rd isn't far off now."

They had tea and went on to discuss their various theories on what the device might do, and how the entities could be tackled. The mood was quite cheerful by the time Jack carefully slipped the device into his jacket pocket and got up to leave. As he held the door for Reggie, he looked back and smiled at the sight of Aaron and Sophia sitting close together.

He thought of Mandy, and about how much he'd missed her the previous week while she'd been away on business. She'd not even been able to get time off to accompany him to the memorial service. Still, she should be on her way back by now and no doubt keen to see him too, so he took out his phone and dialled her number.

Chapter Twenty-One

Despite his good mood, Avaro traipsed a little wearily up the steps to the Pimlico house. He was keen to keep intact the reserves of energy he had built up, and so had withheld from using any to assist him unless absolutely necessary. His construct felt it as fatigue and tiredness, yet the result was that his aura glowed like a furnace. He had surprised himself somewhat at the restraint and commitment he had shown, though in truth he knew that things were nearing the end. His ultimate goal was almost within grasp and it was not for very much longer that he needed to remain disciplined.

He made his way to the kitchen and grabbed a bottle of red wine to decant. He left the last inch untouched, not as a libation but to keep any sediment from spoiling his indulgence. The 1978 Conterno Monfortino swam enthusiastically into the crystal decanter and rewarded him with a rich and spicy aroma. He placed it respectfully on the table, forcing himself to give the wine a chance to chamber properly.

He slumped into a chair, leaned back until its legs creaked and then smiled to himself. Everything was ready, all the elements were in place. Even the warlock's whore was stowed safely upstairs. With two days to go until the 23rd he could relax a little and prepare his concentration for the task ahead.

He had been delighted by the news from *The Streets of Gold*'s development team, more than forty-five thousand players had signed up for the events that had been organised. There was no guarantee they would all turn up, but it was a good omen nevertheless.

He was also grateful for the success both he and the twins had been having through their use of social media. He had been amused to find out how easy it was to get people excited and organised by playing on the public's herd mentality, their desperate desire to be part of something in this belief-starved age. All sorts of groups would be turning out, not just Hetty's APA, but also counter marches by campaign groups of myriad flavours. With luck there would be substantial numbers of opportunistic rioters and looters joining the fray as well. It was going to be some party.

His satisfaction was tempered only by the slight hint of regret that he would not see the ultimate fruits of his labours in person. Still, he was going to be very much a part of what was to come and he looked forward to that.

He was about to reach for the wine to test whether it was ready for consumption when he noticed a small anomaly in the energy field within the house. He got up to investigate and quickly realised that the discrepancy was related to the cellar. There was something not quite right with the shield he had set up, a substantial mask against any intruders they should have, mundane or otherwise.

As he descended the stairs he was welcomed by the warm glow of the coffin, but his eyes opened wide when he saw it was alone. The bomb had gone.

He examined the shield and knew straight away that the clumsy repair job on it was Ferren's handiwork, he had never been able to grasp the technique properly. He really was a useless little shit. Just when success was so near, he had chosen to risk it all. The bomb had been right where it needed to be, doing its damage from afar and being saved for later, better use.

Now was not the time to risk setting it off, or worse still have it captured by the authorities – the tidal wave of relief could very easily ruin their plans entirely. Damn it, a thermonuclear detonation might just be enough to destroy his own construct so completely it would send him back through the veil. That did not bear thinking about.

Trying and failing utterly to keep his temper in check, Avaro went back upstairs and dialled Hetty's mobile. It was answered on the third ring.

"Where is that fucking brother of yours?" he spat.

As soon as he had the reply he cut the call and stormed out of the house, his aura pulsing incandescently.

The twins sat in the trendy Pimlico wine bar Bacchus Again, only a few minutes' walk from their house. It was noisy with the chatter of clipped tones and Hetty had to lean forward to make herself heard.

"He's really pissed you know, and I mean *really* pissed. What the fuck did you do little brother?"

"Just put things back as they should be."

Ferren's nonchalance had been encouraged by the now empty bottle that sat between them, the second of the evening. Hetty channelled a small dart of energy, which stung him like a slap in the face.

"Hey, cut it out," he was starting to slur his words a little. She hit him again, "OK, OK, I gave the nuke back to that group of jihadist wannabes. They'll be irradiating a chunk of North London fairly soon," he checked his watch and giggled to himself.

"You did what! I thought you scrubbed them when ..."

She grimaced when she saw the self-congratulatory grin spread across his face, and then slapped him with yet more energy.

"Ferren, you've really fucked up this time. Why? Why on earth would you do that?"

The smarting caused by his sister's rebuke brought him back into focus.

"Well first up, it was my plan, not Av's. So I get to choose how it all works out."

He drained the last of the wine in his glass.

"And secondly, because it'll scare the crap out of the population, which means I'll have well and truly beaten you. No ifs, no buts, no maybes. I win, you lose."

He saluted with his empty glass and flashed her a lop-sided smirk.

"Seriously," she replied, "you're risking everything just to spite me?"

"Why not? You would, given half the chance. Besides, don't get too full of yourself. The *real* reason," he leaned forward and whispered, "is that the resultant surge from London's masses will still allow our plans to go ahead, but this way the dominant alignment of energy will be mine. Not yours, and not Av's."

"Why you devious little ..."

Ferren raised his voice above his sister's, "Which means that when the time comes, I'll be the one that's turned to, I'll be the favoured one. At the very least I'll be rewarded with a proper construct."

Incredulity turned Hetty's face into an ugly sneer.

"You're insane, you don't even know how to do the rituals, you've no idea how they work."

"No I don't, but Av does, and he can't afford not to go through with things can he? Not after the delay he caused by letting the rift get closed. He'll have to go ahead, just on my terms rather than his."

"You're wrong Ferren, you've so misjudged him. He'll never let you get away with this."

"Screw him, he's too late to stop them now. He'll never get there in time, not during rush hour."

He sat back in his chair and pouted.

"And screw you too sis. It's about time the pair of you gave me the respect I deserve."

"Well at least you grew some balls, I'll give you that. I mean, this is an epic mistake on your part, no doubt about it, but at least you've put yourself first. Maybe too much of Av has rubbed off on you?"

"Fuck off Hetty."

She was about to reply when she saw Avaro's volcanic aura cross the street and enter the wine bar. With a wave of his hand he knocked all the other drinkers and bar staff unconscious, and stalked over to where the twins sat. With no music playing, the tread of his step on the creaky floorboards was the only sound in the room. As he came to a halt beside the table, Hetty instinctively shuffled slightly further away from her brother.

"What have you done, whelp?"

Avaro spoke slowly, his voice guttural and primeval, the syllables tearing at each other as they left his mouth.

"What I should've done ages ..."

"Answer me!"

As Avaro bellowed his command, a lance of energy flew from his mouth and skewered Ferren's head, instantly stripping it of names, places and intentions. A second later the interrogation was dropped, leaving Ferren clutching his temples and whimpering as he squirmed in his seat.

"Fool."

Avaro shook his head in disappointment before turning to Hetty.

"Keep this one at the house, I will deal with him later, and do not let him near the coffin."

Hetty nodded her assent but avoided making eye contact. Avaro then took a pace backwards and closed his eyes, his breathing deep and loud as it hissed through his nostrils, his chest heaving up and down. Energy started to flow from his core to form a sphere around him, a wavering shell at first that thickened and stabilised as he put more and more of himself into it. The surface of his aura cooled to such an extent that it appeared to be made solely from dull patches of rock, only the merest hints of crimson visible at the seams.

The sphere had become coherent and smooth, and for the briefest of instants it gained a gleaming metallic sheen. With a loud bang it vanished, taking a scoop of the floor boards with it and leaving the air ringing with the taste of ozone.

Ferren's jaw dropped.

Hetty poured herself a glass of the perfectly chambered Monfortino and took a healthy swig. She knew it was good stuff but the subtleties were lost on her, she didn't possess Avaro's palate for such intricacies. She licked her reddened lips and sneered at her twin.

"Not so cocky now, are you?"

Ferren was sat in a chair across the other side of the table, his wrists bound to its thin wooden arms by tight cords of energy. He'd given up struggling soon after Hetty had restrained him, she was good at that sort of thing and he knew there was no chance of wriggling free. He'd thought for a moment of trying to overpower her aura but that too was pointless, she was stronger and much better suited to direct confrontation. Desperation clawed its way into his voice, which had developed into a plaintive whine.

"But it should have gone off by now, it should have gone off."

"Come on, we both know he's stopped them. I told you it was a stupid idea. A stupid idea, from stupid little Ferren."

For a moment they were transported back to their childhoods, where numerous conflicts had resulted in them glaring at each other, Hetty having come out on top. She made a face at him and broke eye contact so she could go to the fridge. She took out a leg of cured pork and placed it on the table, letting its aroma taunt Ferren's alcohol induced hunger. She brushed past him and flicked his ear, a petty demonstration of how helpless he was.

She selected a razor sharp cooking knife from the block, sat down again and deftly cut herself several thick slices. She moaned in delight as she ate, the exaggeration for Ferren's benefit. She licked her fingers and laughed.

The loathing on her brother's face stiffened to apprehension as the front door sounded. They could hear awkward shuffling noises and seconds later Avaro entered the kitchen, dragging the heavy suitcase he'd retrieved. His aura was almost non-existent.

"So, you got it back then?" Hetty asked nervously.

Avaro gave her a dry look and she wished she'd kept quiet, it was only then she noticed what looked like a large knife wound to the back of his left leg.

He sat down carefully and reached for Hetty's glass, draining it in one go. For a brief moment he closed his eyes in appreciation and then turned his attention to Ferren.

He waved a hand and the bonds evaporated in a puff of smoke.

"Nice try," he said evenly.

Ferren's quivering lips turned into a grin as relief spread across his face.

"Oh, well no hard feelings ..."

He looked down at his chest.

His heart had stopped.

"I ..." was all he could manage before he slumped forward, his head hitting the table with a wooden thud.

As the human core of his aura began to fade, the tight red coils began to unravel. As they did so, each split into several filaments, which in turn became finer and finer strands until a messy ball of red vermicelli hung in the air. As the last of the human aura vanished, the ball began to crackle and fizz, red sparks arcing and spitting amongst the mass of tendrils, a miniature lightning storm contained within.

Summoning the last of his reserves Avaro leaned forward and extended a hand. With great concentration he stood up and fought to control the ball as it hissed and popped, bringing it closer until it hovered a few inches above his palm.

He forced it to rotate slowly, the motion increasing his level of control and synchronising it to his will. He commanded the ball to shrink, the individual fibres delving deeper towards its centre, knitting tighter and tighter together. By the time it had condensed to the size of a tennis ball it shone intensely, with energy manifesting itself in reality as brilliant crimson sparks that showered the kitchen like a bonfire night sparkler.

Avaro then brought his hand back towards his face, his jaw distended and lips curled back as he directed the sphere into his mouth. The energy was rapidly absorbed and his aura ignited in conflagration, starting with his head and then spreading throughout his body until his entire form glowed with pyroclastic menace.

He shrugged his shoulders back and then flexed all the muscles of his upper body, an elemental snarl accompanying the resurgence of power.

Hetty looked at him, her face a blend of awe and horror.

"He's ... he's gone."

Chapter Twenty-Two

It was a few minutes before sunrise and the floating jetty bobbed slowly up and down in the gentle wash of the river. Sited on Victoria Embankment, just upstream of the Houses of Parliament, its dull grey metalwork looked barren and industrial compared to the majestic architecture lining that part of the Thames. The busy throng of river boats that would normally pester it during the day were still asleep in their moorings elsewhere, and for now just two figures stood looking out over the water. One with his arms outraised towards the other bank, the other huddled inside her jacket against the morning chill.

Avaro concentrated hard as he manipulated strands of energy into a complex ovoid formation in front of him. The arcane shape hung in the air a couple of metres above the water, its desire to enter the murky depths evident by the constant straining downwards that its creator had to contend with.

The intensity of the construction continued to build until the effort began to show on Avaro's face. Just as Hetty started to worry that he might not be able to complete the rite, he raised his arms higher and sent the shape out towards the midstream. He then cast his hands downwards and released the knot of energy to plummet into the river. It caused only the merest of ripples as it disappeared beneath the surface without a sound.

Seconds later vapour began to issue from the water. Thin and wispy at first, it soon thickened until dense rolls billowed up and cascaded over the banks and onto the streets of London. The fog travelled the capital's roads and alleyways for about a mile and a half in every direction, its intensity reducing only a little as it spread out until it settled as a heavy mist that blanketed most of central London.

Detective Sergeant Valerie Tucker left the briefing room and cursed the APA. Just when the police needed to concentrate on finding the bomb in North London, they'd been forced to divert resources to managing a hostile march. She just hoped it wouldn't turn uglier than it already promised. With many other groups assembling in opposition to the APA, it would take the smallest of sparks to set things off.

Having had nine years of level two public order experience before becoming a detective, she'd been drafted back in to help out on the front line. She trudged off to the locker room to get kitted up and retrieve her baton, then called her husband and told him to expect her back late. It was going to be a very long day.

Reggie stepped outside the door and onto the pavement of Henrietta Street.

"What the bleedin' hell is this stuff?"

Jack and Aaron joined him and walked around in the mist, as if expecting it suddenly to part and reveal normality again.

"According to the local news it's just an atmospheric anomaly," said Jack, "but I reckon we can safely say it's down to them, there's a faint aura to it."

Aaron rounded on him and shouted angrily in his face.

"Watch what's happening Jack, or are you blind!"

Stunned, the younger man took a step backwards and raised his hands in protection against the American's huge presence.

"I, I don't know ..."

Aaron's expression softened, as did his voice.

"I meant quite literally *watch what's happening,* to the energy."

The three of them peered at the puff of red smoke that the exchange had generated. Rather than dissipate as it normally would it appeared to hang in the air, clinging to the mist as if a bloody stain upon gauzy fabric.

"Oh, OK. Right you are. Sorry, I didn't get your drift," Jack replied, his pulse gradually slowing back down.

"My apologies, but that was kind of the point."

They went back inside and finished their breakfast while they discussed where their search would start. They'd already established that Jack had the best chance of finding the bomb. He'd experimented using some of the sources at the University – the first time he'd been back in a while – and found that he could sense radioactive material from about twenty metres, though it required some concentration. The other two had no such ability but they guessed they'd be able to detect the negativity that doubtless surrounded it, albeit at a much shorter range.

With Rebecca's plane being delayed, they couldn't afford to wait for her and so set off soon after 8am. Their first destination was Westminster, the political heart of the capital seemingly the epicentre of the mist according to the news reports.

Jack was tired and on edge, he'd not slept much since discovering that Mandy was missing. Learning from her office that her last client before vanishing was Avar Investments had sent him into a blind panic. It had taken Aaron several days to get him vaguely back in focus, and even then he'd struggled to be productive. He'd managed the radioactivity test, but the Book of Ways had remained largely untouched. Aaron tried again to reassure him.

"Look Jack, I know it's hard but you've got to concentrate today. They want you angry, they want you distracted. You're the one they're worried about. You can best help Mandy by stopping the bomb, then we'll work on getting her back. Sophia's keeping an eye on Gresham Street, she'll let us know if there's any movement there. In the meantime, just try and stay cool."

Jack turned to him, his face drained and gaunt from worry.

"That's easy for you to say, what if it were Sophia they'd taken?"

Aaron opened his mouth to respond, but then closed it and walked on. He knew full well how he would cope in Jack's situation, and the thought worried him. It worried him a lot.

Tom lent his voice to the chant that echoed around outside Victoria Station, the mob of Albion Patriotic Alliance members already numbered several thousand and continued to grow rapidly. The simple slogans were alternately anti-government and anti-Islamic, the fervour increasing with each refrain.

He was enjoying the empowerment and liberation of the gathering and wondered when they would get the signal to advance on Parliament. They were one half of a pincer movement being coordinated with the second flank assembling in Trafalgar Square.

Tom peered through the mist at the assorted flags and banners proclaiming which branches of the organisation were present. He made his way towards his local group from east London and shook hands with them as he took his place amongst the rank and file.

Gary Hawkins milled around outside St James's Park station, trying to stay clear of trouble while he waited for his chance. He'd already dodged several police patrols and was eager to get into the special dungeon about to open up within the imposing building above the station. 55 Broadway was formerly the headquarters of the London Underground and it was rumoured that the end of dungeon prize would be a *Season Ticket of Transport Control*, a legendary item giving complete command of the city's transit systems. It was priceless, and it was going to be his.

The portal opened and Gaz_the_Gr8 charged through the shimmering door and into the grime and filth smeared lobby inside. A pack of goblins in Transport for London styled uniforms charged straight for him and he bellowed a mighty war cry as he set about cleaving limb from torso.

Hetty pressed the phone closer and covered the other ear with her free hand.

"Sorry Av, it's really beginning to heat up over here, what was that again?"

"Have you got everything in place?" he pronounced each word very deliberately.

"Oh yeah, of course. We're already up and running, the coordination's proving to be quite easy really. What's it looking like from up there? Is the mist working?"

"It is indeed, energy is accumulating nicely. Give it one more hour and then you may start the next phase."

"OK, will do. Speak to you later."

Tom shouted abuse at the Muslim youths as they ran off down the street, bloodied and broken from their encounter with his much larger branch unit of APA. The House of Commons was where they were aiming for, but they'd moved to the side streets to find a way through the mass of bodies congregating on Westminster. They were also heading off to arm up properly.

They'd had news that the second APA front had encountered heavy police resistance, so for now it was up to them to get the job done, and Tom was determined to do some major damage.

Gaz_the_Gr8 left the dungeon without the Season Ticket but nevertheless his pockets bulged with other valuable loot. As soon as Gary had seen the in-game announcement that player kill codes had been activated, he cut his losses against the TfL goblins and went in search of other competitors for a bit of player versus player action.

One of the advantages of being at a high level meant his kill code was very short, 'g86'. All he had to do was enter it into another player's handset and their character would die, with all their items and wealth passing to him. Lower level characters might have to enter ten or more letters or numbers, making it harder to do so before the owner recovered their smartphone.

The geography teacher pushed his way through the crowds to a small park nearby where he observed a young woman concentrating intently as she played the game. Darting forward he ripped the woman's phone from her grasp, turned his back to shield it whilst he jabbed in his code and then discarded it on the ground. The woman cried in desperation and dived to the floor to retrieve the smartphone, only to be trampled underfoot as the crowd surged in her direction.

Delighted with his haul of items, Gary set off in pursuit of another victim.

Sergeant Tucker brought her shield in closer and regained the overlap with her colleagues on either side. It wasn't easy to keep formation while walking backwards, but the slow withdrawal was necessary if the wavering line across Whitehall was to be stabilised.

The bastards had come armed and masked up, and the day was descending into a pitched battle, she just hoped that baseball bats would be the worst of it. The call had gone out for reinforcements, but whether or not they'd get there before the thrust coming from Trafalgar Square broke through, she couldn't guess.

She barely had time to wipe the sweat from her brow before the next wave of enraged APA emerged through the mist at a run. Her section of the line was called to a halt and she braced herself for the impact.

Reggie pushed back on the crowd of people pressing in behind them as they were swept along Great George Street, which gave Jack and Aaron just enough leeway to dodge up the steps and into the doorway of the Institution of Civil Engineers. They grabbed Reggie as the crowd surged on and hauled him up beside them.

Burly porters looked on from behind thick glass doors, making it quite clear that access to the magnificent neo-classical building was not an option. Jack flashed them a sarcastic smile and turned back to the others.

"This is ridiculous," he shouted, "I can't sense anything with all this going on, it's mayhem out here."

Aaron threw up a quick sound shield to let them speak more easily.

"I know, but what other choice do we have?"

Jack was about to reply when he felt his pocket vibrate. The display on the phone read Mandy. He showed it to the other two and with some trepidation answered the call.

"Mandy? Is that you?"

"Hardly Jack, but it's nice to finally speak, isn't it? Last time we met we rather skipped the introductions, so let's start again. My name's Hetty and I hold in my hands the life of someone who claims to love you. Are you there Jack?"

The woman's voice induced a surge of emotions that Jack struggled to control. He waited until he could keep his response steady.

"Yes, I'm here."

"Good. Now do you want her back, or do you want me to inflict unspeakable pain and suffering upon her?"

"What do you want?"

"Ooh, even better, you understand how this is played. Right, well I want you to make your way to the key works gallery at the Tate Britain, and when you get there I want you to work out which of the two paintings by Millais on the far wall is relevant. If you get the answer right I'll give you further instructions. Get it wrong and I'll start playing with your friend. Got it?"

"Yeah, I've got it."

"Well hurry up then. Oh, and Jack?"

Another pause whilst he breathed deeply to calm himself.

"Yes?"

"I'll be watching you. And if I see so much as a glimmer of one of your companions, or anything other than you, on your own, nice and compliant, then I'll kill her. Slowly. Got that too?"

"Yes."

"Excellent. Good luck."

He relayed the details of the conversation to the others.

"Paintin's? What's she talkin' about?" asked Reggie.

"At best it's another distraction," said Aaron, "at worst it's a trap. You can't go Jack, you simply can't."

"Well of course it's a bloody trap! But it's also the only shot I have to save Mandy."

Again he had to breathe slowly to restore his composure, his aura stabilising so the other two could see it was a decision he hadn't made rashly.

"I'm going. No discussion."

Reggie and Aaron looked at each other, then back at Jack.

"Well then, we damn sure goin' with you boy."

"No, no you're not. Whatever the trap is I need to spring it, and that won't happen unless I play by their rules."

Aaron reached into a pocket and took out the Gorgoneion, pressing it into Jack's hands.

"Well at least take this with you."

Jack shook his head.

"Again, I play by their rules. Besides, I've shown you how to use it and you might need it when you find the bomb."

He placed the amulet around Aaron's neck and turned the symbol so that it glared outwards. Despite the warmth of the day, Aaron zipped his jacket up to obscure it from casual inspection.

"Can I borrow your mobile?" asked Jack.

Aaron handed over the smartphone and Jack spent a few moments synchronising it with his own.

"Right, that'll at least keep you updated as to where I am."

He shook hands with them both, nodded grimly and then headed out through the sound shield and into the crowd. Reggie shook his head as he watched him become absorbed into the masses.

"It's like the ghost's been sayin', he'll betray us all."

Gary Hawkins stumbled through the wreckage inside an electronics shop in Strutton Ground. He tapped furiously on his smartphone as he tried to locate a save point where he could deposit his treasure in safety, but they seemed to have disappeared in the last few hours.

He looked up every second or so to scan the jumble of boxes and broken display cabinets until he saw an intact laptop. Shaking the shards of glass from on top of its lid, he stowed it under one arm, clamping it with his elbow so he could continue playing the game.

As he made his way out of the shop his fingers began to slip on the screen, despite being misty the day had warmed up considerably and he had to wipe the sweat from his hands.

He looked up and spotted a jewellery shop being looted so set off to see what items he could win there.

Sergeant Tucker stooped over as she caught her breath. Her small group of riot officers had been roaming as an independent unit ever since Whitehall had fallen and the APA run amok. They couldn't get to Parliament to regroup so had fought off smaller handfuls of rioters in the back streets. She shook her head in dismay, they'd already chased off several gangs of youths, whose agenda was nothing more than using the opportunity to loot the pubs and shops that served the area. She thought of her own kids and desperately hoped they would never end up having such little respect for themselves and the society they lived in.

Picking up her shield she started getting her team back on their feet. They'd just had the call from Control to force their way through to central Westminster. It wasn't going to be pretty, but they'd damn well give it a go.

Tom tried to back off but couldn't move for those pressing in behind. The mounted police had turned and were preparing for another charge, the clatter of hooves audible above the shouting and screaming in Parliament Square.

While those around him readied their weapons and took a couple of eager steps forward, he used the opportunity to sneak in behind and try to dodge his way to safety.

He thought he was in the clear but shots sounded and the crowd surged in response, crushing him against a set of railings. He jammed his hands against the iron bars and used his elbows to try and create enough space in which to breathe. He started to panic and thought he was done for, then suddenly the surge changed direction and the pressure eased. He clawed his way over the railings and sought through the mist for a path away from the violence.

Jack was out of breath by the time he reached the Tate Britain. Not only had he run the few occasions when there was enough clear space to do so, but he'd frequently had to use energy to move the crowds apart. He didn't have Aaron's ability to influence people subtly, so instead had relied on creating forces to push them out of the way.

He slowed to a swift walk as he approached the building, and was strangely irritated at having to go all the way round to the entrance on the far side. Knowing that he needed to remain calm, he stopped outside for a few moments by a statue to catch his breath and cool down a little. He glanced at the inscription he'd just leant against and raised an eyebrow at seeing it read

JOHN EVERETT
MILLAIS

He took heart from the positive nature of the aura surrounding the artist's image and headed to the main entrance. He was quite surprised to find the gallery still open considering its proximity to the disturbances further north, but didn't stop to enquire as to why they'd not taken the obvious step of shutting for the day.

He consulted a map in the lobby and went directly to the room of key works from the historic collection, located just off the main rotunda. He was so focused that he barely registered the elegant sculptures populating the halls he passed through. What he did notice as soon as he entered the room he'd been sent to were the four large men standing one in each corner. They looked a little suspicious anyway, the hard set of their faces being atypical for museum goers, but it was their auras that made him pause. Already largely negative, they had thick red bands of smoke wrapped around their heads that spoke of control and obedience.

As Jack approached the far wall he didn't have much trouble making out the two paintings by Millais from amongst the group on show. The one on the right was *Christ in the House of His Parents,* The Carpenter's Shop, a healthy purple aura bringing the love and humanity of the scene to life.

The one on the left was Ophelia, the artist's iconic depiction of the deceased heroine floating serenely in the brook. The aura was much more confused, elements of positivity ensnared by the tragedy of Shakespeare's masterpiece.

Jack's phone rang.

"So, have you worked it out yet? Mandy's just dying to know what's to become of her."

"It's Ophelia, OK? I know the story, you've made your point. Now where is she?"

"Interesting. All in good time Jack, it won't be long now.

I'm about to hang up, and when I do I want you to give your phone to the nice man standing next to you and then follow him politely. Do you understand?"

Her question had an edge to it, an insistence.

"I understand."

"Good boy," the breezy tone was back, "see you soon."

Jack looked across at the thug standing beside him and surreptitiously locked his phone as he handed it over. The man stared back impassively, pocketed the device and walked away.

Jack followed him at a steady pace, aware that at least some of the others in the room were also on the move with them. He didn't bother to look round and instead focused on marshalling as much energy to himself as he could, using the mental exercises he'd learned from Aaron and the Book of Ways.

The man he followed was quite adept at pushing his way through the crowds and Jack kept close so as to make use of the brief path cleared for him. It wasn't long before the baroque edifice of St John's Church in Smith Square loomed up ahead of them through the mist. As they reached the corner, the man stepped to the side and opened the door to a redbrick block of offices, some of the most exclusive in that part of London. He led Jack up six flights of stairs, passing several open doors where stacks of boxes could be seen. Jack looked with his aura and found they contained weapons of different sorts, from batons and baseball bats to handguns and petrol bombs. A number of people thralled in a similar manner to his guide were busy either organising equipment or hunched over laptops.

The man opened the door to the roof and stood aside for Jack to go through. As he stepped out he saw a woman standing near the corner of the flat roof, her hands on shapely hips, looking down at the havoc below.

The woman who had killed Sabir.

Jack had a rising urge to push her over the edge, it would be so easy, all he had to do was extend his aura and ...

She turned to face him and laughed.

"I don't think so, not if you want to see her again."

Jack withdrew the tendril of energy and met her gaze.

"I should kill you now, bitch. You know I can."

She tilted her head to one side and considered the power and complexity of his innate energy field.

"But you won't," she said with a grin, "you know you won't."

She walked forward until she was just a couple of feet from him, where her aura proceeded to caress the negative elements within his, her seductive strands encouraging his darker components to express themselves. He wanted to shudder and recoil, but something deep down told him that he mustn't. He stared back, unflinching.

She leaned in close to him and spoke in a breathy purr.

"Just how far would you go for her, this mundane creature of yours who can never understand your secrets, never share in your power and glory. What would you give to get her back?"

His lips almost touched her ear as he whispered his reply.

"Everything. I would give it all."

Satisfied with his response she stepped away, her energies still entwined with his.

"Excellent, you may yet save her then."

She gave him instructions about Mandy's location and monitored his aura closely as she asked where his companions were.

"I don't know, probably still looking for your bomb."

Content with the veracity of his answer she sent him on his way, watching from the roof as he exited a minute later at street level and started to work north through the masses, using energy to fling people aside in the process.

She took Jack's phone from her henchman, threw it on the floor and ground it into pieces with her heel. Taking out her own mobile she made a call.

"He's on his way, might be a little while though, it's pretty crowded out there."

"Is he ready?"

"Yes, I rather think he is."

"My thanks, you have served well. I will see you on the other side."

"Goodbye Av."

She sighed and put thoughts of the future out of her mind, she still had work to do. There was time enough to bring yet more violence to proceedings, so she headed down a floor to see how the incitement was going.

Tom turned and ducked but failed to avoid the volley of missiles thrown in his direction. He'd thought he'd found a safe street, but in the mist and confusion two groups of APA had attacked each other from range.

A half-brick caught him in the back and he fell forward gasping for breath. It was all he could do to crawl into a corner between two walls, narrowly avoiding the stamp of steel toe caps as one of the sides retreated.

Waves of pain shot up his spine as the full extent of the injury became apparent. Tears filled his eyes and he started to weep, clutching his knees to him and curling up as tight as the injury would allow. He wished the shouting and screaming and violence would stop, and he wanted to go home.

Gary sauntered down the alley way and came to a stop by a set of commercial bins with rubbish bags piled next to them. He was delighted to have found a refuge away from the mobs where he could focus on getting back into the safety of a dungeon, Gaz_the_Gr8 had too much loot to stay out in the open any longer.

He'd just located a shimmering portal round the corner when suddenly he slumped forwards, his smartphone clattering to the ground. A teenage girl stepped from her hiding place behind the bins and dropped her improvised club, picking up the phone and entering her own kill code. She then stripped out the device's SIM card, which she threw into one of the bins, and pocketed the mobile.

Gary started to move so she kicked him hard in the ribs several times, and then rifled through his pockets for his wallet. She briefly pondered taking the laptop as well, but thinking it a little bulky she stamped on it instead and then kicked him again for good measure.

Gary lay amidst the scattered remains of the computer and watched helplessly as the girl walked away.

Sergeant Tucker looked up and through the mist could see another group of APA advancing, thankfully no guns this time but there were still an awful lot of them. Her makeshift squad was surrounded by rioters and had no chance of making it any further, all they could do now was try and protect the civilian casualties.

She detailed the youngest member of the team, twenty year old Constable Thompson, to drag the injured man back up the street to the shop where the other wounded had been left and barricade themselves in.

She got the remaining six of her colleagues in a huddle and fired them up for what had to be done, at least they could buy Thompson some time. They turned to face the enemy, formed a line and gathered speed for one final charge.

Hetty finished distributing the last of the weapons, grateful that the flow of APA supporters through the office had ended. Each of them had also received a small impulse of encouragement and she was exhausted. She'd kept her energy replenished from the mist and was glowing brightly, but physically her body still felt the exertion.

She sat down in a leather office chair and was about to put her feet up on the windowsill when she caught sight of a familiar aura in the misty street below. The wiry Negro was heading down Smith Square and making for the main entrance to the building. At first her eyes lit up at the prospect of tangling with him again, she still owed him for besting her the previous time they met. Then she spotted the other guardian a few paces behind him, one she didn't recognise. So there were five after all, and the new one was strong too, with some kind of device she didn't like the look of.

She gathered all the remaining henchmen and sent them down to occupy the two intruders whilst she made for the side exit. Despite all the commotion of the riot outside she could hear shouts and sporadic gunfire coming from the front of the building, as well as feel the waves of energy that were being unleashed by her pursuers.

Hetty chuckled as she reached the ground floor and ran along the corridor, she rounded the last corner and stopped abruptly at the sight that confronted her. Standing between her and the door was another guardian, one whose aura was inflamed and tempestuous, equal parts red and violet swirling in bright unison. Hetty regained her composure.

"You again? Going to fold as easily as your bloke?" she taunted.

Rebecca walked forward in silence, the swirls of negative energy accelerating. Hetty backed up a couple of paces.

"Looks like you're coming around to my way of thinking at least."

Hetty had been hoping for a slip in the other woman's concentration, but when none was forthcoming she drew her gun anyway. She'd not even managed to raise it level when Rebecca lashed out with a blast of energy so strong that Hetty's hand smashed convulsively into the wall, the gun dropping from her fingers.

"OK, so we do this the old fashioned way."

She launched her aura at Rebecca and the two of them grappled, each seeking control over the other's mind. Hetty felt her psyche being ripped into and was astonished at the strength of her adversary. The priest was so much more potent now that she drew upon loathing and revenge.

The struggle between them continued until Hetty realised

she was in danger of the other guardians showing up. She put a large portion of her reserves into a concentrated strike and broke free of Rebecca, then turned and ran back along the corridor and up the stairwell. She could feel the pursuit behind her and didn't look back as she took the stairs two at a time. She burst through the door and onto the roof, pausing to try and conjure the unfamiliar energy effect she needed to make it to the next roof. The pause cost her dearly as Rebecca barrelled into her, sending them both tumbling to the gravelled surface of the roof.

They rolled for several seconds grappling furiously for physical advantage, their auras locked in stalemate. As they came to a halt Rebecca had her opponent pinned, hands securely around Hetty's throat. She squeezed with all her strength and Hetty's face reddened, the veins straining dangerously as the life was choked from her body. She tried to force out a final insult, but Rebecca held her grip all the stronger as Hetty's human aura faded. As the last wisps dispersed into the air, the physical form shuddered and died.

Aaron and Reggie made it to the roof in time to see Rebecca stand up, engulfed in a whirlwind of negative energy. She staggered a few yards before collapsing to her knees, her arms raised in supplication and tears streaming down her face. Opening her soul up to the winds of the positive veil she begged its forgiveness, pleading shame and remorse for what she had become.

Aaron stepped forwards but was forced to cover his eyes by a blinding flash that enveloped Rebecca. He blinked away the retinal afterimage and saw her still kneeling, but this time with head bowed and her aura restored, just a thin trace of red in an otherwise strong collection of violet swirls.

The two men rushed forwards and she raised her head to look at them, her face calm and serene.

"Hadn't we better do something about that?"

She nodded sideways at the stormy sphere of negative energy

that was accumulating above the woman's corpse. Sizzling with animosity it was growing in size and coherence.

"Let's hope Jack was right about this thing," Aaron said as he took off his jacket to reveal the Gorgoneion, its face flawless and smooth, eyes shining with piercing intensity as the snakes hissed at the corpse.

The three of them formed a triangle around the body and started to draw forth positive energy and direct it inwards. With no prompting required, the amulet eagerly fixed its gaze upon the essence of the negative entity and lanced it with a vivid purple beam of energy, sparks flying off like an arc welder. All the positive energy the three poured in was sucked into the beam and accelerated towards the entity, their power focused and concentrated in a single attack.

Crimson filaments were seared and then burned up by the stream of violet energy, the ball shrinking as it desperately sought to maintain its form. It spun and writhed as it got smaller, trying to find a way to break free, but gradually it withered until every last strand had been vapourised.

The face on the amulet licked its lips and promptly turned back to solid, worn metal.

The three friends buzzed with adrenaline as they looked triumphantly at each other. Reggie was the first to frown.

"Ah, but that's not so good."

He pointed at the Gorgoneion, whose aura had reduced to little more than a dull glow.

"Jack thought that might happen," said Aaron, "it likely needs some time to recharge itself."

Rebecca was about to reply when all three of them had an immediate and overwhelming sense of foreboding. They turned as one to face northwards, just in time to see a shimmering red surface race towards them. It was upon them in an instant, passing straight through and knocking them to the floor in the process.

It took them several moments to recover from the shockwave

that had traversed the veils. By the time they stumbled to their feet, they could see that the mist in the street below was flowing very slowly to the north, taking all the negative energy from the day's events with it.

Chapter Twenty–Three

Jack stood at the foot of the clock tower at the north end of the Houses of Parliament, and gazed up at the soaring neo-gothic structure that rose nearly a hundred metres above him. The nickname Big Ben had been given originally to the 13.7 tonne Great Bell, but over the years had come to denote the clock and tower as well. Since its construction in 1859 it had become the defining symbol of London's skyline, visible and audible for miles around, it kept watch over the city and sounded its pulse.

He'd found it remarkably easy to pass the lines of police and security staff that were massed outside the railings of the Parliamentary compound. He'd not consciously used his powers, but instead had simply asked to be let through. His sense of purpose had been so focused that his aura had influenced those on the gates without him even having to think about it.

He ignored the battle that raged behind him in Parliament Square and headed through an archway towards the entrance. The locked outer door was dealt with swiftly, and the inner one labelled *Clock Tower* took only a moment to open. It had a knot of energy woven around it, similar in form to the one he'd encountered at the investment house in Gresham Street. He ripped the strands apart with ease and took hope that at least he'd been sent to the right place.

Jack closed the door behind him and though he could still hear the commotion taking place outside, it was but a dull background noise that left the stairwell eerily quiet. His footsteps echoed up the staircase as he started the long climb, wondering what lay ahead. Was Mandy even still alive? He had to believe so, he couldn't face the alternative, and kept pushing the thought from his mind. It hovered on the periphery, threatening to take hold should he let it.

He'd lost count of the number of flights of stairs he'd gone up when he passed a door leading to a series of displays on the subject of timekeeping. He guessed he was about halfway up the tower and paused briefly to catch his breath. He leaned on the wrought iron handrail for support and tried to ready himself for whatever form the trap might take that he was about to walk into. Why did they want him in particular? Was he just being separated from the others to reduce their strength and make them easier to pick off one by one?

He set off up the stairs again, and cleared his mind by focusing on the physicality of the task. He kept up a brisk pace and was soon breathing heavily. The steps seemed to go on forever but it was only a couple of minutes before his concentration was interrupted as the hairs on the back of his neck stood up. A sense of trepidation rolled over him as he rounded a corner and approached the mechanism room, the heart of the tower that was surrounded by the four huge clock faces. The door was open and as he stepped through he saw a body lying on the ground, its aura just a dull residual glow. It was Mandy.

His heart raced in panic and he rushed forwards to cradle her in his arms. He lifted her head gently from the floor and was about to hug her still warm body to him when he saw one of her eyelids twitch very slightly. At first he thought it some kind of post mortem spasm, but now that she lay within his aura he sensed that something wasn't quite as it seemed. Although she looked superficially like the other recently dead people he'd seen since his awakening, there was something subtly different, a feeling of incompleteness.

He concentrated first on the positive veil, through which her soul surely would have passed if she'd died. He could sense nothing at all, no disturbance, everything was smooth and intact.

He then shifted his focus to the negative veil and straight away he saw it, an after-image, a shadow of her aura. It was as if her essence had been pushed through the veil and into the plane beyond, leaving a vague impression behind, a silhouette of her soul. So she wasn't really dead as such, she'd been artificially separated from her body. If he could get her soul back from the negative plane then maybe she could yet live, all he had to do was open a rift and ...

In an instant it all made sense. He'd closed their gateway to the negative plane, and they wanted another. If he could even create a rift, which he was far from sure of, then it probably wouldn't last for long, so they must be nearby to take advantage of it.

"You might as well show yourselves, I know what it is you want," Jack shouted as he stood up.

A few moments later the air in one corner of the room shimmered as a powerful shield was dissolved and a Mediterranean looking man stepped forward. Beside him was a small lead coffin, the lid of which had been removed to reveal a collection of bones, the lime covered remains of a small boy. A tidy pile of clothes lay nearby and surrounding the coffin was a glittering energy field, unlike anything Jack had seen before.

"Then you had better get on with it Mr Eastwood, before your friend becomes a permanent resident of my domain."

Jack looked down at Mandy and saw that her already dull glow had dimmed a little.

"What did you do to her?"

"A curse of sorts, one that cannot be reversed by me, before you ask."

"But if I open a rift ..." Jack left the idea hanging, "why do you want that so badly?"

"Does it matter?"

"Well I'm guessing it's not so you can invite a paragon of light and virtue through."

"Probably not," chuckled the man.

"And what's that for?" Jack indicated the coffin.

The man paused as he searched for the right words.

"You might call it a template. A familiar form for something to build upon."

"Something worse than you?"

The man's calm demeanour became a mocking sneer.

"Worse than me, Mr Eastwood? In this plane of existence I am but a reflection of yourself and the rest of this city. Worse than me is still just another aspect of you. Worse than me, is nothing more than a fuller expression of your humanity."

With visible effort the man regained his composure.

"Much as I would like to continue discussing the nature of your kind, the woman does not have long left. I suggest you get on with what you know you are going to do."

The giant mechanism that occupied the majority of the room ticked relentlessly, one advance of the escapement every two seconds. The rods, gears, brake shafts and fly fans all moved in perfect synchronisation.

"I can't. There's no way I'd be able to open a rift even if I wanted to."

"Oh, but you do want to, that is the point. Someone of your talents can achieve anything when they want it desperately enough. I have faith in you Mr Eastwood."

The man's calm smile was back and it made Jack feel sick, a hollow sensation that ballooned in his stomach. Inevitability was creeping up on him and he didn't know whether he could run fast enough.

"What would be the point anyway, you'd just kill us both as soon as the rift was open."

"Possibly, but where would be the fun in that? Besides, having you searching around inside will help keep it stable a little longer. I am more than happy to treat with you Mr Eastwood. You open the rift, and I will not interfere with your attempts to save the woman. Do we have a deal?"

"I won't," he pleaded, "I won't be the one to do it."

"Then she will exist in torment for the rest of eternity. Understand Mr Eastwood that for one such as her to reside on my plane is the most pure form of punishment."

The man took a step closer.

"Even now she is being subjected to horrors the like of which you cannot begin to imagine. Do you really want that to be your parting gift to her, the legacy of the love between you?"

Jack fell to his knees, tears welling up as he gazed upon the peaceful face of the woman that meant everything to him.

"But I mustn't," he cried, "I mustn't help you."

The mechanism continued to tick.

"Then I might as well finish her off now."

The man raised a hand that crackled with energy and pointed it towards Mandy's body.

"No!"

Jack instinctively threw up a protective shield. Panting hard he held the man's gaze, the giant clock mechanism ticking over three times before he lowered the barrier.

"I'll do it, you bastard. I'll do it."

The man tilted his head to one side.

"Well done, I knew you would get there eventually."

Jack knelt with shoulders slouched, already feeling the weight of defeat, knowing he was about to betray everything he'd thought he believed in. He sighed and drove the distractions from his mind as he concentrated on what needed to be done.

He stood up and relaxed his body, letting his aura attune to the fabric of the negative veil. He felt the positivity within the barrier itself, holding back the terrible forces of the plane beyond. He focused on the desperate love he felt for Mandy, using her as inspiration to align himself with the nature of the barrier until he felt his consciousness become part of the structure of the veil itself.

He went down the layers, deeper and deeper until he was a single point in the tiniest of threads within the fabric. He searched his own psyche and found the selfishness that was buried within the love he felt. That simple act of acknowledgement was enough to snap the thread. The rupture caused a ripple of energy that he chased back up the levels, causing a cascade of breakages with larger and larger components of the barrier coming apart. By the time his consciousness had retreated as far as his body, he had ripped a small tear in the negative veil. He could feel the raw emotional heat of what lay beyond shining through.

He looked across at the man, fully expecting him to strike, but instead he merely smiled and bowed politely as he gestured that Jack may continue as he please.

With one final glance at the coffin and its remains, he sent his aura towards the rent in the veil and projected his consciousness through the rift.

Jack found himself floating in a formless void. All around him were countless tiny pinpricks of deep red light that coalesced fleetingly into winds of energy, and dissipated as quickly as they had formed. He was aware that he had no body, no eyes with which to actually see anything and therefore deduced that what he was experiencing was merely his own interpretation of the negative energy plane.

He felt the presence of a disturbance nearby, and turned – or so he thought of it – to observe the rift behind him. It was a dark patch where the motes of light seemed to stretch and dilate the nearer they approached, like water gathering speed over a waterfall.

Jack found the absence of an up or down extremely disconcerting and although the rift was an obvious point of reference, there was no indication as to where to go from there. He tried focusing on a particular spot in what he thought of as the distance, but the more he looked at it the more he had the sensation it was both infinitely close and infinitely far away. The duality threatened to overwhelm him and his thoughts started to race. He struggled to keep his consciousness together and knew that if he failed to do so he would lose the link to his physical body and be consigned to the plane forever.

Focus on your goal Jack, and then embrace the void to understand it.

There was no vision this time, but he couldn't help thinking the voice of his subconscious still sounded quite a lot like Alec Guinness. Jack took comfort from the advice and let his awareness fill with memories of Mandy. Once he had a strong sensation of her, instead of trying to maintain coherency of his thoughts, he sent them flying out in all directions to search for what had become lost.

He found himself in a large square room with high white walls and a chequerboard floor. Where the ceiling should have been, the red void shifted and flowed, yet the light in the room appeared bright white and had no visible source. He looked down and – apart from being pleased to find that there was a down – saw that he now had a body. There was nothing else in the room except for a single door in the far wall, so he strode towards it and turned the white doorknob.

The next room was the same size and shape as the first, but this time contained a pair of white leather sofas at right angles to each other, with a low white coffee table in front of them. Sitting on the sofas were two people, both wearing plain white stylised masks such as might be found at a masquerade ball. The masks were identical and androgynous, the expression a slightly manic leer.

From their build, clothing and demeanour, Jack recognised the two individuals as being Mandy's parents. They hadn't noticed him so he walked over to the coffee table.

"Look who it is dear," whispered Mr Richardson, "that bloody Eastwood boy."

"Oh do I have to? He's so tiresome," replied his wife.

Jack felt his neck start to redden. On the previous occasions he'd met them they had always been impeccably polite, but he'd never been able to shift the nagging feeling that they didn't think him good enough for their daughter. Mrs Richardson looked up at him.

"Jack, how nice to see you. What are you doing here?"

"I'm looking for Amanda, have you seen her please?"

"Well yes of course I have, but she doesn't want to see you I'm afraid. Ever again."

"It's really important Mrs Richardson, I have to speak with her right now."

"I don't think that's going to happen. She's finally come to her senses and left you, and I respect her decision."

Jack could feel the room start to get larger, the walls growing further apart. He spotted another door in the far wall and decided to cut his losses, so he ran towards it. As he opened it he could hear Mr Richardson in the distance behind him.

"You know Jack, you were never worthy of her."

He passed through and found himself in a room with a large crowd of masked people talking to each other as if at a party. Most had drinks in hand and the atmosphere amongst the guests was genial and intimate. Jack recognised some of the people as friends of Mandy's from school or university days. He approached the nearest.

"Steve, have you seen Mandy?"

The man ignored him. Jack moved in front of him and grabbed his arm.

"It's Jack Eastwood, Mandy's boyfriend. Steve!"

The man continued his conversation with two other of Mandy's friends. Jack turned from person to person, trying to get them to answer him but none did.

Again he felt the walls start to move away from each other and he looked around in desperation, he saw three more doors, one in each wall.

"Come on you bastards," he shouted, "at least tell me which door to take."

It was as if he didn't exist.

He suddenly remembered a summer's day that he and Mandy had spent at Hampton Court Palace, where they laughed at having got themselves lost in the yew tree maze. She had hugged him and said if in doubt they should always go left. Jack made for the door to the left of the way he'd entered the room and had to sprint to catch up with the retreating wall.

In the middle of the next room stood a bed which he instantly recognised as the one from her flat. The white cotton sheets had been discarded on the floor and a man lay on it, naked save for the mask on his face. He had the well-muscled and perfectly proportioned physique of a Greek statue, though was significantly better endowed than artists normally allowed for.

His skin glistened with sweat and his chest and neck were flushed. Jack couldn't help but notice the man's tumescence as he lay back in post-coital satisfaction.

Not wanting to approach the bed, Jack looked round for other doors and not finding any he turned to leave the room, but the way he'd come in was now a blank wall, and like the others in the room was starting to move further away. Jack ran forwards.

"I don't care who you are, I just want her back."

The man propped himself up on an elbow and despite the mask still managed to look at Jack with contempt.

"Who?"

"Mandy!"

"Oh, that's her name is it? She's quite a lot of fun."

Jack felt the desperation rise and with it he lost control, bellowing at the man at the top of his voice.

"GIVE HER BACK!"

Sound shook the room as the intensity of Jack's fury

momentarily blotted out all other meaning or purpose to his existence.

"Whatever," replied the man, and as he rolled over to go to sleep a door materialised in the far wall. Jack sprinted for it but the nearer he got the faster it retreated. In a last ditch effort he dived forwards and just managed to grasp hold of the doorknob. It dragged him along the floor, legs twisting underneath him, knees smashing into the ground as his body rolled from side to side. He grimaced and held on, forcing the doorknob to turn and willing the exit to open inch by inch. He stretched out a hand to grasp the doorframe and agonisingly pulled himself through.

All was still and quiet.

Except for the sobbing.

Jack picked himself up off the floor and saw that he was in the biggest room yet. In the far corner, huddled with her arms clasped around her legs was Mandy. She wore no mask and her hair hung down in tangled, matted clumps. She was clothed only in the cream silk camisole he had given her the previous Christmas, the simple garment ripped and tattered. The sound of her crying wrenched Jack's heart and he ran over to her. Crouching down he put a hand tentatively on her shoulder, she looked up with bloodshot and exhausted eyes, a thousand yard stare peering straight through him.

As the walls started to retreat, Jack scooped her up in his arms and she fell limply against his chest as he stood. He hugged her close and whispered in her ear.

"Come back with me, my love, come back."

She turned her head to look at him and gradually her eyes started to focus. Recognition spread across her face and the moment she began to smile, everything disappeared.

He was back in the void and the winds of the negative plane had started to gather. The red motes were blustering all around and he could sense their agitation as they gusted to and fro.

He couldn't see her as such, but he felt that Mandy was

with him, her soul clinging to his with an absolute passion. He tried to search about him for the rift, but the movement of the energies within the plane obscured everything. Maybe the entity had tricked him after all, and the pair of them never really had a chance to find their way back.

Then he felt the currents shift, all the movements were aligning themselves in one direction and great clouds of clustered energy started to billow past him.

Run Jack, run.

He needed little prompting from his subconscious, he could sense that something was coming, driving the clouds before it as if even the energy wanted to escape its approach.

He willed himself to move with the retreat and despite knowing that he was gathering pace he could feel himself being gained upon. He focused every thought on going faster and faster, yet still it was closing in on him. Jack felt its presence as a relentless heat and knew that he was about to be enveloped when suddenly he burst through the cloud front and saw the rift before him.

Without pausing even a fraction to consider what was behind him, he flung his consciousness forwards into the tear in the veil, taking Mandy's soul through with him.

Jack gasped and opened his eyes just in time to see a stream of brilliant red energy issue from the rift. It flowed straight through the field surrounding the coffin and into the remains within. It was so bright he had to squeeze his eyes shut against the glare.

He lay on the floor, his head resting on Mandy's chest, which he felt heave as she also took an involuntary gulp of air and started to breathe again. He rolled away from the light and dragged her with him, cradling her protectively on the other side of the room.

Jack heard a voice say something in a guttural language he

didn't understand and forced his eyes open as far as a squint. He saw the man step into the stream of energy and be pierced straight through the abdomen. As the energy flowed through the man and into the remains, it stripped pieces of him away. Chunks of volcanic aura peeled off and become entrained in the flow, more and more breaking apart until only a semblance of the man remained, a mere stick figure drawing. Moments later, that too had succumbed to the conflagration and the man was no more.

Jack could see and feel the rift in the veil had been stretched much wider by the surge of energy coming through. He saw it flex alarmingly as the flow swelled further and then in the tiniest fraction of a second it all changed. The bright red stream stopped and the rift collapsed instantaneously, its frayed edges slamming back towards each other with such ferocity they fused together, creating a massive shock-front in the veil that exploded in all directions.

Jack and Mandy lay unconscious, huddled next to a wooden seat against one wall. Across the other side of the room, the coffin and remains sat quietly within their protective field. The giant clock mechanism continued to tick, one beat every other second. A complicated series of gears and ratchets started to animate and the Westminster Quarters began to sound in the belfry above. They finished their sixteen note peel and after a long moment's pause the strike weights for the Great Bell moved into action. The hour sounded and as the unmistakable voice of Big Ben rang out across London, mist started to creep into the mechanism room. It flowed in through the weight shafts beneath the workings of the clock and in via the open doorway. It even forced its way in through gaps in the windows.

A thick blanket seeped across the floor towards the glittering force field, passing straight through and rolling up the sides of the coffin where it was absorbed hungrily by the remains within.

Chapter Twenty-Four

"This is bad," said Rebecca, fully aware of how inadequate the phrase sounded. The three of them stood at the edge of the roof and looked down into Smith Square at the slow flowing mist.

"Why do I have the nasty feeling that Jack was involved with whatever the hell that was?" asked Aaron.

"Like I said, it's all part of their plan," replied Reggie, "the boy's gone and done exactly what they wanted him to."

He shook his head in disappointment.

"Well whatever's happened, we're not doing any good standing here. We need to go help him, and we need to get hold of that nuke," said Rebecca.

"Follow the mist and I bet we find Jack, but we have no idea where the bomb is. It might not even be in London anymore."

"Actually, I think I know exactly where it is," she said, and proceeded to tell them about the twins' house in Pimlico.

The two men turned and stared at her, eyebrows raised.

"When I was struggling with that thing," Rebecca indicated the corpse lying a few yards away, "we both got quite deep into each other's minds. I didn't have time to make much sense of what was in hers, but I did get an address. I'm pretty sure it's where they've got the bomb hidden. I also got the impression that the other younger one, the one like her, is already dead, or banished, or whatever it was we just did to her."

"Good work Becky, so how do we do this then?" asked Reggie.

The two of them looked to Aaron for the decision.

"Rebecca, you try and find Jack. If he's still alive he may be hurt, and you're best suited to dealing with that. Reggie, you go with her and keep her safe. I'll go after the bomb, if I can get it secured then I'll get the word out as fast and as far as I can."

He took the dull amulet from around his neck and made to give it to Rebecca, but she just smiled and shook her head.

"You keep it, you're the one on your own. Besides, I wouldn't really know what to do with it anyway."

They wished each other luck and then set out from the building, Aaron heading south and west, the other two directly north.

Rebecca and Reggie found the going quite easy at first. Many people were still recovering from the shockwave passing through, and those back on their feet were rather muted. The atmosphere had changed significantly, aggression having been replaced by confusion and worry, and most just milled around aimlessly.

Progress slowed the further north they went as the density of the crowds increased. Rebecca avoided the bottlenecks in the main thoroughfares by taking them through the Dean's Yard at the rear of Westminster Abbey. The gate guards recognised her and let the pair of them pass, and it wasn't long before it became obvious where the mist was going. As they barged through the throng in Parliament Square they could see thick vapour rolling up the sides of Big Ben. It disappeared round about the level of the clock faces, together with the heavy concentration of negative energy it dragged along with it.

Pushing their way to the cordon surrounding the Palace of Westminster, they found the police on duty looking as apprehensive and uncertain as the crowd they held back. None of them wanted to go near the tower, and when Rebecca suggested with total conviction that she and Reggie should be let through, they were ushered straight in. Minutes later, and very out of breath, they reached the doorway of the mechanism room.

The first thing they saw was Mandy. Sitting on a pew like bench at the side of the room she hugged her knees close, keeping her feet out of the deep carpet of mist flowing across the floor. She rocked gently back and forth, her eyes locked in a vacant stare.

As they stepped into the room they saw the coffin in the far corner and its shimmering force field, with Jack pacing to and fro beside it. His aura was severely drained and he had a frantic air about him.

"I'm sorry. I'm so very sorry. I know I shouldn't have, but I had to, I had to. And now it's here and it's coming for us, it's coming for everyone ..."

As he continued to ramble, Rebecca approached him and put her hands on his shoulders. Straight away his speech started to slow and he grew calmer until he stood quietly, letting her sooth his mind and restore clarity to his thoughts.

While she worked on Jack to allay the worst of the shockwave's effects, Reggie eyed the mist with suspicion. The layer on the floor was so dense and its energy so deeply concentrated that it made him very uncomfortable to stand in it. He reached out with his aura and challenged the vapour to approach if it dare. To his surprise it started to divert around him leaving a clear patch of linoleum beneath his feet. He stood by the others to provide them with some small relief from its presence.

As soon as Jack was behaving relatively normally, Rebecca turned her attention to Mandy. It took a few minutes to draw her out of the damaged state she'd been found in, during which time Jack explained what had happened. As the story unfolded he could sense Reggie's disappointment in him, but was grateful the older man withheld from saying anything. Rebecca just provided a reassuring smile.

Jack finished by demonstrating the imperviousness of the force field, which he'd been trying to break through since waking after the blast. He couldn't even get his aura close to it, and physical attacks just bounced off.

They left Mandy sitting more comfortably and went to look at the coffin and its contents. The remains had started to reform, fragments of bone had already knitted together and a thin translucent membrane now covered the skeleton. The child's body was slightly longer than the box it lay in and the legs were hunched up, causing the knees to poke out.

"The entity wasn't lying to me," said Jack, "that thing is a template, it's being used by what came through to rebuild itself a physical form."

"But what is it? What came through?" asked Becky.

"Pure evil, something an order of magnitude greater than the thing that planned all this."

"It's the Devil," said Reggie.

"Don't be melodramatic."

"OK, well call it a bloody great big demon then."

"Whatever it is," said Jack, "when it's fully re-grown, which I guess will be when it's absorbed all the mist, we're properly screwed. I'm so sorry guys."

"Well in that case we'd just better find a way to prevent it ever reforming, hadn't we?"

"How?" Jack's voice regained some of its earlier mania. "That field is impenetrable, there's barely any time left and then everything will change."

"Stop it Jack, just concentrate. First of all, how long do we have?"

Trying to work out an answer calmed him a little, and he led them upstairs to a mesh covered platform above the belfry to get a decent view across the city.

"Judging by where it started this morning and how quickly it's coming in, I'd guess at an hour or so. And then it all kicks off. Those entities had been planning this for ages, they knew we wouldn't be able to stop it, that's what the force field is for. That's why they never bothered coming after us, we weren't ever any threat to them."

"Not true," said Rebecca "we dealt with the female one."

"She was expendable! It was all about this, don't you get it, this was the only thing that mattered, this was ..."

Rebecca slapped Jack across the face, the sharp smack sounding clearly despite the noise of the wind.

"Sorry about that, but you need to keep calm."

She placed a hand on his chest and sent a strong pulse of energy.

"Calm Jack. We need you now more than ever, and you have amends to make."

His eyes refocused and the others saw him come back to them. The three friends stood in silence for a few seconds as if they waited for the gusting wind to provide inspiration. Reggie shifted uneasily from one foot to the other.

"What if there's somethin' that were missed, somethin' not known about?"

"Like what?" asked Rebecca.

He shifted again.

"Well, one of them says there might be a way."

"One of them? A ghost? No Reggie, if we're going to beat this thing the solution will come from us, not from them. They lie to you, they always have."

He practically danced on the spot as Rebecca turned away from him.

"Come on Jack, think. You saw it arrive, it must have a weakness."

"But Becky ..."

"No Reggie! No ghosts. It's just us now."

"But," he stammered again.

"No!"

"But ... the ghost is one of us. It's Sabir my girl, it's Sabir."

She turned in anger and disbelief.

"I'm sorry Becky, I didn't want to tell you, but ..."

"It can't be! He's gone. He died in my arms, I felt him pass over."

"No girl, he did not. He stayed to..."

"Shut up!" she screamed, beating her fists against his chest.

Reggie let her hit him and waited for the attack to slow. When Rebecca started to cry, he pulled her to him and comforted her as she sobbed. The heaves eventually subsided and she looked up at him.

"May I see him please?"

Reggie nodded and lifted her hands, placing them on his temples. He shut his eyes, opened his mind and let her aura into his consciousness.

She approached with caution.

Rebecca found herself standing in a muddy ditch, carved between banks of earth by the tracks of a giant machine. In the distance she heard explosions and the rapid chatter of gunfire, wisps of acrid smoke drifted in the still air. Up ahead was a small crater, and sitting on a burned and twisted tree trunk was Sabir. He was dressed in a sharp suit, its fine petrol blue fabric at odds with the surroundings.

She walked forwards and was just a few paces away when he looked up and caught her staring at him.

"I always wanted an Alexander Amosu," he grinned.

Though she returned his smile, hers was laced with pain and loss. He stood up and moved closer to take her hands in his.

"I am so sorry my love, I had wanted to spare you this."

"But I don't understand, your soul is good. I thought you were content, I thought I made you happy."

"You did, and I was ready, but it got complicated. The forces of the positive plane do not grant our powers for no reason. I still had an obligation, a duty to perform, to try and assist you I chose to enter the other plane as well."

Rebecca squeezed his hands.

"Is it awful?"

"Yes, actually it really is. But do not worry, I can cope with it for now."

He grinned again to reassure her.

"I tried to work out what was going on and how to stop it. Unfortunately I did not manage to do that, but I may have found a chance for you, something I learned from the ancient and twisted spirits still clinging to the oldest parts of the city. It is probably a slim one, but it is a chance all the same. I gave the details to Reggie just before you arrived, and you had better hurry, there is not much time left."

"I don't want to leave you."

"I know, but you must. And anyway ..." he stopped mid-sentence, biting his lower lip in restraint.

"What?"

"It is nothing. Reggie was correct you know, the past, present and future all blur into one."

"Sab, what aren't you telling me?"

"Just be strong my love."

He started to walk away from her.

"Sab? Sab?"

He continued to walk.

"Sab, I'll always love you."

And he was gone.

It took Rebecca a few moments and a couple of deep breaths to regain her composure.

"So Reggie, what's the plan?"

"You need to get to the City, to Cannon Street, and find The London Stone. Sabir said it's the key."

"The what?"

"The London Stone," said Jack, "I know where it is, I saw it on one of those walking tours when I first moved here."

"Well OK then, Reggie can explain on the way. Jack, try

texting Aaron and Sophia, let them know where we're heading."

"No," said Reggie.

"Why not? They might be able to help?"

"I mean no, I'm not comin'."

"What? But we need you."

"I'm stayin' here, I think I can buy you some time."

He turned and headed off down the steps back to the mechanism room. By the time the others caught up, he was standing next to the force field, his feet planted in a wide stance. He projected his aura outwards and commanded the energy laden mist to stay away from the room. He built up his concentration until his whole being was set against the flow. This time no clear patch of floor emerged, but the mist appeared to slow a little. Within seconds the strain upon him started to show, sweat beaded on his forehead and all the muscles of his face became taught.

"Good luck to you, and seal me in boy, I don't want nobody else to stumble in."

Rebecca looked at the older man with affection and stood on tiptoes to kiss him on the cheek. Jack nodded his gratitude in silence and took Mandy's hand.

The group of three left the room and locked the door behind them, Jack placing a ward upon it for good measure. For the first few flights of stairs he could feel the immense exertion of Reggie's aura above and shuddered at the ordeal his friend had chosen.

Aaron looked over his shoulder to check that the camera crew still followed him. He'd been lucky to bump into the three-strong team from the BBC who had been patrolling the edges of the rioting area looking for an angle on the day's events. His assurances of a scoop regarding the bomb had still required some fairly robust persuasion, but he reasoned that under the circumstances it wasn't really an abuse of his powers.

He'd also found a surprising and rather inconvenient lack of police officers en route. Having seen so many earlier in the day he'd assumed co-opting a few would be easy, but somehow had failed to pass any during the entire journey down to Pimlico.

As he walked up the steps of the Regency townhouse, he sorted through the bunch of keys in his hand and was grateful he'd thought to check the woman's pockets before leaving the building in Smith Square. The third and fourth keys he tried fitted the two locks and he pushed the door open.

He couldn't sense anyone's presence and decided not to spend too long being cautious, so he instructed the TV crew to wait outside and headed into the luxuriously appointed property. He reached out with his aura and straight away realised that a lot of energy had been in the house, there were complicated residuals all over the place. It took him a little over twelve minutes to sort through the mess and locate the tell tale signature of a shielding effect in the basement.

It was a subtle and powerful mask that made its subject invisible to the naked eye, as well as cloaking auras and suggesting to people to avoid its presence entirely. Save for Aaron's skill and experience with warding abilities he would have missed it.

He knew he had no chance of unpicking the construction of the shield, so he woke the Gorgoneion up. She yawned at him, her glow still a mere shadow of her true capacity, and it was with heavy eyes that she established a modest beam of positive energy. Aaron fed the attack until it was bright and focused, putting his full weight behind it. A minute into the assault he was trembling and about to abandon the attempt, when suddenly the shield gave way and it dissipated in a colourful collapse. It revealed the suitcase sitting in quiet menace on the floor.

He went back outside, checked his phone and then fetched the camera crew. They took some convincing that it was the missing bomb, but agreed that as soon as they'd got it verified, they'd get the footage and the story to their news desk. Aaron left them standing in the cellar, and some minutes later the slight fog he'd had to place on their minds started to lift.

"Hang on a minute, who did that guy say he was again?" asked the reporter.

"I have absolutely no idea," replied her producer, "more to the point, what the bloody hell do we do with this thing?"

He was about to kick the suitcase to illustrate his point, and then thought better of it.

They'd been struggling to make headway through the dense crowd along Victoria Embankment, when Jack saw something on the river that gave him an idea. He helped the other two over the low railings beside the joint air services war memorial and down to the tiny jetty below the Whitehall Stairs. The gilded eagle perched atop the memorial kept watch as they neared the water's edge.

"Quick you two, jump up and down and wave your arms."

Whilst Mandy and Rebecca did as requested, Jack crafted a narrow tunnel in the air which he then shouted down, projecting his voice out to the vessel some thirty metres from shore. His call for help was answered and the lifeboat *Legacy* motored over to them. It was one of several based at the RNLI station by Waterloo Bridge and was possibly the fastest craft on the river.

The volunteer crew were a hardy bunch but had a keen appreciation for an emergency. The wave of energy that accompanied Jack's genuine plea for their help was enough to secure their services, and moments later the E-class's twin engines roared into life as 480hp of water jet sped them downriver towards the City.

The struggle between Reggie and the mist had become a battle fought in every fibre of his being, his will honed to the singular purpose of slowing its advance. If he'd taken the time to think about it, he would have been pleased with the results of his efforts. He definitely had reduced the rate at which the coffin had been fed.

What he did know however, was that he was weakening rapidly and a new and sinister note had begun to sound at the edge of his awareness. The overtone of another consciousness starting to take form, the nerve scratching crackle of an intent as pure as fire.

Reggie could feel the want, the ambition, the arrogance, the loathing and the cowardice. He dare not turn around to face it, he wasn't scared but he knew that once he let his concentration be shifted from its purpose, he would never recover it.

Must. Hold. On.

He mouthed the words through gritted teeth while behind him darkness approached in the form of a young boy, whose limbs were whole and whose features had started to take shape.

The helmsman steered the *Legacy* to shore and they tied up at Swan Pier, a small commercial wharf just upstream of London Bridge. The three passengers thanked the crew and set off down the lane towards Upper Thames Street. Mandy remarked on how quiet the roads were, even for a weekend the City was unusually muted. She guessed it was the threat of the bomb that had shut everything down and left the place deserted.

Leaving the Clock Tower had perked her up and she'd taken Jack's explanation of recent events in her stride, the days she'd spent with the entities having already introduced her to the 'wider reality' he kept referring to. She knew where Cannon Street was and eagerly led the way.

They passed through some narrow back streets and emerged by the front of the mainline railway station. They saw Sophia across the road and ran over to join her, where Rebecca breathlessly updated her on what had occurred.

"Well I guess that explains why there's been no movement at Avar Investments, if that thing is dead I mean," said Sophia, "or whatever passes for dead in its case."

Jack was already eyeing the resting place of The London Stone, a small grill fronted cavity set in the wall of the building they stood next to. He crouched down to get a better look.

The weathered piece of limestone was about the size and shape of a small piece of luggage, though a little more rounded at the edges. Its yellowish grey surface was stained from centuries of accumulated grime, and it was further obscured by the dirty glass behind which it hid. Jack could detect almost no aura at all from it, certainly nothing more than the surrounding brick work or pavement.

"It's not much to look at," he stood back and frowned.

"What is it?" asked Mandy.

"No one really knows," answered Sophia, "but there are lots of theories and legends. The more romantic of them have it as the stone from which Arthur withdrew Excalibur, or part of an ancient druidic circle on Ludgate Hill. More prosaically it was a Roman marker from which all distances in Britain were measured. I prefer the version where it's the altar stone of the Temple to Diana, which used to be where St Paul's now stands. In any event it has definitely been in London for hundreds of years, possibly even thousands."

"Hmm," Jack pondered, "but on the other hand, that might be leaded glass."

He reached forward with a thought and shattered the pane into hundreds of pieces. Straight away he could see a faint construction of energy radiating from within the stone. He let his aura reach into it and felt a distinct jolt as his mind was pulled into the rock itself. Once there he could see a myriad of lines and shapes pulsating in a three dimensional structure.

He moved himself around, viewing it from different angles and realised it was a map, with the Stone itself at one end and a focal point at the other. He went in closer and could see four tiny auras next to the Stone, two of which were brighter and animated. He weaved a path through to the other end of the map and examined what was obviously the objective. As soon as he started to probe the bright column of light some of the details started to fall into place. He moved his consciousness outwards and with an effort snapped himself back into his own head.

"It's a map, and it shows the way to the rest of the stone, this bit here is just the sister to a much larger piece."

"OK, but where?"

"Oh," Jack looked confused, "that's strange, I don't know. I can't recall the details of the route. I do remember that the other stone is some kind of vault though. I'm certain that's what Sabir was meaning us to go after."

"But we still don't know where it is. Can you take this bit with us?"

Jack eyed the ornate ironwork grill.

"I suppose so, I guess I could break it out of there, but that won't help if I can't remember the details."

"Hang on," said Sophia, "let me try Aaron."

She got out her mobile, selected the number and handed it to Jack.

"It's ringing," she said.

He paced impatiently for several seconds.

"No, it's Jack. She's fine, we're all fine, except for Reggie but that can wait. You're breaking up," he looked at the handset, "let me find a better signal."

He moved off down the street to continue his conversation, while Sophia took a vacuum flask from her bag and shared a cup of lukewarm tea with the others. Mandy had drained the last of it when Jack came jogging back to them.

"Sorry, I was being stupid. I've seen this sort of thing before in The Book of Ways."

The three women looked at him blankly.

"Doesn't matter, I know what to do. You were right, I *do* need to take the map with us, just not the Stone."

He moved his thoughts back inside the rock and this time carried on homing in until he felt himself as one with the point of light that represented the Stone. He waited until he was comfortable with all the lines, locations and features arranged about him, and then yanked his consciousness back into himself as fast he could, taking the whole map with him in the process. As he opened his eyes he saw a faint copy at life-size scale inlaid within the world around him. The effect was particularly strange when he looked at his companions as a point of light shone from within each of them. He was glad however that he could now read the map and knew exactly which direction they needed to go in.

As they set off east down Cannon Street they spotted a black cab coming their way, the first sign of life they'd seen since reaching the City. It slowed to Rebecca's hail and swung round to their side of the street. They jumped in and then sped off under Jack's direction towards the Tower of London.

Sweat poured down Reggie's face and his legs trembled under the strain of holding back the mist. He stayed in the fight through sheer bloody mindedness, using the pain to maintain focus and eek out the final reserves of his willpower.

Behind him in the coffin the youth was fully formed, his skin as white as the powdered lime he'd lain in for more than fifteen hundred years. His body was delicate and bony, as were the features of his face sitting beneath a dark mop of hair. His chest rose and fell as he became accustomed to the atmosphere of the twenty-first century.

The slow and even pace of the clock mechanism sounded loudly in the room, and then hesitated for the slightest of fractions as the boy's eyelids snapped open.

Sophia paid the cabbie and ran to catch up with the others. The large open area on which they stood was part of Tower Hill, the section of the Tower of London's grounds that separated it from the City. The small granite blocks used for paving lent the place an atmosphere as solid and durable as the fortress that overlooked it. Usually it was a gathering place for tourists and sightseers, though on this day it was deserted. The Tower itself was closed and the nearby refreshment kiosks had all shut up shop in response to the bomb.

"The map shows there's something here, something deep underground," said Jack.

"Under the Tower you mean?"

"No, right about where we are now."

Sophia looked puzzled.

"That's weird, I was certain it'd be under the main keep."

"How so?"

"Well, there are many legends about the Tower, but the one that was starting to ring true is about Brutus, the consul of Rome who is said to have founded Britain. The story has him buried under the main keep. I just assumed that was where you were leading us."

"I have no idea what's down there, but this is definitely where the map is pointing to. Give me a moment, there's a kind of key in this somewhere."

Jack closed his eyes and focused his thoughts into the diagram that existed within his mind, he came to rest on a small but complex pattern of energy. It was the final link between him and the end of the route and as he embraced it he felt himself start to change. The components of his aura moved under instruction of the key and his body re-oriented itself, not just in space but also a subtle physiological change.

Involuntarily, Jack dropped to one knee and punched the ground with his fist. The others gasped as the granite blocks split asunder and his hand buried itself halfway up his forearm. Mandy made to step forwards but Rebecca gently restrained her.

A tendril of Jack's aura snaked out from his fist and set off into the ground, weaving its way between the subsoil, delving through clay and dodging rock as it headed downward. Many metres below it came upon a square sectioned column of limestone. The single piece of worked rock was tall and of a regular shape, though one end was rough where a piece had been broken off.

As Jack made contact with the stone he could feel it was not a natural piece of rock. The minerals within had all been purposefully aligned to form one continuous crystal structure, the thought and craft that had gone into its construction was breathtaking. There was a resonance to it, a fingerprint of its maker that spoke of an Awakened from long ago. Someone similar to him, yet of skill and power so great he felt humbled by their echo.

He tried to press past the surface of the stone and though it wouldn't yield he felt a response. A quiet presence was with him, it had a soft quality as if it were a long way away, yet he felt it surround him as it read his soul. The presence spoke to him in his own voice.

You are right to seek my aid, though it will cost you everything. Are you willing to pay that price?

Yes, I am. It was by my action the evil came through and I must atone for that.

Jack felt it consider him, weighing his motives.

It was for love that you were weak, and if for love you can now be strong, you will have my aid.

The filament of Jack's aura touching the stone started to harden and he felt a crystallising effect shoot back upwards with alarming speed. It reached his hand and calcified his fist before he could react. He panicked as the sensation spread up his arm and he fought hard to concentrate on resisting it, breathing life back into his limb. Bit by bit he forced his will down into the strand of energy and it softened and came alive once more. By the time he reached the stone his breathing was steady and he knew what he must do.

Jack opened his eyes and looked up at Mandy, drawing strength and courage from her beauty. He didn't have time to explain, nor to tell her how he felt and what she meant to him. He managed a rueful smile and let her face be the final image for his eyes, before he closed them and directed the full force of his willpower at the stone and its crystalline nature.

He concentrated his aura through the filament until an intense stream of energy poured forth, disrupting the organised pattern of the minerals. He put more and more of himself into it, willing the rock to give up its structure and yield the occupant within. His physical form started to sag and his breathing became laboured as an increasing portion of his aura went into the stone, leaving little to sustain his body.

A tiny crack appeared in the rock.

Reggie couldn't look behind him, his body had become so taut that he wasn't able to move anymore. He just stood and watched as the last wisps of vapour travelled across the floor unimpeded, his strength all spent.

Behind him the boy was dressed in the child-sized pin-striped suit that had been left for him. He rested one foot at a time on the coffin to tie the laces of his shiny black shoes, and then set about putting his tie into a half-Windsor.

As he pushed the silk knot up tight, the clock mechanism suffered a massive failure and shuddered to a halt, the complex series of gears ticking no more.

The boy waved a hand and the force field vanished with an audible pop. He stalked to the middle of the room and looked back at Reggie, tilting his head to one side as he regarded the obstinate Caribbean man. It was all Reggie could do to return the stare.

The child narrowed his eyes and Reggie was thrown backwards, slamming against the wall with a sickening crunch of bones before slumping to the floor. His painfully weak aura dimmed further but persisted to flicker between each of the veils, refusing to call time on its shattered body. The boy raised an eyebrow at the Awakened's stubbornness and decided to save him for later. He would be rebuilt to the child's own design and become a powerful servant in the new order.

Turning his attention to one side of the room the boy raised a hand towards it. As if hit by a freight train, a huge section of the metre thick wall exploded outwards, taking the north clock face with it. Rubble and glass rained down onto Bridge Street, crushing and impaling scores of people unable to escape the debris.

The child walked forward and stepped out through the opening, hovering effortlessly in the air. Below him in every direction Westminster was crammed with a seething mass of humanity and he commanded obedience from them all. To a person they quailed at his presence, many throwing themselves on the ground in supplication.

He paused and looked north-eastwards where he sensed that something stirred, but in his eagerness to soak up yet more energy from this new generation of followers, he chose to ignore it. He knew there was nothing to challenge him and refused to suffer interruptions to this moment of rebirth.

The boy cast his aura far and wide to reveal his true nature to the masses, and as they gazed upon him they recognised the aspects of him that lay within themselves. Every negative emotion and motive, no matter how deeply buried, was ignited and started to consume the crowd.

Friends and colleagues turned on each other, venting all the suppressed jealousies, slights and grievances. Strangers chose spite and bigotry for greetings, using the smallest of differences as catalysts for panic and rage. In a matter of seconds, tens of thousands of people descended into anarchy and a melee began that far surpassed the riots of a couple of hours earlier. The boy smiled to himself and drifted down amongst the crowd where he drank thirstily from the fountains of negative energy that poured forth.

Jack collapsed to the ground and rolled onto his back, his breathing no more than grating rasps. He'd put every last drop he could into breaking the stone, what was left of his aura barely registered and even that was fading fast. He would die with the stone intact, leaving the world to face the consequences of his actions.

"I'm sorry," was all he managed before passing into unconsciousness.

Deep below ground all was still, the tiny crack in the rock the only evidence of his efforts.

Then it widened.

And split down its length.

Back on the surface Mandy cradled Jack in her arms and was being comforted by the other two when the ground behind them erupted. Earth and stone were flung to the side as a figure of dazzling brilliance rose from the depths. It was a glowing purple humanoid of athletic build and androgynous features, composed solely of deep and pure positive energy.

It nodded to the group clustered around Jack and then soared into the air. They watched it climb thousands of feet skywards, its ascension like a searing firework arcing high above the city.

Then it began to sing, a melody as ancient and beautiful as itself. It sang of a challenge to all those who would harm that in its care, to all who would threaten the great city of London.

In Parliament Square, the child walked amongst his subjects as they clawed, gouged and punched each other. In every direction people succumbed to their most base instincts and worshipped him through their weakness and violence.

He walked on blissfully, revelling in the energy and enthusiasm of his new flock, until a painful and terrible sound shattered his concentration. All around him the combatants paused, suddenly uncertain of their actions.

The boy turned to look upwards at the source of the blasphemy, and with an elemental howl of rage he flew into the sky to answer the challenge.

The two beings came together high above the city, the formidable auras of the ancient enemies testing each other as they circled a few metres apart. The first was the guardian spirit of one of the world's greatest cities, a deva who had been the quiet strength of a resilient population as they had suffered through plague, fire and war. The other was a manifestation of pure evil, born of the excesses and weaknesses of that same population, a dark champion for the modern age.

Though thin and reedy, the child's voice had an assured arrogance to it.

"I had thought you returned to your masters following our previous encounter."

The spirit smiled.

"The one who helped me defeat you last time found a way for me to remain, for just such a time as this. Myrddin knew you would come back."

"I always do, I am in their nature," the boy glanced down at the millions of tiny auras in the metropolis below. "They need me, they have been crying out for me."

"Not so. You are just a convenience, an easy path in an uncertain era. Their true nature is good, you are but an aberration."

"And what of their fear, of others and for their own futures? What of their hate, of the different and of the successful? But above all, what of the delicious greed of this city? So many clamouring for more and more, oblivious to anything except their own positions."

"Yet I see the creativity, the passion for life and all the wonders it holds. I see their acceptance and love for each other, the fortitude and strength of character. You and I are both but the products of their free will."

"Maybe," said the child, "but this time I am the one they have chosen, I am the stronger."

He launched himself at the glowing spirit and they began to grapple, their energies struggling for dominance. As they stood locked together, the child drew from the mood of the city beneath them and gained the advantage. He forced one small fist into the chest of his opponent, readying himself to put an end to the contest. He looked the spirit in the eyes and grinned.

It started with a single bulletin issued by the British Broadcasting Corporation, who interrupted its coverage of the London riot to bring confirmation of a tactical nuclear device having been recovered by the authorities. The bomb threat was over. The story was taken up by other networks and agencies, and within minutes had also spread across the social media.

In the capital, mobiles and smartphones buzzed, beeped and rang with the news, causing spontaneous shouts of joy and relief. Strangers hugged and kissed each other, neighbours shook hands over garden fences, opening bottles in celebration, whilst landlords declared drinks on the house and led choruses of Jerusalem and Rule Britannia.

The wave of positivity swept across the whole of the city, washing away the desperation of the previous weeks and lifting the hearts of ten million Londoners.

The child's grin faded as the spirit drew from the surge and thrust a glowing hand into the flesh and blood of the boy's chest. They looked down at the state of mutually assured destruction they had achieved. The spirit broke the silence.

"Looks like we are both leaving this time."

"The difference is that I will be back," said the child, "and when I return they will not have you to protect them."

"True, they will have to look after themselves, but I think they can learn their lessons. They will be ready for you next time."

"I doubt it."

The spirit accepted the suggestion with a shrug, and then focused the sum of all its energies into a single moment of annihilation. A blinding flash saw it vanish from existence as it sent the evil back to the depths of the negative plane. All that was left behind were the ashen remains of the manifestation's physical form, which scattered in the wind and were distributed harmlessly over several square miles.

Mandy stroked Jack's hair, her tears dropping onto his neck as he lay in her lap. Rebecca knelt next to them and injected him with her own energy, the healing effect enough for him to rally briefly. His eyes flickered open and he looked up at his friends. Aaron now stood to one side with Sophia. He was out of breath from his rapid journey but nodded back approvingly.

Jack tried to speak, but didn't have the strength and felt himself start to slip away. He was about to close his eyes for the final time when Rebecca leaned in closer and whispered in his ear.

"Forgive me Jack."

In the space of a heartbeat she urged her aura into a powerful vortex, its rhythmic cycle pulsing as it shed huge quantities of energy that she directed into him.

Jack gasped as his soul was anchored to his body and his aura soaked up the gift of life.

No! he mouthed, unable to produce a noise.

"Don't worry about me, I'm going to a place of love and beauty. I'll be with Sabir."

Jack felt a presence approach, and saw a faint shadow of his friend's aura materialise next to Rebecca. His strength returning a little, Jack managed to call out.

"Sabir, stop her! Aaron!"

She prepared to transfer the last of her energy and whispered to him again.

"Jack, London needs you now, you must live and help it grow better and stronger. And Mandy needs you too, you both have so much yet to experience together."

As she poured the last of her energy into him, her voice started to fade.

"Remember Jack, everything is free will, we all have choices to make. You've made some and learned from them, others need to learn from you. Love and beauty Jack, love and beauty."

Rebecca's body toppled sideways, her soul joining with Sabir's as they passed through the positive veil to the plane beyond. Aaron held Sophia's hand and saluted his departing friends.

Jack clung to Mandy and wept.

Epilogue

The fallout from the events of June 23rd forced Aaron to do something he had carefully avoided in all the years since his awakening, namely contact the authorities. He had to deploy the full range of his powers including the use of direct influence, which despite the circumstances he still felt was rather suspect. Before the following day was over however, he had sought and gained an audience with the Prime Minister of Great Britain.

Their conversation lasted nearly twelve hours, during which time the leader of the country was made aware of the wider reality and exactly what had occurred in London. To Aaron's relief she understood the need to keep the Awakened outside of official channels, the opportunities for abuse of their powers would be too great if brought within the establishment.

The two of them agreed upon a plan that would disassociate himself and the others from recent events and put in place as plausible a cover up as possible. Over the next few weeks all official footage was seized and destroyed, and a series of government experts trotted out to help debunk the amateur recordings circulating on the Internet. Although conspiracy theories abounded, some of which were almost entirely accurate, most people who were actually present had rather vague recollections of what had taken place. The official line of 'a foiled terrorist attack on the Houses of Parliament accompanied by atmospheric anomalies' became the accepted wisdom and the news cycle soon moved onto the next story.

Reggie had been dragged from the rubble in the Clock Tower and spent three weeks in a coma before regaining consciousness. It was Christmas time before he recovered from his injuries, some of which never healed properly, but eventually he went back to watching and walking the streets of the capital. He was happy and content in his work, rising early each day to help clear up after the excesses of the night before.

Sophia moved into the house in Henrietta Street and some months later an inspired Aaron started performing in public again, to much critical acclaim.

Without its creator and financial backer, Streets of Gold was rapidly replaced by a spate of other ultra immersive online games. It passed into cyber folklore and few admitted to ever having played it.

Following multiple appearances on high profile chat shows, Steve Marshall and Michelle Kalendar achieved a reconciliation of sorts, much to the dismay of prominent feminist commentators. Marshall went on to lead England at the next World Cup, though despite his best efforts, the team didn't make it past the group stage.

As for Jack, well he hurriedly finished his research into the Hof-del Pino instability and wrote up a rather slim thesis which he successfully defended. The doctoral certificate was filed away in a drawer and he never set foot in the lab again.

Mandy quit her job at Hamilton & Beach and the pair of them set about experiencing life as per Rebecca's final request. They travelled the world seeing many great sights and cultures, finding wisdom, answers and even more questions in the remotest parts of the globe.

Along the way they visited most of Aaron's network of Awakened, often helping them to deal with increasingly frequent manifestations from the negative plane.

They returned to London the following midsummer to join Reggie and Aaron in remembering their departed friends. Rebecca and Sabir were never forgotten.

It was late evening and an unremarkable man in a beige raincoat stood on Vauxhall Bridge. He rested his elbows on the metalwork handrail, leaning out just enough that he could look straight down at the murky water of the Thames. In his hands was a sizeable deck of Oyster cards spread out in a fan, he pondered each in turn as he recalled the details of their acquisition.

He finished looking at the most recent of them and gathered the collection back into a neat stack. He weighed it in his hand and considered whether to cast the evidence into the water and walk away a new man. After several minutes he had made up his mind and drew his wrist back in readiness. Just as he was about to fling them away for good, two drunken young men staggered past. One of them bumped into him, causing the cards to spill from his hand and scatter into the swift flowing current below.

The men stumbled forward a few paces before one turned and shouted in a barely coherent drawl.

"Watch where the fuck you're standing, you stupid fucker!"

"Leave him be," said the other. "We'll be late for our train."

The pair of them lurched away towards Vauxhall Rail Station and the unremarkable man turned his head to watch their departure, his eyes narrowed in thought. He did his coat up tight against the late autumn chill and set off after the two drunks, ready to start a new collection.

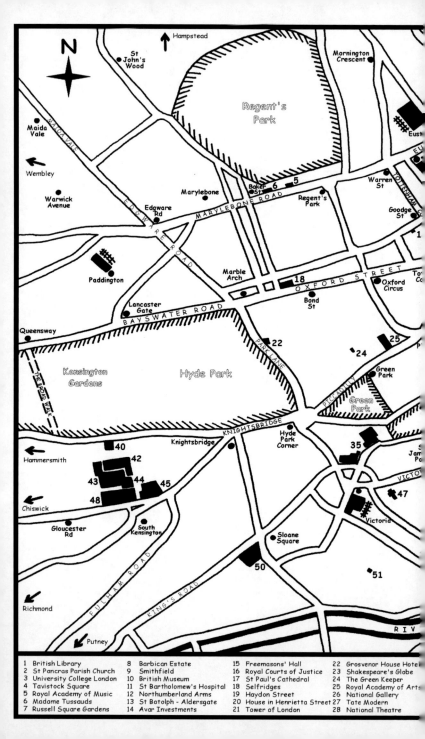

1	British Library	8	Barbican Estate	15	Freemasons' Hall	22	Grosvenor House Hotel
2	St Pancras Parish Church	9	Smithfield	16	Royal Courts of Justice	23	Shakespeare's Globe
3	University College London	10	British Museum	17	St Paul's Cathedral	24	The Green Keeper
4	Tavistock Square	11	St Bartholomew's Hospital	18	Selfridges	25	Royal Academy of Arts
5	Royal Academy of Music	12	Northumberland Arms	19	Haydon Street	26	National Gallery
6	Madame Tussauds	13	St Botolph - Aldersgate	20	House in Henrietta Street	27	Tate Modern
7	Russell Square Gardens	14	Avar Investments	21	Tower of London	28	National Theatre

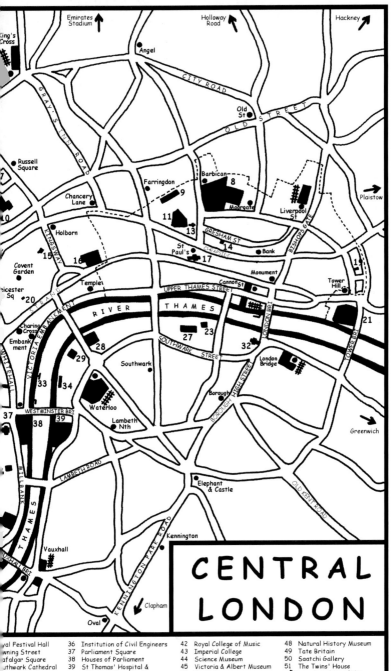

CENTRAL LONDON

Emirates Stadium

Holloway Road

Hackney

King's Cross

Angel

CITY ROAD

Old St

OLD STREET

Russell Square

Farringdon

Barbican 8

Plaistow

Chancery Lane

9

Moorgate

Liverpool St

Holborn

11

13

GRESHAM ST

14

Bank

BISHOPSGATE

Covent Garden

KINGSWAY

15

16

St Paul's

17

CHEAPSIDE

Leicester Sq

20

Temple

Cannon St

Monument

Tower Hill

1

STRAND

UPPER THAMES STREET

Charing Cross

RIVER   THAMES

21

Embankment

VICTORIA EMBANKMENT

27

23

LONDON BRI

28

SOUTHWARK STREET

32

TOWER BRI

29

London Bridge

WHITEHALL

33

34

Southwark

Borough

37

WESTMINSTER BRI

38

39

Waterloo

Lambeth Nth

BOROUGH HIGH STREET

Greenwich

MILLBANK

LAMBETH ROAD

Elephant & Castle

OLD KENT ROAD

THAMES

Vauxhall

KENNINGTON PARK ROAD

Kennington

VAUXHALL BRI

Clapham

Oval

	yal Festival Hall	36 Institution of Civil Engineers	42 Royal College of Music	48 Natural History Museum
	wning Street	37 Parliament Square	43 Imperial College	49 Tate Britain
	afalgar Square	38 Houses of Parliament	44 Science Museum	50 Saatchi Gallery
	uthwark Cathedral	39 St Thomas' Hospital &	45 Victoria & Albert Museum	51 The Twins' House
	itehall Stairs	King's College London	46 Smith Square	Boundary of the
	ndon Eye	40 Royal Albert Hall	47 Westminster Cathedral	City of London
	ckingham Palace	41 Westminster Abbey	48 Natural History Museum	

ACKNOWLEDGEMENTS

Although many people have assisted me in writing this story, I claim all mistakes, errors and factual inaccuracies as mine, and mine alone.

For their technical assistance of various kinds I would like to thank: Lucie Allen, James Bentley, Terry Boon, Bill Broome, Richard Hobbs & the staff of the British Museum, Alistair McCann, Padre Pio & celine dion, Carlos del Pino, Grace Rollason, Steve Watts, and John Yeldham.

For their comments, corrections and suggestions my gratitude goes to: Matthew Allen, Diane Armitage, Ab Haran, May Holmes, and Richard Smith.

I am grateful for the fine work and patience of my proof reader Laura Dingle and Russell Gibson of Gibson Publishing.

My special thanks to Orla Molony, your encouragement and support have meant more than you can ever know.